W r

ELIZABETH GASKELL: 'WE ARE NOT ANGELS'

Elizabeth Gaskell
'We are not angels'

Realism, Gender, Values

Terence Wright

Lecturer in the Department of English
University of Newcastle upon Tyne

First published in Great Britain 1995 by
MACMILLAN PRESS LTD
Houndmills, Basingstoke, Hampshire RG21 6XS
and London
Companies and representatives
throughout the world

A catalogue record for this book is available
from the British Library.

ISBN 0–333–61452–6

First published in the United States of America 1995 by
ST. MARTIN'S PRESS, INC.,
Scholarly and Reference Division,
175 Fifth Avenue,
New York, N.Y. 10010

ISBN 0–312–12649–2

Library of Congress Cataloging-in-Publication Data
Wright, T. R. (Terence R.) 1951–
Elizabeth Gaskell, "We are not angels" : realism, gender, values /
Terence Wright.
p.   cm.
Includes bibliographical references (p.   ) and index.
ISBN 0–333–61452–6 (Macmillan Press).— ISBN 0–312–12649–2 (St.
Martin's Press)
1. Gaskell, Elizabeth Cleghorn, 1810–1865—Criticism and
interpretation.   2. Literature and society—England—History—19th
century.   3. Women and literature—England—History—19th century.
4. Gender identity in literature.   5. Social values in literature.
6. Realism in literature.   I. Title.
PR4711.W75   1995
823'.8—dc20

95–4152
CIP

10   9   8   7   6   5   4   3   2   1
04   03   02   01   00   99   98   97   96   95

Printed and bound in Great Britain by
Antony Rowe Ltd, Chippenham, Wiltshire

For Karon

Contents

A Note on Texts

CP   *Cousin Phillis and Other Tales*, edited by Angus Easson (World's Classics, Oxford, 1981)

CR   *Cranford/Cousin Phillis*, edited by Peter Keating (Penguin, Harmondsworth, 1976)

DNW   *A Dark Night's Work and Other Stories*, edited by Suzanne Lewis (World's Classics, Oxford, 1992)

EL   'My Lady Ludlow' in *Cousin Phillis and Other Tales* (Everyman's Library, London, 1912, reprinted 1970)

L   *The Letters of Mrs. Gaskell*, edited J. A. V. Chapple and Arthur Pollard, Manchester, 1966)

MB   *Mary Barton*, edited by Stephen Gill (Penguin, Harmondsworth, 1970, reprinted 1985)

MM   *The Manchester Marriage and Other Stories* (Alan Sutton, Stroud, 1985)

NS   *North and South*, edited by Angus Easson (World's Classics, Oxford, 1982)

R   *Ruth*, edited by Alan Shelston (World's Classics, Oxford, 1985)

SL   *Sylvia's Lovers*, edited by Andrew Sanders (World's Classics, Oxford, 1982)

WD   *Wives and Daughters*, edited by Angus Easson (World's Classics, Oxford, 1987)

Preface

There has been relatively little serious examination of the works of Mrs. Gaskell, yet she is one of the most firmly 'placed' of all Victorian novelists. I mean by that, that there is an almost unanimous expression of opinion, when it is necessary to say something about her, which stresses her simplicity and sense of compassion, admits that she had talent, is ready to admit also if pressed that some explanation must be found for the diverse nature of her production, and notes finally that because of certain books (the choice may vary within a limited range) she is definitely an important minor novelist. There is generally added a reference to her charm, femininity and some vague quality that is better felt than analysed. Yet any close reading of her work reveals qualities that merit closer attention, and should make us realise that until her art and mode of thought are given a closer examination we lack the criteria necessary for a reassessment.[1]

Thus Edgar Wright, opening his 'basis for reassessment' of the work of Mrs Gaskell one hundred years after her death. In the intervening thirty years, scholarly and critical material on her, as on most writers, has expanded enormously. 1966 saw the publication of Chapple and Pollard's indispensable edition of the letters. Full-length studies have placed her in the context of her age and her religious and social milieu, examined her thematically, attempted to understand her literary inheritance and bequests, related her art to her life and studied her credentials as a semi-paid-up feminist. Two major biographies have appeared, she is now part of the 'Critical Heritage' series[2] and perhaps most significantly a good many of her lesser fictions are now appearing, newly edited, for the first time in many years. She has, on the whole, been well served by her critics, even if few would go as far as Coral Lansbury's claim that

If *Cranford* had never been published, Elizabeth Gaskell's reputation would be as secure today as that of Thackeray and George Eliot, and she would be ranked without question amongst the major novelists of the Victorian period.[3]

Most feel some need to apologise for Mrs Gaskell in one way or another. Her penchant for melodrama, her religiosity, the glibness of her storytelling talent, her supposed Victorian optimism, are all cited as reasons why we should not accord her full honours in the pantheon. Patsy Stoneman sees Gaskell as insisting 'that women share in the creation of values', but defuses her positive assessment by linking Gaskell's achievement with a practical feminist agenda, so that her heroines achieve 'that sense of self-worth which is the pre-requisite for political action' – her genius is left, as it were, in a prophetic role rather than standing on its own terms.[4] Even the admirable and sympathetic Jenny Uglow cannot resist a remark on her inferiority to two of her contemporaries, albeit coupled to a compliment:

> Gaskell does not take one's breath away at her breadth and penetration as George Eliot does, nor can she match the visionary intensity of Charlotte Brontë, but her unforced storytelling power and impassioned sympathy create an unrivalled range of fully imagined worlds.[5]

In part her range of achievement, which is one of the most remarkable things about her, may have hindered an appreciation of her acutely individual voice and sensibility. I felt there was no point in registering her 'points score' against her contemporaries, nor in tackling specifically the negatives felt by other critics. Rather I have tried to work from the 'inside out', beginning from a reading of her texts – the words of a deeply poetic writer – and let these speak for themselves in a context of categories which seemed to me particularly relevant for this novelist and which have formed the subtitle to this study. In adopting this strategy, particularly when dealing with the seductively slippery subject of sex, it is to be hoped that I have avoided the over-enthusiastic exegesis of a Dr Robyn Penrose in David Lodge's novel *Nice Work*, with her knowing allusions to the metaphoric overtones of 'knobstick'[6]. I have, in other words, tried to keep my sense of the novels' artistic structure linked to what seems consonant with her personality (even when the matter may be subconscious) and the time in which she lived (even when we are drawn to deconstruct its assumptions, values and structures).

None of my themes is entirely new to Gaskell studies; it would be surprising if it were, given the treatments of her work in the last thirty years. But I hope to have approached her work in an expansive, open and comparatively unjudgemental way, allowing the reader to assess her achievement for what it *is* rather than for what it might have been or is not. Above all, if I have encouraged reading and re-reading of her fiction with some fresh sense that this was a woman who dealt in the largest issues of love, death and the meaning of life, I shall consider myself satisfied.

Introduction

'I daresay it seems foolish; perhaps all our earthly trials will appear foolish to us after a while; perhaps they seem so now to angels. But we are ourselves, you know, and this is now, not some time to come, a long, long way off. And we are not angels, to be comforted by seeing the ends for which everything is sent.' (WD 140)

I chose the title of this book as an allusion to the above quotation from *Wives and Daughters*, in which Molly Gibson replies to Roger Hamley's slightly conventional words of comfort that 'perhaps in ten years' time you will be looking back on this trial as a very slight one' (140). Very few trials, if any, in Mrs Gaskell's work appear light. Perspective is indeed important, whether it is being able to see your life whole, or indeed see it in the context of eternal life in Heaven. But the latter is chiefly a release from a world of doubt and difficulty, the pain and sorrow of loss.

I shall return to the local context of this quotation and its application to Molly and her story in its proper place, but her words struck me as being particularly apt in identifying some of the major concerns of Mrs Gaskell, and I shall use them as a starting point for a general discussion. The most remarkable thing, then, about this quotation is its resolute, if faintly regretful, pragmatism. The angels are absolute and eternal; they 'see the ends for which everything is sent'. We mortals must live without this gift, trying to accommodate ourselves day by day to circumstance. We live in the 'now', and there is more than one instance which may be quoted to suggest that Elizabeth Gaskell was suspicious of a futile yearning for heavenly visions before our time. The most notable is Bessy Higgins, rebuked by Margaret Hale in *North and South* for turning her face from the world in which she is dying to 'the land o' Beulah':

'Bessy, don't be impatient with your life, whatever it is – or may have been. Remember who gave it you, and made it what it is!' (NS 90)

But more convincing, typically, is the positive presentation given to all those in her fiction who, to quote her own reference to Carlyle's words 'do silently good actions' (L 70). 'I don't call the use of words *action*: unless there is some definite, distinct, practical *course of action* logically proposed by those words' (L 530). This pragmatism dictates, in one way or another, the essential realism which is at the core of all her work; the moral idea is involved with the concrete and immediate. Her work is full of the stuff of life which makes an immediate and significant bond between things and people. 'Just read a few pages of De Foe &c – and you will see the healthy way in which he sets *objects* not *feelings* before you', she advises her daughter Marianne (L 541). It is a lesson she learned herself. The inarticulate grief of John Barton at his wife's death is given voice in the objects hands are set upon, in half-blind gestures and movements:

> He heard the stiff, unseasoned drawer, in which his wife kept her clothes, pulled open. He saw the neighbour come down, and blunder about in search of soap and water. . . .

> He thought . . . of his first gift to her, a bead necklace, which had long ago been put by, in one of the deep drawers of the dresser, to be kept for Mary. He wondered if it was there yet, and with a strange curiosity he got up to feel for it; for the fire by this time was well-nigh out, and candle he had none. His groping hand fell on the piled-up tea things, which at his desire she had left unwashed till morning – they were all so tired. (MB 57)

This is the 'beauty and poetry of many of the common things and daily events of life in its humblest aspect' of which she spoke as early as 1838 (L 33) but it is certainly not the only measure of her realism. Let us consider a passage from the other end of her writing career, in which Mr Gibson, Molly's father, deals with a certain Mr Coxe, one of his medical student lodgers. Having intercepted a love-letter from the young man to his daughter, the Doctor decides to quell the attachment without informing the girl, who knows nothing of the matter. A satirical note is sent, to which Mr Coxe's injured pride responds by demanding an interview with the Doctor. Subsequent events show Mr Coxe to be fickle and silly, though we do not know this yet, and there is no doubt that the comedy of the scene essentially derives from the Doctor's discomfiture of his pupil. The whole episode clearly also has a purpose in the plot – it results in Molly's being sent to stay with Squire Hamley. Yet Mrs Gaskell uses the occasion to bring together two men of different ages and temperaments, with keen but opposing interests in the daughter of one of them, related as teacher and pupil, host and guest, and indirectly, through Mr Coxe's father, as family friend. It is enough to consider for a moment their different temperaments to sense the scope for complex interplay between the two. Nor are their temperaments simple. Mr Gibson is satirical, but his youthful feelings for 'poor Jeanie' moderate his satire. Mr Coxe stands upon his dignity, but he is not *without* dignity; he is a slightly ridiculous figure, but he does not lack spirit or genuine feeling.

It is a scene in which Mr Gibson is manifestly in control. His note initiates the meeting; he is the master, the father, the *in loco parentis*; we are allowed into his thoughts rather than Mr Coxe's. Mr Gibson's control ensures the comic control of the whole scene. Yet the business is one of tactics. Mr Gibson is never dismissive, Mr Coxe never loses respect for his elder, however he may smart. The Doctor first tries to ridicule the younger man, albeit with some consideration for his feelings: 'He'll not like *Master* Coxe outside; no need to put him to unnecessary shame' (WD 49). Mr Coxe, however, takes umbrage, complaining that it is not 'the conduct of a gentleman' to intercept a note not addressed to oneself. Mr Gibson assumes the tones of superior age and higher moral ground:

'And let me tell you, young man,' replied Mr. Gibson, with a sudden sternness in his voice, 'that what you have done is only excusable in consideration of your youth and extreme

ignorance of what are considered the laws of domestic honour.'
(51)

When the threat to remove him from the household startles
Mr Coxe 'into dismay, if not repentance', Mr Gibson is able to
shift his tone to one of fatherly disappointment – 'for I trusted
you, Edward, like a son of my own!' and score again. It is a
scene in which one participant is all words and wit (eighty
per cent of the words are his), certainty and confidence, while
the other is uneasy, standing rather than sitting, 'stammering',
muttering, 'in a hurry of anxiety', 'startled'. Yet there is no
sense of victor and vanquished in the scene. The strongest feeling
is of density – the density of words which convey far more
than the intellectual crossing of swords.

First there is the sense of personality, which carries a rhythm
of mood, of shifting emotional stance, constantly altering the
relations between the participants. And beneath this is a drama
of psychology between youth and age – an older man who is
putting a (rather feeble) young pretender in his place; who is
jealous over his daughter, wishes to be fatherly if the right
respect is shown, wishes to have the advice of wisdom recognised but is prepared to show his teeth if challenged; and a
young man who is untried, awkward because he is in every
way subservient, but yet feels in his youth that he has a right
to recognition, socially and sexually. Yet for all the silliness of
one and the arrogant sarcasm of the other, they reach a truce
by recognising what is a truth for both of them:

> 'You are ridiculing my feelings, Mr. Gibson. Do you forget
> that you yourself were young once?'
> 'Poor Jeanie' rose before Mr. Gibson's eyes; and he felt a
> little rebuked.
> 'Come, Mr. Coxe, let us see if we can't make a bargain,'
> said he, after a minute or so of silence. (53)

The ruefully comic note in the compromise is perfectly adapted
to the timeless comedy of youth, age and love, and the scene
is a type of some confrontations later in the book which end
in a somewhat bleaker compromise. The triumph of Mrs Gaskell's
realism here is that she can give to Mr Gibson and Mr Coxe

the full weight of attention that we owe them; her feeling for
the interaction of personality and her ability to capture it in
mood and temper ensure this. It is profoundly inconclusive,
yet dense with significance, and it is a scene which exemp-
lifies in a minor key all the characteristics of its author's comic
realism – dialogue and situation illuminating personalities as
they establish themselves in mutual relationship.

But she is not only a great realist in details – the separate
minutiae of experience, whether objects and gestures or dialogue. She has a larger sense of the rhythms which mark the
lives of generations, of the poetry of lives dignified simply by
their dedication, their acceptance of all things in due season
and their stubborn reliance on Wordsworth's 'primary laws of
our nature'. Her feel for these qualities in Northern hill farmers
informs her firm, onward-moving sinewy prose in the following passage from her short story 'Half A Lifetime Ago', gathering
up the years and the seasons into the lifetimes of experience
of many families and many generations:

> William and Margaret Dixon were rather superior people,
> of a character belonging – as far as I have seen – exclusively
> to the class of Westmoreland and Cumberland statesmen –
> just, independent, upright; not given to much speaking; kind-
> hearted, but not demonstrative; disliking change, and new
> ways, and new people; sensible and shrewd; each household
> self-contained, and its members having little curiosity as to
> their neighbours, with whom they rarely met for any social
> intercourse, save at the stated times of sheep-shearing and
> Christmas; having a certain kind of social pleasure in amassing
> money . . . the men occasionally going off laking, *i.e.* play-
> ing, *i.e.* drinking for days together, and having to be hunted
> up by anxious wives, who dared not leave their husbands
> to the chances of the wild precipitous roads, but walked miles
> and miles, lantern in hand, in the dead of night, to discover
> and guide the solemnly-drunken husband home; who had a
> dreadful headache the next day, and the day after that came
> forth as grave, and sober, and virtuous-looking as if there
> were no such things as malt and spirituous liquors in the
> world; (CP 61)

Elizabeth Gaskell's is a realism which thrives on inevitability – of suffering, pain and death in her darker works – but it is also always strong with the possibility of adaptation, rebirth and self-discovery. There is a moral pragmatism in the determination with which her people pull themselves from the threat of self-loss, metaphoric death and disintegration, and turn back into life. 'Courage, little heart', says Margaret Hale as she prepares to face life alone. 'And so it fell out that the latter days of Susan Dixon's life were better than the former' are the last words of 'Half a Lifetime Ago'. Phillis Holman resolves to visit Paul's parents, moving out of her sheltered sphere for the first time at the end of her story. Libbie Marsh confronts herself, and, facing the unlikelihood of her ever marrying, resolves to live with the mother of the little boy she had befriended. And it is not by chance that the impetus to such self-redemption is sometimes spoken by down-to-earth, elderly retainers.

Such muted optimism must be considered with some care, since it could easily be mistaken for a want of artistic toughness or integrity. Her realism in these cases is not of the kind which is best exemplified in Wordsworth's 'Michael' or 'The Ruined Cottage'. In these cases suffering and decay are their own aesthetic justification. Wordsworth simply recounts them, and the very telling contains their tragedy. Mrs Gaskell herself is capable of tragedy, as we shall see, but in 'Libbie Marsh's Three Eras', 'Half a Lifetime Ago' and 'Cousin Phillis' her faith above all in the human heart leads unerringly to renewed possibility. The understatement of the phrases of renewal leave unspoken the weight of experience it will be needful to turn round in order to progress.

'Libbie Marsh' closes with a moral, albeit comically framed, directed at those with the 'amiable peculiarity' of reading moral endings: 'She has a purpose in life; and that purpose is a holy one' (DNW 193). The word 'holy' should not surprise us. We may not be angels, but these heavenly beings undoubtedly exist. Could we assume their form we might better understand the 'weary weight of all this unintelligible world' as Wordsworth put it. Faith is fundamental to Elizabeth Gaskell's vision. Brought up as a Unitarian and married to a minister in that faith, her first commitment was to the immediate, humanist

life of works. She denied the co-equality of God and Christ –
'the one thing I *am* clear and sure about is this that Jesus Christ
was not equal to His father; that, however divine a being he
was *not* God' (L 860). At the same time, as this quotation
suggests, she was inclined to equate the human, and particularly the compassionate side of Christ with the divine, at least
as an example. It was an effective equation for one who relied
with Wordsworth on the 'holiness of the heart's affections'. But
this faintly anodyne account does not tell the whole story of
her faith. Her awareness of the power of human passion and
the mystery of mortal suffering could not let her rest easy with
a simply rational and benevolent religion. There was a personal commitment which, to quote Jenny Uglow, led her to
believe 'that the witness to truth should be taken, if needs be,
to the point of martyrdom'.[1] This martyrdom may be, as in the
case of Lois Barclay, to the cause of rational truth, or, as in
Gaskell's own alienation of Dissenting industrialists with the
publication of *Mary Barton*, to the truth of social justice, but
martyrdom is the extent of the price the woman of religious
convictions will be prepared to pay. Uglow speaks also of the
Unitarians retaining 'the self-scrutinizing anxieties of traditional
Nonconformity'.[2] Certainly she had a conviction of sin and, as
we shall see, the place of sexuality in a sinful world provided
her with one of her most imaginatively disturbing and creative problems. Passion in a more general sense both worried
and attracted her, and there seems no reason to doubt that she
was in a quite precise sense a passionately religious woman.
There is no work she ever wrote which is not informed with a
sense of the absolute – of divine sanction for our duty, of the
mirroring of divine love in our earthly charity and compassion,
of sin and the necessity of redemption, of the life-defining nature
of death and the promise of eternal bliss. It is one of the marks
of her greatness that the absolute, far from denying the validity
of realism, gives it a special dimension; together they define
and create values for the individual human being.

The word 'holy' itself clearly possessed a special status for
Mrs Gaskell. It was closely associated in her personal experience
with reconciliation to grief and loss. In 1849 she had thanked
a correspondent for her mother's letters:

I have been brought up away from all those who knew my
parents, and therefore those who come to me with a remembrance of them as an introduction seem to have a holy claim
on my regard. (L 797)

In a letter of 1850 to Eliza Fox she recalls the death of her
baby son, 'that wound that will never heal on earth':

Do come to us soon! I want to get associations about that
house; here there is the precious perfume lingering of my
darling's short presence in this life – I wish I were with him
in that 'light, where we shall all see light,' for I am often
sorely puzzled here – but however I must not waste my
strength or my time about the never ending sorrow; but which
hallows this house. I think that is one evil of this bustling
life that one has never time calmly and bravely to face a
great grief, and to view it on every side to bring the harmony out of it. (L 111)

The house is 'hallowed' by the 'never ending sorrow', but she
adds significantly that it is a grief faced and viewed on every
side so that the harmony is brought out of it. This is as much
an artistic as a religious reconciliation. 'Harmony' is understanding the 'ends for which everything is sent', but it is also
a satisfying sense of beauty, such as may be expressed in art.
The influence we look to, once again, is Wordsworth's as much
as Christ's – the Wordsworth, for example, of 'The Ruined
Cottage':

I well remember that those very plumes,
Those weeds, and the high spear-grass on that wall,
By mist and silent rain-drops silvered o'er,
As once I passed did to my heart convey
So still an image of tranquillity,
So calm and still, and looked so beautiful
Amid the uneasy thoughts which filled my mind,
That what we feel of sorrow and despair
From ruin and from change, and all the grief
The passing shows of being leave behind,

Appeared an idle dream that could not live
Where meditation was.[3]

What is striking about the Victorian writer, as against the Romantic, is that his unified tragic sense is split in her vision into Good and Evil. So 'The Crooked Branch' or 'The Grey Woman' show the stark, hopeless destructiveness of human wickedness, while other shorter fiction expresses the more characteristic upward turn of rebirth or redemption. In the longer fiction there is no loss without a balancing gain. John Barton dies but Jem Wilson is rescued by his true love's dedication and energy. Barton dies in Mr Carson's arms; Christian values are reasserted. Margaret Hale is left alone in the world but discovers her mutual love for Thornton. Squire Hamley loses his elder son, but even in the moment of his feeling that 'it is past human comfort' (WD 587) he is granted the pledge of a little grandson. It is part of an essentially 'comédie humaine' vision which is only perhaps really denied in 'Sylvia's Lovers', where trust for redemption must be satisfied by deathbed forgiveness and trust in eternal life.

In avowing that 'we are not Angels' Molly is not only pointing to the imperfections of the mortal state; she is assuming gender – not merely for herself but for Roger and for all human beings. Angels are traditionally sexless; novelists writing about men and women can hardly avoid dealing with relations between the sexes. But Elizabeth Gaskell has special and peculiar concern with the nature of women, both historically and biologically. 'We' clearly means mankind in general, but in the context of a society of men who conventionally and patronisingly referred to women as 'angels' the twentieth-century reader may see some ironies. These may be unintended, but Mrs Gaskell was perfectly capable of seeing the restriction such labelling could place upon women, and her celebration of female selfhood is a deliberate refutation of such categorising. After *Mary Barton* women become her central characters, and the vast majority of her fiction is seen at least by implication through women's eyes. Even when this is not the case, as in 'Cousin Phillis', the strategy is designed to gain a special view of the main, female protagonist. But the woman is never in isolation; they are always related to men, even when it is in their distant youth, as in 'Half a Lifetime Ago', or when, as in *Cranford*, the male is absent, and even when the commitment is no more than Phillis Holman's barely articulated admission of love for Holdsworth. In *Ruth* the heroine's very aloneness is a direct result of contact with a man. Men define women, initially at least, in all these works if for no other reason than that the male is by tradition the active principle, deciding quite literally what life a girl shall lead by marrying her (or not!) and attempting to define women in general through their experience of particular women. However forceful, ingenious, stoical, honourable women may be, their stories are reactive. Even if this is not so biologically, it was true socially and historically for Elizabeth Gaskell's age, and in some cases may still be so today.

So much is unsurprising. What may be less expected is the ubiquity of sex itself in Mrs Gaskell's work. In the case of men it may be more or less explicit – think for example of Mr Thornton watching the bracelet on Margaret's arm:

> It seemed as if it fascinated him to see her push it up impatiently, until it tightened her soft flesh; and then to mark the loosening – the fall. (NS 79)

and the pains of unrequited passion he suffers later in the novel. Elizabeth Gaskell is aware of the special quality of sex-appeal in women. She distinguishes those who have it by placing them against less inflammatory natures – Cynthia against Molly, Sylvia against Hester Rose. Anyone who doubts the ubiquity of sex in her work need only consider that traditionally least likely candidate for sexuality in any form, *Cranford*. The message may be parodic of excessive female apprehension about the aggressive male, but when Matty rolls a ball under the bed as a precaution, and confesses to jumping from ground to bed every night in one bound for fear of being caught by the heels, she fears a male intruder, and the implications of man and bed cannot be denied. The pathos of Matty's childlikeness is compounded by her concomitant stunted sexual development, aware of men as an exciting threat, but denied the full relationship which would make them human companions.

MOI : Many B's only power over men is in her sexuality

It is hardly surprising that a woman who called sex *'the* subject of a woman's life' (R 44) should give the matter thought, and some prominence in her writing. It is a matter fraught with problems and ambiguities. Female passion is seldom directly admitted, but a climax of commitment on the woman's part sometimes suggests it, and sex is constantly evoked by the implication of its very absence. Sylvia feels a sexual repugnance for Philip, Lois for Manasseh. These are not of the intensity that could make a Sue Bridehead jump from a window rather than receive the embraces of her husband, but the shudder of distaste at the prematurely stooping Philip's pressing upon Sylvia – literally quite as much as metaphorically – and Lois's fear of the tall, gaunt, obsessive Manasseh, pressing himself with divine rather than social sanction upon the orphan girl, are pictures in which female sensibility is repulsed and distressed rather than wooed, and turns cold in indifference or dread.

Mrs Gaskell is thoroughly aware of the need for this necessary quickening within a woman's breast if she is to awaken sexually, and she sets much store by it. At the same time female sexuality is constantly kept at arm's length by an emphasis on reserve and pride. Among the author's favourite phrases are 'maidenly', 'maiden modesty', 'maiden pride', all implying that lack of sexual experience is the specially female virtue, carrying overtones of integrity and proper pride. Yet with typical ambivalence it is again a virtue which can only be defined in relation to a man. As novelists recognised as long ago as *Pamela*, the very state of chastity for women is complicated by opposite but complementary implications. Chastity's worth is only to be proved in its loss. It is exciting to the other sex simply because of its anticipatory opposite. The more the woman remains aloof in her 'proud maidenhood' the more she is presenting herself as sexually provocative. So John Thornton discovers when he is ensnared by the haughty Margaret Hale

> She handed him his cup of tea with the proud air of an unwilling slave; but her eye caught the moment when he was ready for another cup; and he almost longed to ask her to do for him what he saw her compelled to do for her father, who took her little finger and thumb in his masculine hand, and made them serve as sugar-tongs. (NS 79)

A function of the woman's reactive role is her constant association with secrecy. This may be comically played with, as in
the gossip of Cranford, but more often the matter is serious,
with heroines who must tell lies, find their public reputations
questioned, or in one case live with possibly the most damaging secret in her society – the illegitimacy of her child. It is the
nature of chastity to be self-contained. A woman who 'gives
herself away' by admitting her love for a man is approximately
'giving herself away' to him as a possession – sexually if in no
other way. Yet every woman is capable of such a thing. In
denying her angelic status, Molly Gibson is speaking for women
specifically, who are labelled 'angels' by a patronising and hypo-
critically idealising male society. It is a label associating radi-
ant, even transcendent beauty with sexual purity. But in fact
real female beauty is sanctioned and consummated by sexuality. Is it then a God-given faculty totally in tune with nature
or a 'charm' derived from another ambiguous label men have
accorded women – 'witch'? This is a theme pursued in 'Sylvia's
Lovers', *Wives and Daughters* and, most terribly, in 'Lois the
Witch'.

There can be no doubt that for Mrs Gaskell sex outside wed-
lock is a sin, but how far would she account female sexuality
itself as, if not a sin, at least a dangerous impulse needing to
be harnessed to good man, home and family? Such an assumption seems to be implied in Mary Barton's refusal of the up-
standing Jem Wilson. Her resourceful, intrepid rescue of her
lover could be seen as a kind of penance for her earlier dismissal of a good man with whom, it is implied, any decent
girl should be glad to ally herself. But if we turn to 'Sylvia's
Lovers' we encounter a heroine who might have followed her
heart but for the duplicity of her future husband, and who is
condemned to an unnatural and repressed marriage as a result of gratitude and dependence upon the opposite sex.

Yet women are far from being only exploited victims. 'We
are ourselves' says Molly, and the discovery, definition and
creation of the self is a key theme of Elizabeth Gaskell's fiction. The forthrightness and certainty with which Molly makes
this declaration suggests her own deep-rooted, articulate
'centredness' within herself, despite her distress at her father's

marriage. Cynthia, by contrast, knows herself only too well, but is incapable of being pleased with what she is. Other women must establish themselves in a world which inadequately establishes it for them. Is Lois Barclay a witch, an angel or a martyr? No, she is what she herself decides. Her one pragmatic certainty in a completely unstable world is the sense of self.

Women are not without knowledge and power. In their darker forms the supposed powers of the female have terrified our ancestors, as witness the hanged witches of Salem and the all-too-effective curse of Bridget Fitzgerald in the short story 'The Poor Clare'. Knowledge of the 'booklearning' kind occupies a rather ambiguous position for women. While Phillis eagerly pursues the classics, and is clearly capable of considerable imaginative development, Paul's father suggests that a houseful of children will cure her of such fancies. Sylvia, a complete, if charming dunce, despises learning as it is bestowed on her by the pedantic would-be lover Philip, but when he has left her, humbly asks to learn to read. Is this the kind of self-martyrdom that the woman must pay to the man she has 'wronged'? But more important in the novelist's eyes is a knowledge that is instinctive, a power that is built into women's makeup. They are shown caring with compassion for children, holding families together, watching and waiting, organising. Their native powers are not always a blessing, proving on occasion as fatal as the witchcraft Lois Barclay is supposed to have practised. Sylvia Robson has an innate, unconscious power of sexual attraction which, despite its naturalness, ultimately destroys the spontaneous humanity that makes her what she essentially is. We are here trespassing on the edge of forbidden knowledge, which is carnal. It is forbidden to women except in strictly defined circumstances. Ruth Hilton clearly transgresses this rule, but her ignorance of sex would seem to be blamed in part for this; paradoxically one kind of knowledge would keep her from another.

Other women are allowed to use their powers for self-assertion and development. There are few women in Mrs Gaskell's works who are not at least the equal of the men about them. In many cases – Margaret Hale, Ruth Hilton, Molly Gibson, Bell Robson – they are inherently the stronger sex; only social convention obscures this fact, to the extent, for example, that at the death of Daniel Robson, his wife, by far the stronger, more intelligent partner, collapses simply because the habit of deferring to her man has convinced her of the necessity of his presence for her own survival. It is often necessary for women to establish their own self-worth and thereby assert or create values by which, it is suggested, their whole society may live. Miss Matty's humble charity and sense of honour morally far outstrip the know-how and worldliness of Drumble. Lady Ludlow's patrician charm, firmness and conciliation not only reconcile the classes and divisions about her, but help her to accept change in spite of herself.

I have drawn attention to the moral, semi-humorously appended to 'Libbie Marsh's Three Eras'. The tyro author could not resist spelling out her point, but the story itself has already acted out a great deal more than can be contained in a moral. Elizabeth Gaskell is far from being a didactic writer. Libbie Marsh may well be living life with a purpose, but this tells us nothing in human terms of what is involved in living with a purpose. Essentially, binding together realism, gender and religion, there is in Mrs Gaskell's fiction a sense of values. These are not external, imposed standards of behaviour but internal discoveries and creations. They are the parameters by which we live, implying certain kinds of contingencies implicit in our being, and which, between our own personal resources and the exigencies of time, place and matter, give meaning to our lives. It is not the least of Mrs Gaskell's resemblances to Wordsworth that she makes us feel the weight of words in human terms. To say that Libbie Marsh has a purpose in her life which is holy is to sum her up from the outside, as it were, but when we understand the full implications of the experience contained in the tale we *know* what 'purpose' and 'holy' mean as values, as 'lived ideas'.

'Libbie Marsh's Three Eras' is simply the story of a girl who finds herself alone and plain in new lodgings at one year's end, and by the next year's end is living with a neighbouring widow whose little boy, now dead, has been the means of bringing the two women together. It might be said that the central factor in the whole business is Libbie's plainness. It is the intractable cost of things which we cannot alter, the hard truth of realism beyond which we cannot go. The burden of this truth for the girl is captured in the casual brutality of passing comments.

> Libbie had often and often been greeted by such questions as – 'How long is it since you were a beauty?' – 'What would you take a day to stand in the fields to scare away the birds?' &c., for her to linger under any impression as to her looks. (DNW 169)

Shy of the good-natured bluntness of the family with which she is lodging, Libbie turns her attention to the crippled Franky Hall, the feverish movements of whose listless arm she sees through an opposite window. She makes the little boy her Valentine, in default of any other, by sending him the gift of a canary. In her second era they take Franky on a day's Whitsun holiday to the countryside, and finally when Franky has been buried, in the last era, Libbie decides to make her home with his mother. The symbol of her commitment is her choice of staying with Mrs Hall on the day after the funeral, rather than participating in the public festivity of Anne Dixon's wedding as a bridesmaid. Anne is vexed, and tells her she will never be married with such behaviour, but Libbie has already faced this fact:

> 'I know that as well as you can tell me; and more reason, therefore, as God has seen fit to keep me out of woman's natural work, I should try and find work for myself. I mean,' seeing Anne Dixon's puzzled look, 'that as I know I'm never likely to have a home of my own, or a husband that would look to me to make all straight, or children to watch over or care for, all which I take to be woman's natural work, I must not lose time in fretting and fidgeting after marriage, but just look about me for somewhat else to do. I can see many a one misses it in this. They will hanker after what is ne'er likely to be theirs, instead of facing it out, and settling down to be old maids; and, as old maids, just looking round for the odd jobs God leaves in the world for such as old maids

to do. There's plenty of such work, and there's the blessing of God on them as does it.' (DNW 189)

Her words come tumbling out, plain and forthright; an explanation of the self, awkward in phrasing yet eloquent in being 'the outpouring of what had long been her inner thoughts'. Although the choice made here is an immediate and apparently pragmatic one, it is really the expression of a course of life we have seen decided by her actions throughout her 'eras'. Though her self-assessment may seem to assume a low horizon by twentieth-century standards, this is in no sense a gloomy or depressing tale; it is active and positive, celebrating the possibilities of practical human endeavour. The gift of the canary is a true Valentine – an act whose love is felt in the thought and care which goes into the choice of bird and the hoarding of her money to pay for it, and which gives the sender delight in her own giving. She directs a lover's joy into another channel of fulfilment. By various means they manage to convey Franky into the countryside for his day out. The thoughtless comment of the Dixon father immediately leads to practical expedients:

'Hast never been to see the deer, or the king and queen oaks? Lord, how stupid.'
    His wife pinched his arm, to remind him of Franky's helpless condition, which of course tethered the otherwise willing feet. But Dixon had a remedy. He called Bob, and one or two others, and each taking a corner of the strong plaid shawl, they slung Franky as in a hammock, and thus carried him merrily along, (DNW 183)

It is also a celebration of the sociability of man. The three eras are marked by festivals; Libbie begins alone, and the story ends with her quiet, private companionship juxtaposed with the public, social harmony of a wedding. When one of the holidaymakers in the second era has eaten his dinner too early, all the others contribute something from their store to help him out. It is certainly no idyll. Franky is in almost constant pain until his death. His mother is distraught, Anne is vexed by Libbie's refusal to be a bridesmaid. But Franky's day out gives him a vision of happiness which could be a foretaste of heaven, and all the holidaymakers a distant view of their smoky home which puts it into a new perspective, if only for a few hours. Anne comes round next day and is reconciled with her friend, thanking her for her humble gift – 'Thou'rt a real good un, Libbie, and I'll keep your needle-book to my dying day, that I will' (192). Libbie is in no doubt of the difficulties facing her in going to live with Mrs Hall. 'She's such a Tartar!' says Anne. 'Sooner than not have a quarrel, she'd fight right hand against left. Thou'lt have no peace of thy life' (192–3). But her 'resolution was brave and strong' and in fact her courage is rewarded:

> Margaret Hall is a different woman to the scold of the neigh-
> bourhood she once was; touched and softened by the two
> purifying angels, Sorrow and Love. (193)

Does such a reward undermine the realism of Libbie's stoical commitment? I believe not. It simply enacts the realistic truth that kindness may breed kindness and love be returned for love given. Yet the shape implied by the reward and the possibility of an ending clinched by a moral reflects a further important aspect of Mrs Gaskell's fiction. Complementing her realism – the ordinariness, probability, understatement, pragmatism and 'poetry of objects' – is the sense of shape and significance bestowed by the story told. The primary drive of her genius was the art of the storyteller. She begins her last novel with a nod of acknowledgement to all stories:

> To begin with the old rigmarole of childhood. In a country
> there was a shire, and in that shire there was a town, and in
> that town there was a house, and in that house there was a
> room, and in that room there was a bed, and in that bed
> there lay a little girl; (WD 1)

And the amusing little fantasy 'Curious, if True' plays off realism against the fairy story by imagining a Mr Whittingham who, while benighted in the French countryside, comes across a chateau whose inhabitants seem to recognise him. Being themselves some of the more famous characters from fairy story, they have in fact mistaken him for Dick Whittington, both of which truths the attentive reader may well become aware of before the narrator. The story is interesting for the interaction it produces between these eternal figures of the imagination and the particularities of individual experience. Asked about his cat, the narrator thinks of his own 'tailless Tom, born in the Isle of Man, and now supposed to be keeping guard against the incursions of rats and mice into my chambers in London' (CP 248). The Seven League Boots are being superseded by the 'new fashion of railroads' (250) and Cinderella suffers from sore feet, which are 'now taking their revenge for my cruelty in forcing them into such little slippers' (251). The room in the chateau is 'curiously full of pale light, which did not culminate on any spot, nor proceed from any centre, nor flicker with any motion of the air, but filled every nook and corner, making all things deliciously distinct' (244). This is the timeless atmosphere of the fable, its truth universal and immutable, and it is contrasted with the 'slanting glory of the dawning day' as Mr Whittingham wakens from his dream.

The truth of fairy stories was important to Elizabeth Gaskell in supplying her with some sets of circumstances which gave form to her shorter fiction, with its orphans, secret heroes, lost children, cruel stepmothers and sibling rivalries. But in a more generally pervasive way the fabular structures of her fiction imply values of a mythic or archetypal kind. Among such structures may be mentioned the test (notably, in these novels, of a young woman falsely accused of deception), the choice of suitors, and the reward. Some repeated themes are clearly felt so profoundly by Mrs Gaskell because they were part of her own experience – the exile beyond the sea reminiscent of her own lost brother, the love of a daughter for a father who is devoted but removed from her by circumstance. Most powerful and pervasive of all is perhaps the lost idyll, used again and again to evoke childhood, spontaneous human freedom or eternal peace after death. All such motifs and patterns suggest the meaningful life; and the general question of the shape and significance of individual lives is one which preoccupied this writer, especially in her shorter fiction.

Mrs Gaskell frequently repeats her situations, and her care-
lessness with lesser characters' names is notorious. No one of
course could mistake Ruth Hilton for Margaret Hale, or either
of them for Sylvia Robson or Cynthia Kirkpatrick. The Christian names of these women seem rather carefully chosen to
suggest their natures, but among minor characters names recur or are echoed with apparent indifference. Hester Rose occurs in two works, Dixon is a surname in at least three; Holmans,
Holdsworths and Holcrofts jostle each other and the first names
of old female servants seem more or less interchangeable. The
very lack of importance we feel inclined to attach to this matter indicates how characteristic of Mrs Gaskell's writing is the
tendency towards a general rather than particular appeal. The
female servants' names appear unimportant because they generally are of the same type, and perform the same function in
the story. More centrally, individual, indeed unique, experiences of *women* constantly lead us towards the generality of
woman. A girl alienated from her father suggests all father/
daughter relationships. We seem not to require the details of
her heroines' childhoods – it is a symbolic time. It is seldom,
indeed, that we have a complex pattern of motivation unique
to that person and their relations with others. Personality is
'given' broadly according to type, or large values. For example
Sylvia's choice is between ways of life as much as between
lovers – the exciting or the cautious, the sexual or the protec-
tive, the liberating or the enclosing. They determine each other
by what they are rather than by what they are becoming.

Yet, as I hope to show, Elizabeth Gaskell's intense evocation
of particularities animates and fleshes out the abstractions
towards which her fiction seems always to be tending. Most
importantly there is an outward impulsion of self-testing, discovery and creation which makes 'value' part of a movement
rather than a situation, and allows us to understand how intimately it is bound up with the process of living.

1
Realising Christianity: *Mary Barton*

'I have tried to write truthfully' (MB 38), wrote Elizabeth Gaskell in the Preface to *Mary Barton*, and an early reviewer of the novel remarked that 'The great beauty of this "Tale of Manchester Life," consists in its self-evident truthfulness.'[1] What kinds of truth are evident in this near-contemporary tale with which the author first made her name? At the most immediate level there is the factual truth of 'reportage' such as is found in the description of the Davenports' appalling slum – the kind of truth recorded in Engels' *Condition of the Working Class in England*. But the very manner in which the scene is handled suggests that these horrors are to be seen in terms of human rather than statistical or objective truth:

> After the account I have given of the state of the street, no one can be surprised that on going into the cellar inhabited by Davenport, the smell was so foetid as almost to knock the two men down. Quickly recovering themselves, as those inured to such things do, they began to penetrate the thick darkness of the place, and to see three or four little children rolling on the damp, nay wet, brick floor, through which the stagnant, filthy moisture of the street oozed up; the fire-place was empty and black; the wife sat on her husband's chair, and cried in the dank loneliness. (MB 98)

The stench is rendered through the reactions of the two men, the filthy dampness of the floor by the children rolling on it. The woman cries in the 'dank loneliness'. The 'truth' of this book, as most early reviewers realised, is not political or

21

economic. The aim of this writer who claimed 'I know nothing of Political Economy or the theories of trade' was to evoke truths of the human heart. But in what terms do we understand this truth? I quote again from the Preface:

> The more I reflected on this unhappy state of things between those so bound to each other by common interests, as the employers and the employed must ever be, the more anxious I became to give some utterance to the agony which, from time to time, convulses this dumb people; the agony of suffering without the sympathy of the happy, or of erroneously believing that such is the case. (MB 37–8)

Despite the cautious hedging of the last phrase, thrown perhaps as a sop to Establishment political views, one must feel the extremeness and intensity of her words – 'some utterance', 'agony' 'convulses', 'dumb', 'suffering'. On one side is all this and on the other 'the happy'. In this novel Elizabeth Gaskell has created a man who sees this divide and asks with bitter vehemence why this should be:

> If I am sick, do they come and nurse me? If my child lies dying . . . does the rich man bring the wine or broth that might save his life? If I am out of work for weeks in the bad times . . . does the rich man share his plenty with me , as he ought to do, if his religion was not a humbug? Don't think to come over me with the old tale, that the rich know nothing of the trials of the poor. I say, if they don't know, they ought to know. We are their slaves as long as we can work; we pile up their fortunes with the sweat of our brows; and yet we are to live as separate as if we were in two worlds; ay, as separate as Dives and Lazarus, with a great gulf betwixt us: but I know who was best off then. (MB 45)

The context into which the telling truth of these rhetorical questions is put is Christian. Christ's own exemplary parable is being lived out in a nineteenth-century city at this very moment. With a single reference Mrs Gaskell lifts the 'problem' out of the realm of Political Economy and makes it a moral outrage of timeless and religious dimensions. Again from her Preface, the author speaks of 'helpless love in the way of widow's mites'. The immediate action of John Barton when he and Wilson have surveyed the wretched condition of the Davenports is to provide practical help:

> So he strode, and ran, and hurried home. He emptied into the ever-useful pocket-handkerchief the little meal remaining in the mug. Mary would have her tea at Miss Simmonds'; her food for the day was safe. Then he went up-stairs for his better coat, and his one, gay, red-and-yellow silk pocket-handkerchief – his jewels, his plate, his valuables, these were. He went to the pawn-shop; he pawned them for five shillings; (MB 99)

He 'sells all that he has' and bestows his mite of five shillings to relieve immediate suffering. It might be compared with the five shillings casually if sympathetically given by young Carson when Wilson calls for an Infirmary order on behalf of Davenport.

Christ's ministry takes on the reality of values for the people of *Mary Barton* because they live it out in states of question, demand and confrontation. John Barton is driven to murder by his outrage at the gulf fixed between rich and poor. His victim's father finds he must face in practical terms the real implications of forgiving one's enemy. The religious ethos extends at times into the very language of the book, the Lancashire 'thees' and 'thous' combining homeliness with Biblical overtones and scriptural turns of phrase:

> I'm but a frabbit woman at times, but I've a heart within me through all my temper, and thou shalt be as a daughter henceforward, – as mine own ewe-lamb. Jem shall not love thee better in his way, than I will in mine; and thou shalt bear with my turns, Mary, knowing that in my soul God sees the love that shall ever be thine, if thou'lt take me for thy mother, and speak no more of being alone. (MB 448)

This is a confrontational book of great starkness and even savagery, and in this it is at the opposite extreme from the author's last novel, *Wives and Daughters*, where the atmosphere is one of evasion, language hiding real motives and feelings. Yet *Mary Barton* is also filled with the warmth of love – between neighbours, lovers, family members – and of hospitality and shared pleasures. The two aspects are interdependent, each embodied in its own images, and together forming a complementary vision of human possibilities.

The Preface holds further clues as to the nature of this novel, especially to its tangible human realism and its sense of common humanity. After contemplating a story in 'some rural scene ... more than a century ago ... and the place on the borders of Yorkshire' (MB 37) she considered 'how deep might be the romance in the lives of some of those who elbowed me daily in the busy streets of the town in which I resided'. The word that catches the attention here is 'elbowed'. A few lines later she naturally metaphorises a general reflection on the state of the working classes into physical gestures:

> At present they seem to me to be left in a state, wherein lamentations and tears are thrown aside as useless, but in which the lips are compressed for curses, and the hands clenched and ready to smite. (MB 38)

These passages are the work of a writer who almost unconsciously thinks poetically; the intimate physicality of gesture, humanising and bringing close to us all those faceless crowds who are our 'neighbours' is crucial to the meaning of *Mary Barton*. Neighbourliness is suggested in the opening chapter when 'Wilson expressed a wish that they were still the near neighbours they once had been' (MB 46) and suggests Alice might drop in to keep Mrs Barton company. A few chapters later the concept assumes its more specific Christian meaning when, as we have seen, Wilson and Barton go to relieve the suffering of the Davenports. The suffering is particularly focused, here and elsewhere in the book, on children. Some of the impetus towards writing the book came from the words of a millworker, who asked her 'have you ever seen a child clemm'd to death?' and the question must surely have associated itself in her mind with the images of the suffering child she had recently experienced in the loss of her own nine-month-old son from scarlet fever. In a letter written to Elizabeth Holland in 1841 she observed that the 'greatest \ & only / happiness' of a 'helpless child' . . . 'is in having a body free from pain' (L 41). In the Davenports' filthy den the image of the child is far from that of conventional piety or sentiment:

> In that dim light, which was darkness to strangers, they clustered round Barton, and tore from him the food he had brought with him. It was a huge hunch of bread, but it had vanished in an instant. (MB 98)

Driven by hunger, these children respond as animals. The fact of hunger is crucial to this novel of the 'Hungry Forties', and it bears a human face in the children who cry aloud for bread 'in their young impatience of suffering' (MB 96). The eloquence of this phrase is not merely rhetorical. As Dostoevsky recognised, there is something specially terrible in the suffering of children. They 'have not eaten of the apple' as Ivan says in *The Brothers Karamazov*, and their lack of experience to understand their human lot distresses us more. The children's 'young impatience' has no defence against hunger which adults could, and did, train themselves to endure. 'I've seen a father who had killed his child rather than let it clem before his eyes; and he were a tender-hearted man', says John Barton (MB 239), and specifically refers to the innocence of suffering children as the barrier between the working man and self-annihilation:

> We want it for daily bread, for life itself; and not for our own lives neither (for there's many a one here, I know by myself, as would be glad and thankful to lie down and die out o' this weary world), but for the lives of them little ones, who don't know yet what life is, and are afeard of death. (MB 239)

Like Dostoevsky again, Mrs Gaskell presents men and women at the extreme of suffering, at which point only the most radical of human responses apply – despair and hatred, or compassion. If the nineteenth-century English writer is not capable of the transcendent insight of her Russian contemporary, she does oblige her characters to live out the implications of an existence on the edge of death by starvation.

Mary Barton, preoccupied with her own troubles, meets a little Italian boy on the street who appeals to her with the words 'Hungry! so hungry' and points to his mouth 'with its white quivering lips' to enforce his plea:

> Mary answered him impatiently,
> 'Oh, lad, hunger is nothing – nothing!'
> And she rapidly passed on. But her heart upbraided her the next minute with her unrelenting speech, and she hastily entered her door and seized the scanty remnant of food which the cupboard contained, and retraced her steps to the place where the little hopeless stranger had sunk down by his mute companion in loneliness and starvation. (MB 284)

The encounter presents us with a paradoxical crux very typical of Mrs Gaskell. To the adult, wrestling with the torment of a guilty conscience, hunger is indeed 'nothing'. To the child, physically starving, it is all. And Mary responds to that pitiful call upon her charity. The boy, 'with the elasticity of heart belonging to childhood' soon recovers his spirits and thanks Mary with natural grace. For Mary, spiritual release is only temporary; the soul's hunger for spiritual solace cannot be so easily satisfied as the bodily pangs of starvation. Yet troubled though she is within, the outward action may be her security for that final soul's peace she is seeking, when· her deed is registered in Heaven:

> The vices of the poor sometimes astound us *here*; but when the secrets of all hearts shall be made known, their virtues will astound us in far greater degree. Of this I am certain. (MB 96)

The immediacy of association between human succour and Heavenly judgement is of course sanctioned by Christ himself:

> Inasmuch as ye have done it unto one of the least of these my brethren, ye have done it unto me.[2]

More specifically bread itself as 'the staff of life' has a powerful mythic status through the Lord's Prayer, the feeding of the
five thousand and of course the Last Supper. Mary goes on,
absorbed in her own woes, feeling she has done only an act of
physical charity, but the episode, like bread itself, has a physical, mortal and a spiritual dimension. The same sense of contingency and absoluteness informs many of the most powerful
moments of a book which relies for a substantial part of its
power on crises. For much of the time, indeed, when we read
Mary Barton there seems little intermediate space between what
people do now at this particular moment, and that state out of
all time, at which we shall be judged eternally. Speaking of
the impossibility of 'read[ing] the lot of those who daily pass
by you in the street' (MB 101) Mrs Gaskell tells us:

> You may push against one, humble and unnoticed, the last
> upon earth, who in Heaven will forever be in the immediate
> light of God's countenance. (MB 101–2)

John Barton, reading only the immediate impression, is con-
sumed with hate, for he is filled with a different absolute –
the divide between rich and poor, Dives and Lazarus. Yet even
in his citation of the parable the 'now' and 'then' is invoked,
and he spells out the importance of seeing events in the sight
of God when he speaks to the policeman on his ill-fated journey to London as a Chartist:

> 'Which business is of most consequence i' the sight o' God,
> think yo', ou'n or them grand ladies and gentlemen as yo
> think so much on?' (MB 144)

As I have suggested in my introduction, Elizabeth Gaskell is
not the woman to see life as something simply to be transcended.
Eternity is not an escape. Her realism listens for the echo of
eternity which will reinforce a commitment to the mortal; we
are, as it were, in the eye of God, and this elevates all our
actions to a divine commitment, a transcendent value. The very
brevity of the moment, the transience of the word, means that
they take on an absoluteness of their own. There is a structure

of intense moments, of confrontations, informing this novel – between neighbours, masters and men, adult and child, murderer and the father of the victim, chartists and government. It is one aspect of *Mary Barton's* immediacy and abruptness – the sense of a foreshortening of life which delineates people, passions and actions with a stark intensity unlike any of her other novels. One need only consider for a moment the contrast with her other novel of contemporary Manchester life, *North and South*, to see that there is a special knowledge of suffering in *Mary Barton* that comes from an imagination which has put itself into the lives of another class. However sympathetic Margaret may be to the Higginses, she ensures that her point-of-view remains outside with the genteel poor who have the leisure to complain of a hideous wallpaper in their new lodgings. The foreshortening we feel in *Mary Barton* is in part a literal foreshortening of time, because even when immediate succour is not necessary to prevent starvation, as in the case of the Davenports, there is a general uncertainty, often a daily uncertainty, about life; quite literally, daily bread may not be given. The point is in fact a very telling social corrective. It was a frequent complaint that the workers were improvident. The immediacy of need, the foreshortening imposed by necessity, shows such a view to be an error of perspective. It is well brought out by contrast with the Carson household, whose easy relaxedness, late hours, long breakfasts and idle reading of reviews and newspapers contrasts with the urgency of Wilson's errand for an Infirmary order, and the intensity of his hunger.

The temporal foreshortening of the lives of the poor is matched by a physical enclosure. The novel opens with a holiday in fields outside Manchester. The images evoked in the preliminary description of the countryside suggest a past age of the 'old black-and-white farmhouse, with its rambling outbuildings, [speaking] of other times and other occupations than those which now absorb the population of the neighbourhood' (MB 39). There are gardens 'crowded with a medley of old-fashioned herbs and flowers, planted long ago, when the garden was the only druggist's shop within reach, and allowed to grow in scrambling and wild luxuriance'. (40) It is spring, and nature is trembling on the edge of rebirth. The freedom and potential are associated with things which, for the millworkers at least, are past and gone. They return to nature as strangers, holiday-makers from their normal lives of urban enclosure. I do not suggest that Mrs Gaskell is being sentimentally romantic about a lost Eden; her picture of the rural poor in *North and South* would give the lie to such an idea. But there is an obvious contrast between this half-day of freedom which opens the book and the gradually intensifying enclosure of starvation, despair and murder which follows, and out of which some of the leading figures escape at the end to an absolutely new and distant land, empty of all associations, good and bad.

As an image of the narrow and oppressive lives led in Man-chester's streets and mills the idea of enclosure is so obvious as to need no elaboration. It images, in this capacity, the more general sense of immediacy and confrontation I have already mentioned, and as a highly-charged mood connects the pres-sure of Mary's urgent search for Will Wilson with the urgency of the socio-political themes of the novel. The confrontation between Harry Carson and Jem Wilson, so nearly fatal to the latter, takes place in a narrrow, enclosed lane:

> in passing along a lane . . . he encountered Harry Carson, the only person, as far as he saw beside himself, treading the unfrequented path. Along one side ran a high broad fence, blackened over by coal-tar, and spiked and stuck with pointed nails at the top, to prevent anyone from climbing over into the garden beyond. . . . On the other side of the way was a dead brick wall; and a field after that, where there was a saw-pit, and joiner's shed. (MB 226)

The wall with its spikes suggests the restraints imposed by authority upon these urban dwellers – an authority biased towards the privileged, as the action of the policeman in the subsequent scuffle demonstrates. The narrowness of the way forces the young males to face each other in a bitter clash of class and interests from which there is no way out except mutual violence. When lots are drawn for the choice of who is to murder Carson, the light is extinguished, and in their separate worlds of darkness each man chooses a lot known only to himself:

The gas was extinguished; each drew out a paper. The gas was relighted. Then each went as far as he could from his fellows, and examined the paper he had drawn without saying a word, and with a countenance as stony and immovable as he could make it.

Then, still rigidly silent, they each took up their hats and went every one his own way. (MB 241–2)

As with the meeting in the lane, there is a feeling of inevitability in this secret choice of personal destiny, and the loneliness of the choice foreshadows the loneliness of the burden to be borne by the murderer. Unsociability would seem to be almost the ultimate curse for Mrs Gaskell, if we think of Margaret Hale's comments on 'sending to Coventry' in *North and South*:

'Why!' said Margaret, 'what tyranny this is! Nay, Higgins, I don't care one straw for your anger. I know you can't be angry with me if you would, and I must tell you the truth: that I never read, in all the history I have read, of a more slow, lingering torture than this.' (NS 232)

In *Mary Barton* the individual concern is constantly threatening to overpower the sociable. Man is set against man, even woman against woman (Mary and Sally Leadbitter, Mary and Mrs Wilson). The ultimate confrontation, murder itself, is the violent reversal of master and man, unmitigated by any distance or detachment, no words spoken, even of mutual recrimination. Again it takes place in a narrow way 'lonely and unfrequented' (261). The policeman remarks that the murderer 'must have been close upon him'. (261) The importance of an intensity of human contact, whether for good or ill, is absolutely characteristic of Mrs Gaskell. For if closeness may mean enclosure and confrontation, it can also mean warmth and sociability. The Bartons and Wilsons, returning from their half-holiday, in the opening chapter, agree to share a meal together, and in the generosity of hospitable plenty invite Alice Wilson from her cellar room. The first act of the returning master of the house is to bring light and warmth into darkness by breaking up the coal on the fire to produce 'warm and glowing light in every corner of the room', as he and Wilson later bring light and warmth to the Davenports. It is the lack of warmth, light and food that characterise Barton's outcast state when he has committed the murder. Now, in these happier times, a strong feeling of simple human pleasure is evoked by the shared meal. The foreshortening of expectations is now seen as a cause of spontaneity, sharing and making-do:

'Run, Mary dear, just round the corner, and get some fresh eggs at Tipping's (you may get one a-piece, that will be five-pence), and see if he has any nice ham cut, that he would let us have a pound of.'

'Say two pounds, missis, and don't be stingy,' chimed in the husband.

'Well, a pound and a half, Mary.'

The victuals are bought in for the occasion, there is just enough for each person, and yet that enough is sufficient for human happiness. Even old Alice Wilson who 'If she comes . . . must bring a tea-cup and saucer, for we have but half-a-dozen, and here's six of us' and whose worldly possessions can be sum-marised in a few lines, is able to contribute a few nettles for 'spring drink'. As with temporal foreshortening, spatial enclosure is a positive at the Bartons' tea. Crowdedness is warm and hospitable rather than oppressive.

It is from this sociability that John Barton gradually with-draws into silence and solitude. He is a man of intense passions which are steadily frustrated. The words he wields at the be-ginning of the novel are reductive – a series of rhetorical ques-tions and answers that express the impossibility of bridging the gulf between the classes. For a period he is articulate, unit-ing with his fellow-men in action as a Chartist to bring under-standing between the classes, but on his return the pain and bitterness of disappointment deprive him of words

'If yo please, neighbour, I'd rather say nought about that. It's not to be forgotten or forgiven either by me or many another; but I canna tell of our downcasting just as a piece of London news. As long as I live, our rejection that day

will bide in my heart; and as long as I live I shall curse
them as so cruelly refused to hear us; but I'll not speak of it
no more.' (MB 144–5)

From this time onwards he withdraws into a morose self-
absorption interrupted only by mute gestures calling him to
secret meetings:

> for there were not seldom seen sights which haunted her in
> her dreams. Strange faces of pale men, with dark glaring
> eyes, peered into the inner darkness, and semed desirous to
> ascertain if her father were at home. Or a hand and arm (the
> body hidden) was put within the door, and beckoned him
> away. He always went. And once or twice, when Mary was
> in bed, she heard men's voices below, in earnest, whispered
> talk. (MB 162)

After the voice of the gun has spoken, he lapses into almost
complete silence. Having left the sociable world of words he is
reduced to the inarticulate cries of inward torment:

> At night he feebly clambered up stairs to bed; and during
> those long dark hours Mary heard those groans of agony,
> which never escaped his lips by day; when they were com-
> pressed in silence over his inward woe.

Thus he reduces language for himself to a point where the
only form it will be able to take is confessional.

I have dwelt upon this journey from articulacy to silence because, as we shall see in due course, the significance of human
utterance is crucial to Mrs Gaskell's art. 'What a single word
can do' sings Margaret (138) and words are used to heighten
our sense of the moments when a crisis of confrontation occurs – often a confrontation with the self. After she has rejected Jem, Mary reflects on the moment lost, it would seem,
for ever, and regrets her words of but an hour ago:

> It was as if two people were arguing the matter; that mournful,
> desponding communion between her former self and her

present self. Herself, a day, an hour ago; and herself now. For we have every one of us felt how a very few minutes of the months and years called life, will sometimes suffice to place all time past and future in an entirely new light; will make us see the vanity or the criminality of the bye-gone, and so change the aspect of the coming time, that we look with loathing on the very thing we have most desired. A few moments may change our character for life, by giving a totally different direction to our aims and energies. (MB 176)

But the moment is enough to make her see her life clearly and change its direction absolutely – 'in the clear revelation of that past hour, she saw her danger, and turned away, resolutely, and for ever' (177). Jem in turn regrets his rejection of the proffered moment when a word to Esther might have turned her destiny:

He had not done enough to save her. One more effort and she might have come. Nay, twenty efforts would have been well rewarded by her yielding. He turned back, but she was gone. (MB 214)

We have seen how Mary repents of her 'unrelenting speech' to the little Italian boy. The terrible paradox that she may have to expose her father's guilt in order to save her lover is framed as an unthinkable question and answer:

what ought she to do, possessed of her terrible knowledge? Surely not to inculpate her father – and yet – and yet – she almost prayed for the blessed unconsciousness of death or madness, rather than that awful question should have to be answered by her. (MB 311)

And it is in the form of question and answer that she courageously commits herself to Jem in the witness stand:

'And pray, may I ask, which was the favoured lover? You say you knew both these young men. Which was the favoured lover? Which did you prefer?

. . .

suddenly her resolution was taken. The present was everything; the future, that vast shroud, it was maddening to think
upon; but *now* she might own her fault, but *now* she might
even own her love. Now, when the beloved stood thus, ab-
horred of men, there would be no feminine shame to stand
between her and her avowal. (MB 390)

Upon his acquittal Jem, assured of Mary's love, feels how life,
'suddenly bright with all exquisite promises, hung on a breath,
the slenderest gossamer chance'. Upon this time-bound, contingent moment hangs the knowledge that 'her love would soothe
him even in his dying hours'. (399)

Mary's avowal of her love is probably the most striking
example in the book of those immediate crisis points which
include past and present even as they transcend them. It is so
powerful because it is self-defining, bringing together the pragmatic to answer a specific demand, and the eternal. It is a life
commitment in a moment when Mary is in control, words are
available and articulation possible.

Mary's succour of the little Italian boy is not the only instance of a significant encounter with a child. It cannot be co-
incidence that two other major protagonists feel the power of
children to influence their lives. At the very moment when John
Barton is going to commit the murder he meets a lost child:

A child's cry caught his ear. His thoughts were running on
little Tom; on the dead and buried child of happier years.
He followed the sound of wail, that might have been *his*,
and found a poor little mortal, who had lost his way, and
whose grief had choked up his thoughts to the single want,
'Mammy, mammy'. With tender address, John Barton soothed
the little laddie, and with beautiful patience he gathered fragments of meaning from the half spoken words which came
mingled with sobs from the terrified little heart. (MB 251)

The epithet 'poor little *mortal*' suggests a common humanity,
his grief 'chok[ing] up his thoughts to one single want' speak
of immediate self-absorption, and it is, like his daughter, im-

mediate relief that Barton brings, calling on the memory of his own dead child. Thus past associations combine with present want in the form of an act of 'beautiful patience'. The child's mother, on his restoration, bestows 'an eloquent Irish blessing', to which Barton shakes his head and proceeds on his way, but the blessing reminds of the eternal home in which his act will be given its true worth. The episode is a part of what he is, what he is making himself, of the values which confer on him value as a human being, just as much as the frightful act of unnatural violence he is on his way to commit.

Mr Carson also meets a child, but in his case he is a watcher rather than participator in the action. The incident occurs after he has left Barton, prostrated by the effort of confession and all the weight of guilt he has borne for so long, but above all crushed by Mr Carson's blasphemous words and the 'blasphemous action' conveyed by them: 'Let my trespasses be unforgiven, so that I may have vengeance for my son's murder' (436). He tries to regain his balance of mind, in which he can remain satisfied with his own justness, and witnesses a little scene in which a delicate 'fairy child' is knocked down by an unheeding 'rough, rude errand-boy'. The child's nurse threatens the boy with the police, and he, though looking 'hard and defying' is terrified at the threat. At this point the little girl intervenes, not only pleading for her injurer, but putting up her mouth to his to be kissed. But the words which strike home to Carson are 'He did not know what he was doing.' At home he finds the words of Christ of which the girl's are an unconscious echo, and is changed in his resolve.

If, as a Unitarian, she could not accept the divinity of Christ, Mrs Gaskell felt the human example of his ministry on her own pulses, as it were, and found in the Gospels a ready-made fund of images for the values of the human heart. The incident of Mr Carson's 'conversion' is the climax of a pattern of Christian and Biblical reference that inform the whole book, from bread to the widow's mite to Dives and Lazarus to admitting strangers to one's house (379) and innumerable casual references besides. John Barton bears the curse of Cain, but is redeemed – in part by his own fundamentally compassionate nature and in part by the Christ-inspired forgiveness of his chief accuser. The two are brought together as father and child, one cradling the other in his arms. Physical closeness finally expresses not confrontation but tenderness. By contrast with the gentle enfolding of the embrace, the characteristic human gesture of *Mary Barton* is the tight grasp – the 'hand clenched' of the Preface. As Davenport passes from delirium into death he finds a gesture more eloquent than the words he has lost:

> He could not speak again. The trump of the archangel would set his tongue free; but not a word more would it utter till then. Yet he heard, he understood, and though sight failed, he moved his hand gropingly over the covering. They knew what he meant, and guided it to her head, bowed and hidden in her hands, when she had sunk in her woe. It rested there, with a feeble pressure of endearment. (MB 110–11)

His handgrasp, which symbolises farewell, is also the relaxation of that tenacious grip on life which even the poor at the end of their physical and mental endurance possess. Esther holds fast in her hand the piece of paper she feels might implicate Jem in the murder:

> And ever and always she clenched the scrap of paper which might betray so much, until her nails had deeply indented the palm of her hand; so fearful was she in her nervous dread, lest unawares she should let it drop. (MB 291)

Mrs Wilson holds the summons to attend Jem's trial as a witness in an iron grip:

> 'What is this? Will you tell me?'
> 'Yo'd better give it me at once, Mrs. Wilson, and let me put it out of your sight. – Speak to her, Mary, wench, and ask for a sight on it; I've tried, and better-tried to get it from her, and she takes no heed of words, and I'm loth to pull it by force out of her hands.' (MB 325–6)

And Mary in court clutches the iron rail before her:

Mary never let go her clutched hold on the rails. She wanted them to steady her, in that heaving, whirling court. She thought the feeling of something hard compressed within her hand would help her to listen, for it was such pain, such weary pain in her head, to strive to attend to what was being said. (MB 393)

All are instances of how the living hold on to life, and the metaphor characterises the desperate extremeness of that state in *Mary Barton*. Death itself is frequently defined by the desires of the living, as when Mary is told that the second of Mrs Wilson's twins cannot die as long as his mother is 'wishing' him.

The hold of the living upon the dying, of contingency upon eternity is an appropriate note on which to turn to an alternative dimension in the novel. Were I to leave the reader with the impression of a work of crises and confrontations, imaged by 'lips . . . compressed' and 'hands clenched' I would be ignoring its full significance. In her long short story 'A Dark Night's Work' Elizabeth Gaskell characterises the variety of individuals' lives as follows:

There are some people who imperceptibly float away from their youth into middle age, and thence pass into declining life with the soft and gentle motion of happy years. There are others who are whirled, in spite of themselves, down dizzy rapids of agony away from their youth at one great bound, into old age with another sudden shock; and thence into the vast calm ocean where there are no shore-marks to tell of time. (DNW 115)

The duality is not exactly parallel with the action of *Mary Barton*, but it suggests a counterpoint in the earlier novel which places a life of crises against a more relaxed and reflective journey, both being finally assimilated in that state which is beyond the measures of time, whether abrupt or leisurely. *Mary Barton* is far from being a book of unrelieved anguish. We have already seen the Barton family in happy comfort with their neighbours, relaxing in bustle and hospitality, and there are other interludes, such as Margaret's beautiful singing, or the breath of the sea that comes with Will Wilson. There is, too, a repeated pattern of reconciliation which balances the confrontational scenes – reconciliation between Mary and Mrs Wilson, Mary and Job and Margaret, Mary and her father. They all act as pointers to that supreme confrontation and reconciliation between Barton and Carson.

Two older characters in particular carry the burden of a more measured rhythm, punctuating the intensity of much of the novel's action. Job Legh is an unlooked-for, but evidently not uncommon representative of the working classes – a self-educated amateur scientist. His quiet, ruminative presence is an alternative to the precipitate events in the story around him. Mary's words 'Dear Job Legh!' spoken 'softly and seriously' close the book. When John Barton has given his report from London, full of bitter recriminations, Job comes to the rescue of the shocked and dispirited audience with an account of his own trip to London with his friend, and their return bearing a little baby. It is a tale comic and pathetic together, circumstantial narrative with an appeal to human sympathy. It reveals the humanity of the teller and the actors in it, and is an assurance of the providential trust in human nature which underpins Mrs Gaskell's writing.

That providence is given a special articulation in the person of Alice Wilson, whose eyes close upon the world after a life of quiet, faithful service. The transcendent serenity of her old age and death again counterbalances the struggle for daily survival. The opening holiday in the fields is a glimpse of the inheritance the workers have lost – a prelapsarian idyll from which they return into imperfection. Only occasionally thereafter do Mary and John, Jem and Mrs Wilson, Job and Mr Carson and all the other sufferers see this peace, reflected in death. Alice's life, poor and unmarried, uprooted from the country since her childhood, has been a kind of coda to that childhood, a patient attendance upon the call of the Lord. The absolute and the contingent have come to a truce in her life, as she explains how her return to the idyll was constantly scotched by the practicalities of everyday life:

'Why have you never been in all these many years?' asked Mary.

'Why, lass! first one wanted me and then another; and I could not go without money either, and I got very poor at times. Tom was a scapegrace, poor fellow, and always wanted help of one kind or another; and his wife . . . was but a helpless kind of body. She were always ailing, and he were always in trouble; so I had enough to do with my hands and my money too, for that matter. (MB 70)

She was once about to 'go home for good and all' to live with some cousins on a farm, but 'Little did I think how God Almighty would baulk me, for not leaving my days in His hands, who had led me through the wilderness hitherto' (117–18). Serene in her faith, she tells Margaret 'an anxious mind is never a holy mind' (84) and that 'the Lord is against planning'. That faith is rewarded when her nephew returns from the sea before her death, yet her way of life cannot be shared by most other characters, for whom 'life' is family life, and living it is the constant compromise of hopes, defeats, wishes and anxieties. And yet that intimation of the transcendent which Alice's presence represents never quite leaves the consciousness of other sufferers. It is there even at the moment of Davenport's death in his squalid cellar. Death is the sleep in which Job leaves his 'blessed child' when he returns with the baby from London. It is Alice's return at last to the home she left so long ago, and the security of childhood. Mary reflects on how changed Alice's real home in the country would now be, but the 'blind and deaf' old woman has already withdrawn to her eternal home. Blindness seems to give an inward sight, as with Margaret, who has greater serenity for the loss of vision, troubled perhaps by one less of the physical connections with the world. In the same way, as Jem explains to Margaret, the living can be close to the dead when they are 'falling off to sleep or very quiet and still' (412).

In terms of its social and political implications *Mary Barton* is scarcely a revolutionary book, despite the outrage of some of its first readers. Egalitarianism is dismissed as 'absurdity':

'You mean he was an Owenite; all for equality, and community of goods, and that kind of absurdity.'

'No, no! John Barton was no fool. No need to tell him that were all men equal to-night, some would get the start by rising an hour earlier to-morrow. (MB 455)

It is taken for granted that market forces must prevail in human affairs:

'Now, how in the world can we help it? We cannot regulate the demand for labour. No man or set of men can do it. It depends on events which God alone can control. When there is no market for our goods, we suffer just as much as you can do.' (MB 456)

But here comes the sticking-place as far as the author is concerned. The poor suffer in their bodies, not in the fall of capital, and the central thrust of the book is an intense evocation of bodily living. As her most committed and occasional work, addressed to the problems of a time and place she knew well, *Mary Barton* might be simply categorised as 'social realism'. What I have suggested is that insofar as it is a great work of 'social realism' it is such not because of its account of institutions or conditions of life and labour. We scarcely see anyone at work; some houses are described, but pleasant domestic conditions are almost as common as appalling ones. The weight of the book, as with all Mrs Gaskell's fictions, is carried in human values, and the particular, tangible object is always informed with a metaphoric potential that has a universalising tendency. Bread, light and fire bear the implication of all human sociability, deprivation of these things is a deprivation of humanity. Pity for children is pity for all suffering, and reflects Christ's compassion. John Barton is Cain, with all men's hands against him, but he is also confused and embittered Man, refused his fellows' sympathy. 'Still, facts have proved and are daily proving', says Mr Carson, 'how much better it is for every man to be independent of help, and self-reliant' (457). But Job says, 'Now to my thinking, them that is strong in any of God's gifts is meant to help the weak, – be hanged to the facts!' (457).

That Job Legh can reject the principle of self-help in favour of mutual support, putting the hunger for human love before worldly ambition, 'goods and wealth' and social equality is dependent as an idea on the whole story's articulation of human values. The poetic embodiment of the discovery and creation of these values is the real 'truth' of *Mary Barton*.

2

'So runs the round of life from day to day': *Wives and Daughters* and Comic Realism

Wives and Daughters is a *tour de force* of comic realism. Its unmistakably comic quality is easily detected in the frequently ironic narrative mode, the focus of interest on romantic love, culminating in the heroine's (imminent) marriage to the man she has long admired in secret, in the breadth of social perspective and the emphasis on manners as the principal formal medium of the book.

But this is not easy comedy, relaxing us into laughter and reassuring us of a general providential wellbeing. Realism and comedy react upon each other to suggest special values which deny despair, but evade any easy solution to the problems of daily living. Moral realism suggests the intractability of such problems; moral comedy indicates compromise with the intractable. Below all is a palpable rhythm of comedy, expectant and expansive, despite fears and disappointments, informing the whole novel. This rhythm, which takes its measure from the triumphs and reversals of days lived outside catastrophe, is felt as a kind of overture in the first two chapters. Molly is here a child of twelve, so excited by the prospect of her first visit to the Hall that she is awake before six in the morning, wishing the time away so that she may begin this most wonderful day. But by evening, when her beloved father comes to take her home, she must say, 'I shall never forget the morning in that garden. But I was never so unhappy in all my life, as I have been all this long afternoon' (WD 26). In between she has been overwhelmed by experiences that seem nothing to the adult world, but are deeply disturbing to the shy, uncertain, home-loving child. At first she sees nothing but an unbroken expanse of landscape from the park:

> if there were divisions and ha-has between the soft sunny sweeps of grass, and the dark gloom of the forest-trees beyond, Molly did not see them; and the melting away of exquisite cultivation into the wilderness had an inexplicable charm to her. (11)

Such is the secure child's happy view of its future life. In her mind there is no clear dividing-line between reality and fantasy. She wanders away and falls asleep in an enchanted garden, wakening to find herself among strangers – one of them 'the most beautiful person she had ever seen' (13). They give her food and drink, but when she awakes, the enchanted world has darkened. Her friends have left, her father cannot know where she is, she may have to sleep in a strange bed. The inhabitants of this world are threatening, and she does not have the key to defusing their anger:

> Lord Cumnor caught the words and the tone.
> 'Oh, ho!' said he. 'Are you the little girl who has been sleeping in my bed?'
> He imitated the deep voice of the fabulous bear, who asks this question of the little child in the story; but Molly had never read the 'Three Bears,' and fancied that his anger was real. (19–20)

Above all, she feels she is an intruder, who has no right or place in this world. When her father arrives to rescue her the reaction is extreme but understandable:

> She threw her arms round her father's neck. 'Oh, papa, papa, papa! I am so glad you have come!' and then she burst out crying, stroking his face almost hysterically as if to make sure he was there. (23)

It is the cry of the child escaping from a nightmare, and relieved beyond belief to find its usual life still there, secure and stable. Molly is on the edge of the divide between childhood and experience. Is the future a dream or a nightmare? The mornings of our lives may be serene, but the afternoon brings the disturbance and problems of maturity, together with intimations of that unknown night we must all eventually face. From this fearful wonder the child is rescued by her father, but when that father is no longer all that is secure, or may even prove our betrayer, then we must discover and create our own security, in order that we may grow and face the world.

Molly's intense disappointment after the morning's promise of fulfilment of her greatest desires sets the tone for much of human experience in the rest of the novel. Mr Gibson professes himself disappointed with Mr Coxe, Mr Coxe is disappointed at the failure of his suit to Molly, and later to Cynthia. Cynthia herself is a disappointment to those who know her abilities. Both parties are disappointed in the marriage of Mr Gibson to Mrs Kirkpatrick, though he more than her, since his is the greater imaginative intelligence. Osborne disappoints his father in almost every way, but on a larger scale it might be felt that the whole Hamley clan is disappointed. They have a kind of household or genetic tiredness which Molly feels the first time she dines with them. There is an answer to this, of course, in Roger, the new lover and New Man; the rescuer of his father's name and estate, who brings fresh stock and vital ideas of the world as it is in the mid-century. For others there remains only compromise with what cannot be altered. The pragmatism which this involves is one of the most notable features of the book's pervasive comic mood. It is embraced by most of the leading characters at one time or another, though with varying degrees of satisfaction. A brief but interesting exchange will illustrate how the central character views the matter.

After her first outburst against her father's remarriage, Molly must try to live with a situation she does not like, but which is now a reality – the engagement of her beloved father to a woman whom Molly would find unsympathetic under any circumstances. As she reflects on her misfortune Roger Hamley appears, as he did once before at such a crisis, and gives her his usual sensible advice: 'It is difficult . . . but by-and-by you will be so much happier for it' (139). In reply, Molly asserts:

> 'It will be very dull when I shall have killed myself, as it were, and live only in trying to do, and to be, as other people like. I don't see any end to it. I might as well have never lived. And as for the happiness you speak of, I shall never be happy again.' (139)

She counters Roger's suggestion that 'perhaps in ten years' time you will be looking back on this trial as a very light one' (140) with the reflection which has given its title to the present study:

> 'I daresay it seems foolish; perhaps all our earthly trials will appear foolish to us after a while; perhaps they seem so now to angels. But we are ourselves, you know, and this is now, not some time to come, a long, long way off. And we are not angels, to be comforted by seeing the ends for which everything is sent.' (140)

The immediate implication is that we should not live our lives in the context of eternity but, as Roger remarks a little later, as 'a mass of trials, which will only have to be encountered one by one, little by little' (140).

No English novel of the nineteenth century conveys this truth so thoroughly in its form as *Wives and Daughters*. Its texture is dense with the daily trivia of human intercourse upon which lives turn. It is part of Mrs Gaskell's genius to make every nuance of mood, tone and gesture a significant part of that 'little by little' process Roger describes.

At this moment of truth between heroine and lover-to-be, they stand 'steadily looking at each other' and Roger loses 'the sense of what she [is] saying in the sensation of pity for her'. Such moments are striking in this novel, because they are not common. The cataclysmic confrontation or public revelation of the self which marks a good deal of her early work is not found here. Much of the human intercourse is evasive, not directly communicative, in a book which is filled with secrecy. Such secrecy is not necessarily bad. It is prized by Molly and her father as a kind of intimacy. As they ride home from her childhood escapade at the Towers

> He rode close up alongside of her: he was not sure but what she might be afraid of riding in the dark shadows, so he laid his hand upon hers.
> 'Oh! I am so glad to feel you,' squeezing his hand hard. 'Papa, I should like to get a chain like Ponto's, just as long as your longest round, and then I could fasten us two to each end of it, and when I wanted you I could pull. (24–5)

But in many more cases secrecy suggests a moral failing, or at least a confusion. The most manifest example is, of course, Osborne's concealment of his marriage. Preston and Cynthia share a secret into which Molly is drawn, albeit innocently. Mrs Kirkpatrick is, as might be expected, deeply implicated in secrecy, since she is constantly concealing feelings and motives – about her personal circumstances, her desire to exclude her daughter from her wedding, in living by 'principles' when in fact she is fundamentally unprincipled. The ladies of Hollingford are fond of secrets as a source of gossip. Mr Coxe, the student, attempts a clandestine affair with Molly, only to be intercepted and told to bury his feelings by the sternly sceptical doctor. But is that would-be paragon of rationality, Mr Gibson, who says that, unlike Cynthia he 'hates mysteries', so clear and decisive in his judgement of others, free of the taint of secrecy? Assuredly not. His feelings are secret – he 'rarely betrayed what was passing in his heart'. And if the realisation of the mistake he has made in his second marriage is not the most tragic secret in the book it is perhaps the most painful, and certainly the least tractable. In attempting to evade the fact that he, the rational judge of human value, has thrown himself away upon a shallow woman, he convinces himself of the doubtful truth that his daughter will benefit, and indeed alienates himself from that daughter with a kind of stubborn self-justification, over-riding her feelings and sacrificing a dear servant to his own pride. The way in which self-evasion and secrecy are the very stuff of intercourse in this book cannot be better illustrated than in the manner of Mr Gibson's revelation of his engagement to Molly. His true feelings have already been sufficiently hinted at only half an hour after his proposal, in a Freudian slip, responding to his new fiancée's complaint that her first husband 'did so dislike the notion of second marriages':

> 'Let us hope that he does not know, then; or that, if he does know, he is wiser – I mean, that he sees how second marriages may be most desirable and expedient in some cases.' (111)

and he thinks 'that his daughter would require sympathy . . .' (112). He comes upon her sleeping and takes her hand in his, feeling full of love:

> She opened her eyes, that for one moment had no recognition in them. Then the light came brilliantly into them and she sprang up, and threw her arms round his neck, exclaiming, –
> 'Oh, papa, my dear, dear papa! What made you come while I was asleep? I love the pleasure of watching for you.'
> Mr. Gibson turned a little paler than he had been before. (113)

There is an instant implication of something unusual – that he is, as it were, encompassing her, when previously the reverse had been the case. She pulls her hand away to turn his head so that he 'should exactly see the very bit [of sky] she meant'. In doing so she disarms him of the kind of intimacy he had wanted and controls his attention outwards rather than in upon themselves. He feels the awkwardness of his position, but determines to 'plunge on', capturing her hand again. .But she anticipates his news. ' "You're going to be married again," said she, helping him out, with a quiet dry voice, and gently drawing her hand out of his' (114).

The withdrawal of the hand belies the help she is giving him. It is an instance of one of the most significant details in this and many other scenes. We have observed how the child Molly's hand is sought in the darkness by her father, and she

in return grips his hand. Touch is here a more speaking gesture than any words. It suggests a special intimacy. Mrs
Kirkpatrick, standing with Molly before Lady Cumnor, 'fondled
her hand more perseveringly than ever, hoping thus to express
a sufficient amount of sympathy to prevent her from saying
anything injudicious' (136). But Molly is not deceived by the
gesture: 'the caress had become wearisome to Molly, and only
irritated her nerves. She took her hand out of Mrs Kirkpatrick's,
with a slight manifestation of impatience' (136). The author
applies to their later handholding together as they walk round
the garden the ludicrous description 'like the babes in the wood'.
When returning from his honeymoon, Mr Gibson takes his
daughter's hand while at the same time helping his wife de-
scend from the coach, suggesting his divided loyalty and his
attempt to bridge the gap. Squire Hamley shakes the new bride's
hand with the fervour of direct honesty. Molly takes Cynthia's
'passive hand and [strokes] it softly – a mode of caressing that
had come down to her from her mother' (344). But when final
honesty is required, she takes the girl's two hands and faces
her directly, 'holding her off a little, the better to read her face',
as she asks her step-sister if she truly loves Roger (a directness Cynthia evades) (395). When, finally, Cynthia is about to
be married, she implies the depth of her feeling for Molly by
taking her hand 'in a very quiet way', an action which brings
her closer to Lady Harriet than they had ever been before (644).
By contrast Mr Gibson grasps Molly's wrists in his anger at
the suspicions she has allowed to fall upon her reputation:

> He had taken hold of her two arms just above her wrists, as
> she had first advanced towards him; he was unconscious of
> this action; but, as his impatience for her words grew upon
> him, he grasped more and more tightly in his vice-like hands,
> till she made a little involuntary sound of pain. (543)

Imaging, as it were, the social secrecy of the book, is a pervasive sense that the dialogue is not conveying direct intelligence or emotion, but is a means of evasion, concealment, coded
messages. This is not merely the idle chatter of Mrs Gibson,
largely beside the point, or the imbecilities of her politeness,

or indeed the soporific use made of Molly's voice by her step-mother: 'If you will talk to me, the sound of your voice will soon send me off' (180). Molly finds herself dissembling to her friends and hosts the Hamleys concerning that very stepmother, 'her loyalty to her father forbidding her to reply fully and truth-fully' (153), and also to the Miss Brownings over the curtains they have ordered, since 'in the first renewing of their love Molly could not bear to contradict [them]' (156). Her telling Roger of her father's forthcoming marriage is an impulse she never anticipated: 'She could not have said why she told him this; an instant before she spoke, she had no intention of do-ing so' (119). She finds herself concealing her concern for one person in order not to give herself away to another:

> Her father's depression, which was still continuing and ren-dering him very silent, made her uneasy; yet she wished to conceal it from Mr. Preston; and so she talked away, trying to obviate the sort of personal bearing which their host would give to everything. (160)

Or is caught between pleasure and a sense of duty, her indeci-sion rendered in a question:

> 'Then I may go?' said Molly, sparkling with the idea of see-ing her dear Mrs. Hamley again, yet afraid of appearing too desirous of leaving her kind old friends. (172)

Mixed emotions are very common, as in this exchange between Mr Gibson and Cynthia:

> 'Well, well, we'll not talk of such gloomy things, and you shall have some sweet emulsion to disguise the taste of the bitters I shall be obliged to fall back upon.'
> 'Please, don't. If you but knew how I dislike emulsions and disguises! I do want bitters – and if I sometimes – if I'm obliged to – if I'm not truthful myself, I do like truth in others – at least, sometimes.' She ended her sentence with another smile, but it was rather faint and watery. (327)

The whole manner of Mr Gibson's arriving at matrimony is something done almost by default rather than direct communication. First he is provoked by the poor showing his household makes when he gives a scratch lunch to Lord Hollingford, and feels he might do worse than find a second wife. On the day of proposal Mrs Kirkpatrick's belief that he might offer is apparently dashed when he seems to be speaking only of medical matters, unaware that he has made up his mind even as she is speaking, because:

> her voice was so soft, her accent so pleasant, that it struck him as particularly agreeable after the broad country accent he was perpetually hearing. Then the harmonious colours of her dress, and her slow and graceful movements, had something of the same soothing effect upon his nerves that a cat's purring has upon some people's. (107)

The very moment when the irrevocable deed is done is permeated with doubt, uncertainty and an intellectual self-awareness that counterpoint Mr Gibson's lover-like stance:

> There! he had done it – whether it was wise or foolish – he had done it; but he was aware that the question as to its wisdom came into his mind the instant that the words were said past recall.
>
> . . .
>
> 'My dear – my dearest,' said he, trying to soothe her with word and caress but, just at the moment, uncertain what name he ought to use.
>
> . . .
>
> 'We ought to tell Lady Cumnor,' said he, thinking, perhaps, more of the various duties which lay before him, in consequence of the step he had just taken, than of what his future bride was saying. (109)

Both participants in the scene are hiding something of themselves, and are consequently dismayed when Lady Cumnor reveals that the possibility of their marriage was not confined to the imaginations of the interested parties, but had been the property at least of two other people:

> They were neither of them quite as desirous of further conversation together as they had been before the passage out of Lord Cumnor's letter had been read aloud. (111)

Non-communication is not always such a sign of alienation as it is here and proves to be throughout the marriage. On the subject of that very marriage, Molly and her father attain a kind of negative bond of silence which is the more powerful for the terrible truths they know it conceals:

> 'Nothing, dear, dear papa – nothing now. It is such a comfort to have you all to myself – it makes me happy.'
>   Mr. Gibson knew all implied in these words, and felt that there was no effectual help for the state of things which had arisen from his own act. It was better for them both that they should not speak out more fully. (419)

The bond is, nevertheless, one of unspoken things, and even the straightforward Molly finds herself answering obliquely when she is minded for a moment to speak some home truths to Roger concerning the woman with whom he is infatuated. '"Bitter beer" came into Molly's mind; but what she said was, "And are you coming?"' (256). Fundamentally, however, Molly yearns for straightforwardness and clarity:

> She had always wished to come into direct contact with a love story: here she was, and she only found it very uncomfortable; there was a sense of concealment and uncertainty about it all; and her honest straightforward father, her quiet life at Hollingford, which, even with all its drawbacks, was above-board, and where everybody knew what every body was doing, seemed secure and pleasant in comparison. (220)

It is these qualities she employs to defeat Mr Preston. It is the lonely strength of conscious integrity which enables her to keep silence in the face of a condemnatory society and her beloved father's doubts about her honour. Yet as I have been at pains to suggest, the texture of experience in this novel is peculiarly one of indirectness and concealment in the minutiae of daily intercourse, of oblique rejoinders and truths mutually avoided. Such evasiveness represents the constant and essential compromise of social existence – a comic pragmatism. It is an evasion of the defeat with which the trivial constantly threatens our life in the daily round. How near defeat can be is demonstrated by the repeated occasions on which, feeling the hopelessness of further expenditure of words, people lapse into silence. Roger tells Molly that it is beyond his power to help her as far as facts go, when her father has remarried, and 'it's best not to talk about it again' (121). Mr Gibson feels that there is 'no effectual help for the state of things which had arisen from his own act [in marrying again]. It was better for them both [he and Molly] that they should not speak out more fully' (419). Faced with the fact of Roger's love for Cynthia, Molly 'turn[s] away her head, and was silent; it was of no use combating the truth' (430). Mr Gibson finds himself avoiding 'all actual dissensions with his wife, preferring to cut short a discussion by a sarcasm' (431), and Molly reflects that it seems 'as if there was not, and never could be in this world, any help for the dumb discordancy between her father and his wife' (432). Squire Hamley complains that he and his elder son 'have lost each other's language' (365), graphically capturing the distance that time, culture and personal problems have put between them.

These are the bleakest points of confrontation in a novel whose characteristic note is in a minor key of protest, captured in the frequent appearance of words such as 'querulous', 'petulant', 'plaintively', 'testily', and 'tearful pettishness'. All except the last are applied to Mrs Kirkpatrick, and that last is given to her daughter, but they are part of a mood of complaint which runs through the book. Osborne and the Squire in particular complain of each other in a long-running war of daily misery, aptly summed up in all its wearing triviality by the old butler's complaints about who should berate a lower servant for not attending to the fire. Osborne dismisses the servant's grievance as nonsense, and he in turn is offended, recalling that his dead mistress 'had always a becoming respect for a butler's position, and could have understood how he might be hurt in his mind' (267). The business is painful and ludicrous at the same time, just as Mrs Kirkpatrick's moral vacuousness – ruthlessly exposed in her encounter with her husband over knowledge of Osborne's state of health – is both stupid and comic.

'Realism' for Mrs Gaskell involves a challenging of absolutes which is innately comic. But there is also a recognition of the dimension afforded by absolute principles and ultimate realities when related to a pragmatic life-view. Molly claims that 'we are not angels', applying the epithet to both sexes. And yet for mankind in general, and in a more narrow sense for women alone, the play between angelic and non-angelic, absolute and compromise, is a fertile source of depth and complexity. The other side of the kind of female integrity represented by Molly's untainted refusal to betray her stepsister, despite the sexual suspicions she would normally repudiate with horror, is represented by that stepsister herself. Despite her necessary secrecy with regard to Mr Preston, Cynthia Kirkpatrick is capable of recognising duplicity – perhaps with a sharper eye than her step-sister. She cuts through her mother's pretensions with a ruthlessness which would be cruel if practised on a more imaginative creature. Speaking purely morally it is clear that she wants 'principle', 'steadiness' ('I must be a moral kangaroo' (229)), uprightness (she accuses Molly of being 'pedantically truthful' (230) and is described as 'flexible' in the art of piano-playing (231)). She could not be accused of rigidity, forcedness, artificiality. Cynthia is a more dangerous and intellectually acute version of Sylvia Robson. She shares the Yorkshire girl's ability to make people like her, but in her case it takes the more sexual and compromising form of a desire to please men. If naturalness is a virtue, then Cynthia's attraction of Roger, despite the shallowness of her affection, must be a virtue – in other words the secret, elusive, evasive sexuality by which a woman attracts a man must be approved. But the moon-goddess is a more cold and dangerous figure than is suggested by the sylvan overtones of Sylvia's name.

Molly herself attracts attention from Mr Coxe, but the author is careful to exonerate her from any suggestion of active involvement. Cynthia has charm and animal magnetism for men. Even the sceptical Mr Gibson, whose daughter's reputation has been threatened by Cynthia's exploitation of her step-sister, cannot resist her for long. 'You have the happy gift of making people love you', says Molly, apparently seeing no irony in their having just brought to an 'end the traumatic affair with Mr Preston (633). But her very magnetism is somehow predatory – a part of the 'old Eve'; she is a temptress and she is weak. In common with a number of Mrs Gaskell's heroines, she cannot escape some suggestion of guilt simply by virtue of femaleness. Mary Barton should never have attracted young Mr Carson, but reciprocated Jem's love. Sylvia Robson, more ambiguously, rejects a good man's care and love until it is too late. Both these women, like Ruth, do penance. Cynthia, by contrast, escapes more or less unscathed, her moral evasiveness rescuing her from the kind of confrontation of the self Mrs Gaskell generally reserves for her heroines.

Paradoxically, perhaps, considering her want of principle, the most damning condemnation of Cynthia is her shying away from the moral realism of commitment to an imperfect world. When admonished by Mr Gibson she rushes from the room, locks herself up and refuses to respond, even to Molly. To be judged and found wanting is unthinkable. Mrs Gaskell clearly appreciates the insecurity her upbringing has produced. She wants love and approval, and believes any swerving from such devotion must be a total rejection of herself. Hence she will not compromise, for fear of losing everything:

> 'You have been in fault, and have acted foolishly at first, – perhaps wrongly afterwards; but you don't want your husband to think you faultless?'
> 'Yes, I do,' said Cynthia. 'At any rate, my lover must think me so. And it is just because I do not love him even as so light a thing as I could love, that I feel that I could not bear to have to tell him I'm sorry, and stand before him like a chidden child to be admonished and forgiven.' (577)

She escapes by taking an inferior man, satisfied with what she can grasp rather than the danger of that reach which involves daily struggle with intransigent reality, but which is the only true way to a glimpse of heaven. *She* believes that she, at any rate, ought to be an angel ('heroine' is her own word) but this is a self-excusing withdrawal from the world, not the pursuit of moral idealism. Pragmatism and compromise are not here the product of a self and a life faced, challenged and reflected upon, but of moral cowardice.

Yet Cynthia in some ways is closer *instinctively* to the mystery of reality than is Molly, for all the latter's gritty pragmatism. She is given, as it were, the last word when she tells Molly:

> 'Molly, Roger will marry you! See if it is not so! You two good –'
> But Molly pushed her away with a sudden violence of repulsion. 'Don't!' she said. She was crimson with shame and indignation. 'Your husband this morning! Mine tonight! What do you take him for?'
> 'A man!' smiled Cynthia. (578–9)

Molly's shocked reaction is the conventional response of maiden modesty to the shrewdness of sexual instinct which persuaded Pope to claim that 'every woman is at heart a rake'. Who is to say that Cynthia's wisdom, including its practical counterpart of duplicity and moral compromise is any less 'natural', and to that extent 'absolute' in the sense of deeply true to human nature, than her step-sister's integrity? Molly, like her virtues, seems asexual. Her love is given as a daughter, sister, or even, to Cynthia, as a mother, understanding instinctively what her half-sister has most needed in her life: 'She took Cynthia into her arms with gentle power, and laid her head against her own breast, as if the one had been a mother, and the other a child' (578).

Molly's pragmatism leads her to question any kind of idealism, even prescribed didactic principles. Looking for some argument which would help Molly overcome her distress at the remarriage of her father, Roger tells her a little story, climaxed with the remark that:

'Harriet thought of her father's happiness before she thought of her own' (120).

At that moment, 'Molly needed the bracing', and Roger justifies the words to his mother, who says he should have comforted Molly, with 'I think that if advice is good it's the best comfort' (122). But a few days later, reflecting on her likely future, Molly sees that

> Thinking more of others' happiness than of her own was very fine; but did it not mean giving up her very individuality, quenching all the warm love, the keen desires, that made her herself? Yet in this deadness lay her only comfort; or so it seemed. (138)

And speaking to Roger she repeats the image of self-slaying:

> 'It will be very dull when I shall have killed myself, as it were, and live only in trying to do, and to be, as other people like. I don't see any end to it. I might as well never have lived. And as for the happiness you speak of, I shall never be happy again.' (139)

The idea of putting oneself second is raised a number of times in the book; sometimes proclaimed with fatuous inappropriateness, as when Mrs Gibson takes up the phrase on her own behalf – 'One must not think about oneself, you know' (179) – but often enough when applied to Molly or Mr Gibson to show that it does not result in death for its practitioner. And yet Molly is instinctively, with a typical realism, touching on a truth, namely that total self-abnegation *is* a kind of death for the human being who would practise it in life, and is a denial of the importance of a sense of self ('we are ourselves, you know, and this is now'). It is another example of her rejection of an artificial code which would deny our humanness. She resolves to be as good as she can, but no more than will be an expression of her living personality. It is unnatural to kill oneself.

Death as a reality, rather than an image, is present in this, as in all Mrs Gaskell's works, but its presence feeds back into the metaphor in a complex way. Shortly after Mrs Gibson's glib remark, quoted above, her husband is called out to attend a dying man, and in complete contradiction she wonders that the doctor could not have put off his visit:

> I think your dear papa might have put off his visit to Mr. Craven Smith for just this one evening.'
>   'Mr. Craven Smith couldn't put off his dying,' said Molly, bluntly. (179)

A page later, overcoming her original repugnance to the idea, and endeavouring to please her father, Molly makes a decision about her step-mother:

> All at once she said, –
>   'Papa, I will call her "mamma"!'
>   He took her hand, and grasped it tight; but for an instant or two he did not speak. Then he said, –
>   'You won't be sorry for it, Molly, when you come to lie as poor Craven Smith did tonight.' (181)

This associates death and self-abnegation again, but in a positive way – at least for Mr Gibson. In the context of one's whole life the little act of selflessness will seem worth doing. This does not contradict Molly's pragmatism, but says that it is only at death (that is, in proximity to the angelic state) that we can see all things clearly, the whole pattern of our lives. Thus the 'little, nameless, unremembered acts', as Wordsworth called 'them, are linked in this novel to the final reality of our existence, the apparently trivial to the certainly absolute. In works of major realism, as this is, relative and absolute, changing and unchanging, enhance each other.

Death has two aspects in *Wives and Daughters*. On the one hand it is 'the death of the heart', the state which Molly fears may overtake her if she lives too much for others. It appears again when she understands that Cynthia and Roger are to be engaged:

> For a few minutes her brain seemed in too great a whirl to

comprehend anything but that she was being carried on in
earth's diurnal course, with rocks, and stones, and trees, with
as little volition on her part as if she were dead. (391)

And when she contemplates the future she must lead between
her father and stepmother, understanding the lack of love and
respect on one side and the lack of depth of imagination and
principle on the other:

> Her heart beat more feebly and slower; the vivifying stimu-
> lant of hope – even unacknowledged hope – was gone out
> of her life. (432)

This contingent sense of 'life in death' is complemented by that
extinction of being against which our lives are measured, as
we see Mr Craven Smith's measured, or Squire Hamley's at
the death of his elder son. It is the final measure of sincerity,
the equivalent of the directly confrontational glance, so seldom
seen in the novel:

> Her face was very white, but it bore the impress of the final
> sincerity of death, when the true expression prevails with-
> out the poor disguises of time. (544)

Thus without a word Molly vindicates herself to her father
when all the town has condemned her and he himself is driven
to unworthy doubts about her integrity.

The evasiveness in the details of human intercourse which I
have been at pains to point out might be taken as typical of
Mrs Gaskell's sense that life is an elusive and mixed experience, ultimately intractable. We understand this in Molly's reflections on her father's marriage:

> It seemed as if there was not, and never could be in this
> world, any help for the dumb discordancy between her father
> and his wife. . . . It was all hopeless, and the only attempt at
> a remedy was to think about it as little as possible. (432)

Yet the same idea causes the author to immediately reverse

Squire Hamley's words on the death of his eldest son that 'it is past all comfort' (587) by introducing his little grandchild. Loneliness, hopelessness are not to be wished away, but they are not *of necessity* the final word. Life is infinitely variable and may surprise us. We have seen this in the ambiguous attitude to women and femaleness, and it is to be observed also in the impossibility of coming to any easy conclusions about guilt. Mrs Gibson, for example, is contemptibly shallow, pretentious and self-centred. And yet when Molly tries to find a definite moral stance, nothing seems so clear:

> It was a wonder to Molly if this silence [her father's] was right or wrong. With a girl's want of toleration, and want of experience to teach her the force of circumstances, and of temptation, she had often been on the point of telling her stepmother some forcible home truths. But possibly her father's example of silence, and often some piece of kindness on Mrs. Gibson's part (for after her way, and when in a good temper, she was very kind to Molly), made her hold her tongue. (380)

And when Mrs Kirkpatrick goes 'groping about to find the means of reinstating herself in his good graces – really trying, according to her lights', Molly is 'often compelled to pity her in spite of herself' (431).

All is circumstance, peculiarities of temperament, subjectivity. How does the rational, sceptical, intelligent doctor make the mistake which is central to the whole action? By reacting to a poor lunch he is forced to give a friend, by convincing himself that his daughter needs a mother when she has done perfectly well without one for a great part of her life, by giving weight to general opinion as he sees it, and by finally finding himself proposing, even as he has doubts about the whole enterprise. There is an inclusiveness in this which marks the novel as a whole, and which seems central to the concept of comic realism. Marriages for the young people are the beginning of a new phase of their lives. For their elders who married in haste, their leisurely repentance will be moderated by acceptance of their lot. Childhood, youth and age, life and death, sexuality are the parameters of one aspect only of the world. We are constrained also by class and social change (tea-parties decline as dinners get later) and money, both on the large scale of Squire Hamley's fortunes and in the small but solider manifestation of ten-pound notes from Mr Gibson to help his daughter, or twenty pounds that bind Cynthia to Mr Preston.

Such inclusiveness extends the vision of life to give yet a further dimension which has not hitherto been mentioned, but whose impact is an important counterbalance to the novel's characteristic sense of compromise and acceptance. Roger tells Molly the little parable of 'Harriet' because he feels she needs 'bracing', and in fact it does her good. His more relaxed and passive mother would not have resorted to such activity. Similarly her father takes an abrupt leave of her when he sees that she is getting sentimental over his marriage, and 'His commonplace words acted like an astringent on Molly's relaxed feelings' (419). Both male role-models in Molly's life embody a kind of pragmatism which is active rather than reactive. Both are placed against figures who are complaining, passive or languid, but unlike the Doctor who is tied to his wife, Roger can outstrip his brother and stand for positive change, contemporary values, theoretical knowledge and practical venturesomeness. This self-commitment is, needless to say, a vital value for Mrs Gaskell. It is the one redeeming feature in Mr Preston, taking the form of a kind of integrity which will not allow him to pursue any other woman than Cynthia:

> Cynthia was Cynthia, and not Venus herself could have been her substitute. In this one thing Mr. Preston was more really true than many worthy men; who, seeking to be married, turn with careless facility from the unattainable to the attainable, and keep their feelings and fancy tolerably loose till they find a woman who consents to be their wife. (533)

In more positive guise it takes the form of Lady Harriet's practical support of Molly when her name is being taken lightly, and indeed informs the whole outgoing, 'gritty' style of that lady. Mrs Kirkpatrick, by contrast, is fearful, cautious, always looking for the line of least defence and restrained by a propriety which will not, for example, allow Molly to live fully until she has 'come out'. The full consequence of the inclusiveness that tells us there is a surprise for every disappointment, that for every muddled, well-meaning Lord Cumnor there is a sharp, astringent Lady Cumnor, that for Cynthia's beauty there is Molly's faithfulness, is an inconclusiveness marking this kind of realism. It is typical of her whole feeling for values as a matter of realistic self-creation that nothing is *finally* said. Unlike angels, we cannot know 'the ends for which everything is sent', and that sense of surprise which Molly so vividly celebrated when her father arrived to rescue her from the Hall is alive for us all if we are open like the author to the way things are and the way they might yet be. Perhaps the tone of shrewd but not unkind scepticism and note of reconciliation in Mr Gibson's remark to Cynthia (the last reference to angels in the book) captures most aptly the mood of this great novel, in manner if not in matter: 'We are all angels just now, and you are an archangel' (636).

3

Women, Death and Integrity 1: 'Lois the Witch'

> In the year 1691, Lois Barclay stood on a little wooden pier steadying herself on the stable land, in much the same manner as, eight or nine weeks ago, she had tried to steady herself on the deck of the rocking ship which had carried her across from Old to New England. It seemed as strange now to be on solid earth as it had been, not long ago, to be rocked by the sea, both by day and by night; and the aspect of the land was equally strange. (CP 105)

Two sensations are apparent in these opening lines of 'Lois the Witch'. The first is the girl's feeling of the land's stability after her weeks at sea, the second the strangeness of that land. The two sensations form a core of opposition in the story, since although Lois's first feeling is of steadiness, the alien environment in which she finds herself is anything but firm and dependable, and she is not to feel that security within herself again until she is shackled with iron in a jail, awaiting an ignominious death. Death has been a final stability for her parents in England, buried in the graveyard of the 'little village church of Barford (not three miles from Warwick – you may see it yet), where her father had preached ever since 1661, long before she was born' (105–6). From that assured, long-founded background of family, faith and worship she has set out to claim kin in a community newly-founded in a wild, strange and inhospitable land. Lois, having only herself to rely on, is a type of the wanderer who is launched into new experience of

63

necessity by the death of her parents; but whereas a Margaret Hale discovers herself in love and is rescued by this, Lois is persecuted and destroyed – though, as we shall see, she also has an important experience, of self-definition. Love is not outside Lois's experience, of course. But Hugh Lucy, the faithful lover, is left behind only to appear in person for the first time after her death. In place of his sheltering love, Lois is exposed to the obsessive passion of the unbalanced visionary Manasseh and the unwelcome attentions of Mr Nolan, which put her in the position of a rival to her cousin Faith.

In the Hickson family, where she finds a home of some kind, the general instability of the New World community is most apparent as mental illness. Although only Manasseh is manifestly mad, we are told that 'if Lois had been a physician of modern times, she might have traced somewhat of the same temperament in his sisters as well – in Prudence's lack of natural feeling and impish delight in mischief, in Faith's vehemence of unrequited love' (147). Certainly this is a family where everyone appears abnormal in some way, from the masculine, self-repressive Grace, to the impish Prudence. Grace, Faith and Prudence, names of abstract spiritual virtues, calm and contained, contrast alarmingly with these women's dispositions. We are prepared for a world in which appearances may deceive by the story of the log which turns out to be an Indian in disguise – a tale to which 'all were breathless with listening; though to most the story, or others like it, were familiar' (113). Even a short journey is a doubtful undertaking. The forests are a dangerous mystery, not only because of the savage animals and humans lurking within them, but for the spells which may transform the good into evil:

> Or there were spells – so Nattee said – hidden about the grounds by the wizards, which changed that person's nature who found them; so that, gentle and loving as they might have been before, thereafter they took no pleasure but in the cruel torments of others, and had a strange power given to them of causing such torments at their will. (127)

The seemingly calm and obedient Faith reveals to Lois that

she 'hates' Father Tappau. The apparently devout Manasseh, the model of religious young men, who studies theology and the works of the Fathers, contains within him a reservoir of darker thoughts which at the climax of the tale bursts forth in a torrent of blasphemy. The subversion of that faith which is the mainstay of an enclosed colony by the outpourings of a madman has also more tangible manifestations. Within New England there are alternative sources of power and authority to those which apparently dictate the shape and ethos of its society.

'Patriarchal' has become a commonplace of contemporary critical discourse, but the society in which Lois finds herself when she arrives in Salem is a theocracy with a truly patriarchal structure. God is represented in a very direct form by His (male) pastors, who carry His word into every home and family, not merely as a precept but as the ground of organisation and action. Male rule is unquestioned and absolute. We should not feel, however, that this in itself accounts for the disease which appears in the society. Patriarchs there had been who were wise and beneficent, but they had died only shortly before Lois's arrival. The problem for Salem is one of confusion and dissension among its leaders; division among the representatives of an absolute Authority. When a community is so self-sustaining in its body-politic, functioning in a kind of closed-circuit with the Absolute, schism is bound to lead to unhappiness, if not evil. The Hickson household is an interesting version of this society's structure and ethos. Here the father, who should be head of the family, is weak in body and personality, and his role is taken over by a wife with 'a deep voice, almost as masculine as her son's' (119). As a non-blood relation, deeply hostile to the homeless orphan whose one defender dies early in the story, Grace Hickson is a type of the wicked stepmother, but she has particular manifestations of her type which define the kind of authority she represents. She is upright and virtuous in the narrow sense that makes her minister dutifully to her husband even when she does not love him – 'I do my duty where I read it' (122). Her first response to Lois's arrival is denial of her existence: 'I know nothing of her' (119) and her second is to abuse the girl's parents' memory on sectarian

grounds. More deeply within herself she is partial and emotional, despite her appearance of grim detachment. She favours
Manasseh and Prudence over Faith, and hides the 'shame' of
her son's madness. Her hostility to any suggestion of union
between him and Lois turns to unwilling reconciliation when
it is apparent that the girl can soothe the young man's dis-
eased imaginings, and finally she begs on her knees that Lois
will release her beloved son from the spell she thinks has been
cast upon him.

We may contrast this authority with that 'happy power' ex-
ercised by the Widow Smith, whom Lois encounters on her
first night in New England. By contrast to Grace, though she
has no kinship laid upon her, 'she kissed Lois on both cheeks,
before she rightly understood who the stranger maiden was,
only because she was a stranger and looked sad and forlorn'
(109). Her test of strangers is not theoretical but human:

> Widow Smith was guided in these matters by instinct; one
> glance at a man's face told her whether or not she chose to
> have him as an inmate of the same house as her daughters;
> and her promptness of decision in these matters gave her
> manner a kind of authority which no one liked to disobey,
> especially as she had stalwart neighbours within call to back
> her, if her assumed deafness in the first instance, and her
> voice and gesture in the second, were not enough to give
> the would-be guest his dismissal. (109–10)

She has 'prompt authority' and 'happy power' (110), and she
stands out in the tale because we find very little other happiness associated with power and authority. Widow Smith is a
woman, yet she can wield a public kind of power, not with
narrow prejudice or partiality, but with human kindness tem-
pered by judgement, backed ultimately by the judicious threat
of force.

In Salem a different kind of power is in evidence – or, one
should say, powers, since the societal and familial authority I
have already described is only one aspect of the matter. This
is the power which society openly wields, and is a model of
how such power is sanctioned and made to operate – from

divine decrees to public laws through personal precept, supported by the paraphernalia of law and justice. Yet in the idea of witchcraft there reside other, secret powers which are personal and unreasonable, but have an authority of their own which is subversive of the publicly acknowledged state.

Most obviously, the hysteria induced in an unhealthy, enclosed society by a belief in witchcraft shows a power of mass self-destruction which the authorities not only are unable to check, but which involves them in its frantic search for victims. More particularly interesting, however, is the fact that, in this tale at least, 'witch' means 'woman'. The power of witchcraft is a female power, and it bears all the marks of subversion. It is secret; it has an alternative source for its power; it is the means of expression for an 'inferior' or oppressed group. The most obvious manifestation of power is in the supposed ability of the Indian woman Nattee to bring the person, and perhaps capture the love, of Mr Nolan for Faith. For the Christian girl to be availing herself of such arts is clearly contrary to her faith and her morality, but such is the torment of frustrated love that she will resort to the black arts to win the man. The efficacy of Nattee's spell is non-proven, but this is of course unimportant. She herself believes in it, and it gives a pleasing sense of power to a female member of an oppressed and scorned race. When Nolan does in fact appear, Nattee takes the credit to herself, and glories in her power over a white man:

> 'Old Indian woman great mystery. Old Indian woman sent hither and thither; go where she is told, where she hears with her ears. But old Indian woman' – and here she drew herself up, and the expresion of her face quite changed – 'know how to call, and then white man must come; and old Indian woman have spoken never a word, and white man have heard nothing with his ears.' (142)

Her subversive act is also one of self-definition, an assertion of her secret knowledge and power. If the black arts may be used in relations between the sexes, witchcraft of a more natural kind may also play its part – 'for there be many kinds of witchcraft abroad' (165). Innocently one may say that a woman has bewitching eyes, that she can charm men, or has cast a spell upon them, but all these metaphors bear a sinister overtone in the case of innocent Lois. She does not court the sexual power she possesses, but it is there mysteriously. The words are used quite unthinkingly by Captain Holdernesse and the widow Smith:

> 'And I don't doubt but what the parson's bonny lass has bewitched many a one since, with her dimples and her pleasant ways – eh, Captain Holdernesse? It's you must tell us tales of the young lass's doings in England.'
> 'Ay, ay,' said the captain; 'there's one under her charms in Warwickshire who will never get the better of it, I'm thinking.' (116)

But they have a terrible irony, not merely in the context of her ultimate fate, but as regards her influence upon Mr Nolan and her power over the deranged Manasseh. Faith's jealousy with regard to the former leads directly to the execution of Hota, while Manasseh sees Lois as part of a fate predestined with himself. He tells her he has dreamed of her being offered two lots, one of marriage to him and one a violent death. When she chooses the latter he puts on her the symbolic black and red garment, 'And when [it] fell to the ground, thou wert even as a corpse three days old' (145). Although he may be mad, Manasseh is possessed of the most mysterious power in the book, since he would appear to dream the truth, albeit by default. She does *not* marry him, and she *does* die a violent death. The choice he offers is a peculiarly disturbing one for Lois, since she herself is aware of a curse laid upon her from her childhood that no one should rise up to protect her when she is taken up as a witch. It is part of that unsettling power of suggestion which insidiously undermines Lois's self-confidence. Her innocence and unassumingness cannot deny the power of her sexual attractions. It is a real force, and one mysterious in its origins and autonomy. Gentle and pure in its personal manifestation, her beauty causes death, madness and destruction. In the advances of the repulsive Manasseh is made manifest the supernatural terror of the double-headed serpent:

that had such power over all those white maidens who met
the eyes placed at either end of his long, sinuous, creeping
body, so that, loathe him, loathe the Indian race as they would,
off they must go into the forest to seek out some Indian man,
and must beg to be taken into his wigwam, adjuring faith
and race for ever. (127)

'I cannot marry anyone from obedience', says Lois, avoiding
direct declaration of her feelings towards one she 'loathed':

He might be good and pious – he doubtless was – but his
dark, fixed eyes, moving so slowly and heavily, his lank,
black hair, his grey, coarse skin, all made her dislike him
now – all his personal ugliness and ungainliness struck on
her senses with a jar, since those few words spoken behind
the woodstack. (134)

In Lois we find the self subverted by a variety of means
which she finds it very difficult to resist. We are constantly
reminded of her loneliness and the strangeness of that world
in which she finds herself. She is alone as no other of Mrs
Gaskell's heroines is alone. Margaret has her family and Mr
Thornton, Sylvia and Ruth their children, Molly her father and
a close and sympathetic society. Lois is totally abandoned in a
country which is already alien to those living there. It would
seem that her fate has been decided by other wills than her
own – by a voice beyond this world, indeed, since she has
been entrusted to the New World by her dying mother's words.
The cry of the woman captured by pirates: 'Lord Jesu! have
mercy on me! Save me from the power of man, O Lord Jesu!'
(113), and Nattee's hints at human sacrifice reinforce the impression of a lack of self-determination in Lois's life. But the
central factor of this subversion of the self is auto-suggestion.
If it is possible for a whole community to suffer a mass de-
lusion, how much more likely is it that a lonely, disorientated
individual will succumb. Were Lois to be accused of theft or
murder she could refute the charge from experienced fact, but
no such solid ground is available to her. In one sense, as we
have seen, she *is* a witch, and the fact that her attractiveness

to men seems beyond her own control only makes the realisation of her power the more devastating. She is capable of feelings of hatred, even though her temperament is naturally loving.
When her aunt has led her on to commit herself to the extent
of almost opening her heart, Grace 'would turn round upon
her with some bitter sneer that roused all the evil feelings in
Lois's disposition by its sting' (125). Such malicious deception
is yet another destabilising influence to add to the suggestions
of the son, who seems at times like the voice of the Evil One.
As she comes down from the loft with a load of flax, not hearing 'the breathing or motion of any creature near her ... she
heard some one – it was Manasseh – say close to her ear; "Has
the voice spoken yet?"' (139) Manasseh's approach is as
unlooked-for, surprising and insidious as those demons' voices
supposed to be heard by witches. He combines in his persist-
ence and his disembodiedness the qualities of deluded and
hysteric auto-suggestion and the supernatural tempter.

There is a special meaning attached to the designation of a
person as a witch. Unlike 'murderer' or 'thief', it is a name
designating a whole type of person with a life in an alternative world. 'Witch Lois! Witch Lois!' cries Prudence (168). The
designation is as intimate as one's own given name; it is a
definition of the woman, just as much as 'angel'. Manasseh, in
particular, would like to define Lois by naming her, just as he
would like to define her by relating her to himself in a fated
marriage. For Grace she is the repository of power 'akin to
that which the shepherd David, playing on his harp, had over
king Saul sitting on his throne' (162) but in his paroxysm
Manasseh turns her from angel into witch. It is little wonder,
then, that when she is accused, and all cry out upon her, Lois
herself has doubts about her innocence:

> 'Aunt Hickson,' she said, and Grace came forwards. 'Am I a
> witch, Aunt Hickson?' she asked; for her aunt, stern, harsh,
> unloving as she might be, was truth itself; and Lois thought
> – so near to delirium had she come – if her aunt condemned
> her, it was possible she might indeed be a witch. (173)

In prison her imagination has free range to believe that she might be what she cannot grasp – that her self is lost to another power without her even recognising the theft. But she is brought back to sanity by the weight of iron upon her leg.

> They feared, then, that even in that cell she would find a way to escape! Why, the utter, ridiculous impossibility of the thing convinced her of her own innocence and ignorance of all supernatural power; and the heavy iron brought her strangely round from the delusions that seemed to be gathering about her. (178)

In part her conviction of her innocence is based on a solid mid-nineteenth-century belief in rational scientific method – to this extent Lois outstrips her age – but less consciously the weight of the manacles represents a centredness and stability which no power of authority or suggestion can subvert. Armed with this surety she in turn becomes the subversive, undermining the assumptions of those who condemn her by refusing to lie to save herself. The truth comes 'out of her lips, almost without exercise of her will. "I am not a witch," she said' (183).

'Lois the Witch' is a tale with implications beyond its individual statement. In it we find rehearsed most of the matter and interest which its author has expressed at greater length elsewhere on the subject of women. They are victims of society, religious prejudice, men, and other women's jealousy over men. They have power and knowledge – some of it imagined, some real, and this power is secret, pervasive and largely subversive. Lois is alone, but her courage, compassion and clear-sightedness allow her to establish a sense of self which cannot save her life, but preserves her integrity for herself, in spite of the corrosive sense of guilt which is the greatest threat for her and for other of Mrs Gaskell's heroines. Lois's self-assertion is of a minimum kind – no immediate positive arises from her death, but as we shall see, women are capable of a more creative role in different circumstances. First, however, we shall examine in the person of Ruth Hilton a curious and disturbing variation on the theme of woman and death.

4

Women, Death and Integrity 2: *Ruth*

Ruth is a novel concerned with a problem – that of the unmarried mother in mid-nineteenth century society. But far more disturbing are the problems it raises less self-consciously – problems of credibility, values and interpretation. There can be no doubt of Mrs Gaskell's indictment of her society's hypocrisy. The whole emphasis in the first chapters is on the falsity of appearances. It is particularly associated with Mrs Mason, that 'adept in the species of sophistry with which people persuade themselves that what they wish to do is right' (R 8). Her 'ideas of justice' are contingent rather than absolute:

> they were not divinely beautiful and true ideas; they were something more resembling a grocer's, or tea-dealer's ideas of equal right. A little over-indulgence last night was to be balanced by a good deal of over-severity today; (19)

and she shuts her eyes to unpleasant realities such as the question of where her young employees are to go on a Sunday if they have no family or friends, since knowing that they had *nowhere* to go might make it necessary to 'order a Sunday's dinner, and leave a lighted fire on that day' (35). This is the woman who condemns and casts off Ruth in one moment without consideration or compassion. But this dismissal, despicable though it is, represents only the culmination of a larger process. Ruth is betrayed by Bellingham, but also suffers a persistent betrayal by her own society. Before the novel opens she has been left without sexual instruction and turned over to the notoriously abuse-prone life of a seamstress by an indifferent guardian.

73

She believes the strictures of her employer, and has no idea of the hypocrisy and neglect concealed in Mrs Mason's words. She is seduced by a thoughtless, comparatively worthless young man whom she sees as a figure of romance, the daring rescuer of children from floods, and her reward is to be abandoned in a Welsh inn, pregnant and totally without friends. The seducer feels some guilt, but is too weak to override the self-righteous outrage of his mother. The landlady is afraid her reputation will suffer. As Ruth turns away 'like a chidden child' (86) Mrs Morgan's heart softens, but she continues to patronise Ruth, with one eye to her own interest. There is a terrible pathos in the girl's running after Bellingham's coach until she realises she will never catch it.

Even when she goes to live with the Bensons, their want of faith in their own actions leads them to placate worldly prejudice by dissembling about Ruth's real status, forcing a wedding ring upon the unwilling girl and designating her a widow. The kindly Bensons in fact cause Ruth a good deal of pain through their concern with the propriety of what they have done. The contrast with the honest servant Sally's open attitude is obvious:

'It's truth there will be more trouble, and I shall have my share on't, I reckon. I can face it if I'm told out and out, but I cannot abide the way some folk has of denying there's trouble or pain to be met; just as if their saying there was none, would do away with it.' (139)

The most striking corollary of the hypocrisy, indifference and bad faith of those around Ruth is the emphasis it places on her childlike innocence. She never questions even Mrs Mason, but relies implicitly on her justice and judgement with absolute trust. Inexperience may be seen as a closed state, waiting for enlightenment; in Ruth's case it is a positive condition of wonder and openness. Images throughout the early chapters emphasise this. The other girls in Mrs Mason's establishment yawn and stretch. Ruth rushes to the window 'and press[es] against it as a bird presses against the bars of its cage' (4). She looks out on a scene which had once been natural but is now

repressed. The larch, now 'pent up and girdled with flagstones'
once had stood in a pleasant lawn (5). Ruth feels the impulse
to break out of this imprisonment, preferring the idea of 'one
blow in the fresh air' to eating supper. She still possesses the
vital interest in life and liberty, unlike her workmates, whose
spirits are deadened by experience. 'Most new girls get impatient at first', says her friend Jenny 'but it goes off, and they
don't care much for anything after awhile' (8–9). The implication is that one *may* continue to care, as Ruth in fact does. Life
does not suppress her instinctive openness. When Mrs Mason
declares that Ruth is to go to the ball, despite her lack of that
diligence which the lady had declared to be requisite for attendance, the other girls receive the news with indifference,
knowing the choice to be made on other than moral grounds.
But to Ruth it is 'inexplicable'.

There is a yearning towards freedom in Ruth which, like
her openness, inheres in her whole life and being. The warmth
and oppressive languour of the interior, preferable to most of
the girls, would willingly be exchanged by Ruth for the bracing cold outside, suggesting that she craves not merely escape,
but the vital contact with experience which is essential to life
and growth. The world would seek, by hiding her, to deny
her a social role which might give her the opportunity for real
identity.

The distinction made between Ruth and her fellow-workers
is more than a localised poetic device. It demonstrates that she
is a superior creature, more sensitive, born for better things
perhaps. Taken with the magically inexplicable permission to
go to the ball, we may detect overtones of Cinderella. The hints
are reinforced when she first meets Bellingham. The ballroom
at first seems magical to her – the voices of the musicians sound
'goblin-like', the candles carried around remind the girl of the
will-o'-the-wisp – until lights and the voice of Mrs Mason call
her back to immediate reality. The 'Prince' Bellingham recognises
his princess, despite her humble role:

not before his attention had been thereby drawn to consider
the kneeling figure, that, habited in black up to the throat,
with the noble head bent down to the occupation in which

she was engaged, formed such a contrast to the flippant, bright, artificial girl who sat to be served with an air as haughty as a queen on her throne.

The 'ugly sister'-like cruelty of Bellingham's partner is almost parodic, as is his bestowal of the flower, but the clichés serve to draw our attention to the fairy-tale dream which is to be itself so callously parodied in reality.

Ruth's innocence is the source of at least two of the book's problems. On the level of sheer credibility it seems unlikely that the Ruth of Wales should be as totally childlike as the 'prelapsarian' Ruth. But more profoundly disturbing is the clash between morality and nature implied in the heroine's innocent spontaneity. Miss Benson complains, after the discovery of Ruth's pregnancy, that the girl is not 'seeing the thing in a moral light as I should have expected' (118), complaining that though the news was broken with as 'cold and severe' a manner as Miss Benson could manage, Ruth burst out with a natural joy:

'just as if she had a right to have a baby. She said, "Oh, my God, I thank Thee! Oh! I will be so good!" I had no patience with her then, so I left the room.' (118)

There is a good-natured mockery of Miss Benson's attempts at moral rigidity here, and we should not doubt that Mrs Gaskell was quite capable of seeing the clash of values involved, but the problem remains. If Ruth is all natural and spontaneous, and if her rejoicing at her pregnancy is good because it is the natural product of motherhood, then why is that spontaneous, natural act which brought the baby into being a sin, as the author and the heroine and by implication everyone else not lost to 'depravity' in the book clearly believe it is. Is it not grossly unnatural to condemn a girl to a sense of owing a life-time's redemption for the neglect of a form of words, especially when the need of those words was, as far as we can judge, unknown to the victim? Mrs Gaskell would doubtless reply that what is involved is not merely a form of words, but is, first, the sanction given by society as a necessary authority to govern the family unit, and thereby the social structure, and secondly the word of God in the form of a sacrament, or at least a vow, without which a union is not blessed.The difficulty, perhaps impossibility, of reconciling sin and nature is a vital tension in the novel, and reflects a larger problem concerning the relative and the absolute, meliorative and condemnative, life-affirming and death-inclining, as we shall see.

In Chapter XXIX Thurstan Benson is characterised as follows:

> it was that early injury to his spine which affected the constitution of his mind as well as his body, and predisposed him, to a feminine morbidness of conscience. (378)

There is more than one interesting implication contained in this passage, but to take the most obvious first, we have here a strong hint that Thurstan is less than completely male. His injury, by incapacitating him for an active life, has made him sensitively inturned in what is seen as a rather feminine way. The consequent implication is that Leonard, the boy, will find himself brought up by a family of women, implicitly, if not in fact. Not the least practically engaging side of this novel is that Elizabeth Gaskell demonstrates how a boy may be brought up in a female environment and not be essentially the worse for it. A good demonstration of how this upbringing works may be observed when it is proposed that Leonard should be beaten, as discouragement to an overactive imagination. The episode is a mixture of the pathetic and amusing. Ruth 'close[s] her ears and pray[s]' (202); Miss Benson 'having carried her point, was very sorry for the child, and would have begged him off' (202–3). But Mr Benson ('the executioner – the scene, the study') feels his determination as the man of the family is on the line, and prepares for action. At this moment Sally bursts in and in typical fashion upbraids the unfortunate Thurstan:

> 'Go away, Sally,' said Mr. Benson, annoyed at the fresh difficulty in his path.
> 'I'll not stir never a step till you give me that switch, as you've got for some mischief, I'll be bound.' (203)

Finally the boy himself disarms the would-be executioner by telling him 'If you want to whip me, uncle, you may do it. I don't much mind' (204). After which, throwing his arms round his mother's neck, he says 'I will be good – I make a promise; I will speak true – I make a promise' (204). The confusion of feeling and idea here, and the practical and humane outcome is a nice example of a family resolving a problem which is quite new to it in a pragmatic and ultimately loving way.

We may contrast this matriarchy with the unnatural repression of Mr Bradshaw's family, where the man is king, his judgements are unquestioned, his wife and daughter repressed, and where, of course, his own son goes to the bad. Paralleling Sally's Biblical reference to the son of Solomon, who did not, of course, 'spare the rod', the rod of narrowness, strictness and oppression results only in hypocrisy and covert wrongdoing on the part of Richard Bradshaw.

A good deal of the account of life in the Benson household is of this sensible, diurnally realistic kind. 'It is better not to expect or calculate consequences', says Mr Benson.

> 'We know that no holy or self-denying effort can fall to the ground vain and useless; but the sweep of eternity is large, and God alone knows when the effect is to be produced. We are trying to do right now, and to feel right; don't let us perplex ourselves with endeavouring to map out how she should feel, or how she should show her feelings.' (128)

Like most of the old servants in Elizabeth Gaskell's novels, Sally urges the practical pursuit of present duties upon Ruth, telling her how, when she began worrying about her soul she also found her puddings turned out heavy. The importance of puddings as against an over self-absorbed conscience is an amusing practical example of the lesson in life whose practical equivalent is the specialised knowledge she determines to acquire in order to educate her son. We cannot doubt that whatever else may happen in the novel, Leonard has grown up a healthy boy, even to the extent of being able to relax his hold on his mother and ultimately accept his illegitimacy. To this extent the tale is positive, clear-cut and healthy. A girl who

has been seduced and abandoned can bring up her child in a
positive moral climate and in the course of the upbringing define
herself. This self-definition extends to rejecting her suitor when
he reappears.

From her initial dependence on him it might be hard to proph-
esy that she will be capable of such independent action a few
years later. But Ruth, even in her most downcast state, has a
certain strength of purpose. She returns the £50 left her by Mrs
Bellingham as a 'paying-off' sum ('I have a strong feeling against
taking it'). She also would like to return the fine piece of
cambric-muslin which is a present from Mr Bradshaw to 'Mrs
Denbigh' 'Because I feel as if Mr Bradshaw had no right to
offer it me' (156). Even more imprudently, considering their
relative positions, she says it is a right which must be earned.
She is in fact dissuaded from sending it back by Thurstan, who
gives the following explanation of how he dealt with such problems of conscience himself:

> It was a time, of all others, to feel as you are doing now; but
> I became convinced it would be right to accept them, giving
> only the very cool thanks which I felt. This omission of all
> show of much gratitude had the best effect – the presents
> have much diminished; but if the gifts have lessened, the
> unjustifiable speeches have decreased in still greater propor-
> tion, and I am sure we respect each other more. (158)

The more subtle worldliness of Benson is an interesting contrast to Ruth's absoluteness which, as we shall see, marks her
off from the Benson family and from most other people around
her. But it is not only the innate strength of Ruth's nature that
makes her able to reject Bellingham. It is the life she has lived
in the intervening years. She tells him 'We are very far apart.
The time that has pressed down my life like brands of hot
iron, and scarred me for ever, has been nothing to you' (302–3).
Time to him has meant nothing, but she has given it value by
living it. Most obviously she has shaped her immediate daily
experience by adjusting to the ways of the family she lives
with, but she is also a creator of that family in a new mould
by her introduction of a child and her conscientious rearing of

him. A good example of this is her determination 'to acquire the knowledge hereafter to be given to her child' (177). 'Those summer mornings were happy, for she was learning neither to look backwards nor forwards, but to live faithfully and earnestly in the present' (177). It is a practical use of time, where there is no gap between requirement and action. All parents of young children will know this rewarding but exhausting employment of time. But value is conferred on time in another way, when Ruth sees past, present and future as giving a special kind of meaning to her life, one closer to God's vision – as when she re-encounters Bellingham:

> It seemed now as if she could not think – as if thought and emotion had been repressed so sternly that they would not come to relieve her stupified brain. Till all at once, like a flash of lightning, her life, past and present, was revealed to her in its minutest detail. And when she saw her very present 'Now,' the strange confusion of agony was too great to be borne, and she cried aloud. (272)

Her 'very present "Now"' here is not the totally absorbed 'now' of her daily life with the Bensons, but a moment of self-appraisal in which a great decision is to be made. Thurstan Benson tries not to plan for eternity, but Ruth cannot live a life measured only by each day's demands. Perhaps in some way Thurstan's lie about her marital status is a culpable compromise resulting from a reluctance to anticipate the future. His sister says 'And now we wash our hands of these Bellinghams' but we cannot live as though our past had never existed. When it is time to return from Wales:

> Ruth could not sit still. She wandered from window to window, learning each rock and tree by heart. Each had its tale, which it was agony to remember; but which it would have been worse agony to forget. The sound of running waters she heard that quiet evening, was in her ears as she lay on her death-bed; so well had she learnt their tune. (131)

Again:

Her thought about money had hitherto been a child's thought; the subject had never touched her; but afterwards, when she had lived a little with the Bensons, her eyes were opened, and she remembered their simple kindness on the journey, and treasured it in her heart. (133)

When she has met Bellingham again, in the guise of Mr Donne, she fixes her mind upon Leonard, not daring to 'look before or behind' (285), such is her immediate fear of the consequences of the father's reappearance. Ultimately her rejection of Bellingham relies heavily on both aspects of time. She has lived enough, in bringing up Leonard, to change. Her former lover wishes that 'those happy days might return' (298); she knows they cannot. And in maturing through experience she has faced the past and built for her future – at the very least, vicariously through her son.

We have, as far as this account has taken us, a positive, humanistic, satisfactory story of youthful errors made good, of maturity and sense triumphing, of a personality developing an understanding of itself and finding a meaning in its life. But we also have only half a book, for Ruth has sinned, and in recognising this we not only admit a whole spritual dimension to the novel, but a spirituality of a very intense and peculiar kind.

The remark of an early reviewer that the heroine could only be condemned by 'a superstitious and exaggerated estimate of physical virginity',[1] while doubtless incompatible with the author's own view of her heroine's guilt, does suggest a morbid obsessiveness which strongly characterises some aspects of the book. We have already encountered the word 'morbid' in relation to Thurstan Benson's conscience. It is a 'feminine' morbidity, and is associated with his injured spine. The implication seems to be that lack of masculine activity leads to this kind of feminine introversion. It is also associated with maiming. At the same time it must not be forgotten that Benson was the one person who offered practical Christian aid to Ruth when she most needed it. And that extreme sensitivity to matters of conscience is clearly preferable to the self-righteous moral brutality of Mr Bradshaw. Mr Benson is also accused of morbidity by Mr Bradshaw (351) and his sister (362), and Ruth herself is adjured by Bellingham not to 'let any morbid, overstrained conscientiousness interfere with substantial happiness'(303). The very fact that this accusation is levelled by such a worldling is an indication that if this is morbidness the author is not, at any rate, unsympathetic to it.

There is a particular morbidity in the enormous disparity between the act – what Joyce called the 'preordained frangibility of the hymen'[2] – and the almost hysterical sense of disaster which affects a whole life, and indeed whole lives, indirectly. For this moment of physicality, Ruth must commit her whole life to a spiritual redemption amounting ultimately to martyrdom. Associated with this morbidity is a sense of overheated emotions, or at least a lack of perspective – a sense not confined to one person or family but pervading the whole atmosphere. Of the episode when Leonard faces punishment for inventing stories, Mrs Gaskell remarks

> Education was but a series of experiments to them all, and they all had a secret dread of spoiling the noble boy, who was the darling of their hearts. And, perhaps, this very intensity of love begot an impatient, unnecessary anxiety, and made them resolve on sterner measures than the parent of a large family (where love was more spread abroad) would have dared to use. (202)

This is not mere unworldliness but the faintly unhealthy centring of the love of a number of adults, none of them married, on a single child. The boy himself is called on more than one occasion 'holy', and while, as I have said, he is brought up in practice as a healthy boy, he must also stand in trust to his mother, and perhaps in a lesser way to the Bensons, as a pledge from Heaven. In her first moments of motherhood Ruth loses all sense of time; 'That one thought excluded all remembrance and all anticipation, in those first hours of delight' (162). And the gift of the child brings her nearer eternity – 'so near, so real and present, did heaven, and eternity, and God seem to Ruth, as she lay encircling her mysterious holy child'. We are told, after she is found out, that 'The child and the mother were each messengers of God – angels to each other' (369).

This intense spirituality is accompanied by physical mani-festations of an emotional over-wroughtness that sometimes borders on hysteria. People gasp, faint, quiver, are convulsed. A fair specimen of this overheated manner is to be found when Ruth has to tell Leonard of his shameful birth. She gazes into his face with the 'agony that could not find vent in words. At last she tried to speak; she tried with strong bodily effort, al-most amounting to convulsion' (342). She bids him kiss her 'once more in the old way' and their lips 'clung together as in the kiss given to the dying' (343). The air of hysteria is not confined to Ruth. This is a novel about conscience and moral outrage, and even Mr Bradshaw can succumb to emotional extremes in moments of stress. But the morbidity and hysteria are centred on the heroine and her situation, and lead us ulti-mately to consideration of the meaning contained in the 'value nexus' of women, sexuality, spirituality and death.

The spiritual equivalent of error and reform is the pilgrim-age from sin to redemption. Ruth's rearing of her son and her acceptance by society is adequate in social and psychological terms, but the role of martyr alone may atone for the sin she has committed against God. The inclination to the martyr's role is ingrained in Ruth's nature in a passive form quite early in the book. When the child calls her a 'bad naughty girl' (71) Ruth turns away 'humbly and meekly, with bent head, and slow, uncertain steps' (72). When Bellingham upbraids her with want of cheerfulness she decides 'I must not think of myself so much' (73). When he is ill she abases herself at his door all night. She has no idea of reproach for him, let alone for de-mands of care or support. Her first instinct on being left alone is to commit suicide, and Faith Benson declares 'It would be better for her to die at once, I think' (112). But she later commends Ruth as 'so meek and gentle . . . so patient, and so grateful' (124).

Ruth patiently allows Sally to clip her hair (symbolic of pen-ance and unsexing?). Her whole life from seduction onwards could be said to be a kind of penance, culminating in her ulti-mate sacrifice. Death as it is contemplated early in her story is the conventional alternative to dishonour, but the completion of that story *is* death, and seems to me to be part of that general morbidity which feels that only death can pay the debt fully, since sin is a transcendent debt.

Ruth's association with the timeless and transcendent is strongly reinforced by her experience of nature. Just as the Cinderella overtones suggested that she was destined for higher worldly things, this profounder Romantic myth constantly reminds us that her real home is in the 'beyond'. As a 'child of nature' we first see her longing to be outside in the snow. Later she visits the deserted garden of her innocent childhood with its obvious associations of Eden. The Welsh landscape is a source of awe and wonder to her. She rejoices in every mood and aspect of the mountainous landscape, unlike her more prosaic companion who is unspeakably bored on a rainy day. This experience, it is suggested, opens up new prospects for her inward as well as her outward eye, even in the days when she is 'living in sin':

> It was opening a new sense; vast ideas of beauty and grandeur filled her mind at the sight of the mountains now first beheld in full majesty. She was almost overpowered by the vague and solemn delight; but by and by her love for them equalled her awe, and in the night-time she would softly rise, and steal to the window to see the white moonlight, which gave a new aspect to the everlasting hills that girdle the mountain village. (65)

This larger vision sustains her throughout her subsequent ordeal. As she waits outside her lover's room for news of his fate, she looks out of the window at the mountains 'shutting in that village as if it lay in a nest. They stood, like giants, solemnly watching for the end of Earth and Time' (83). When with her lover, she had thought that she could exist outside time in a 'land enchanted into everlasting brightness' (83) but 'Now she knew the truth, that earth has no barrier which avails against agony' (83). The implication is that it is only beyond earth that we will be beyond agony. She looks through the window at nature's reminders of eternity, but must then return to her vigil indoors, measured by the weary hours of night.

All aspects of the natural world incline the watcher towards
the Heavenly state:

> A heron was standing there motionless, but when he saw
> them he flapped his wings and slowly rose, and soared above
> the green heights of the wood up into the very sky itself, for
> at that depth the trees appeared to touch the round white
> clouds which brooded over the earth. . . . In the very middle
> of the pond the sky was mirrored clear and dark, a blue
> which looked as if a black void lay behind. (73–4)

The bird soars, the trees appear to touch the skies, which themselves are mirrored on the earth. Even when Ruth lies by the
roadside, abandoned by Bellingham and in despair, the minute
progress of the meanest insect is matched by the ethereal song
of the skylark:

> Yet afterwards, long afterwards, she remembered the exact
> motion of a bright green beetle busily meandering among
> the wild thyme near her, and she recalled the musical, bal-
> anced, wavering drop of a skylark into her nest near the
> heather-bed where she lay. (94)

Her capacity for the transcendent vision remains even when
she has descended into the plains of practical duty:

> A low grey cloud was the first sign of Eccleston; it was the
> smoke of the town hanging over the plain. Beyond the place
> where she was expected to believe it existed, arose round,
> waving uplands; nothing to the fine outlines of the Welsh
> mountains, but still going up nearer to heaven than the rest
> of the flat world into which she had now entered. (133)

It might be said that her life's progress is marked by the different scenery her eye encounters – first the snowy landscape
beyond the window pane, next the bright lights of the ballroom, followed by the idyllic interlude in her father's garden.
From the safety of this enclosure she is transported to wild
nature in Wales and thence to an urban setting in the plains of

duty and parental responsibility. The loneliness of her renewed acquaintance with Bellingham is emphasised by the seclusion of their meeting on the almost deserted sea-shore, eternity now marked by the presence of the sea itself. Finally she is enclosed again, but she now needs no sustaining vision in the world outside her, for she is fulfilling her own transcendent destiny which, as I have indicated, has been reserved for her by implication since the opening pages.

It is to that destiny that I would now like to turn my attention, and particularly to its final manifestation which is of course her death. This strikes many people as the most morbid, and indeed puzzling aspect of the whole book. First, it seems unnecessary, in terms of poetic justice, that Ruth should die at all. If it is expiation, can it be necessary after all her exemplary conduct and the universal forgiveness, indeed celebration of her virtues, that has been bestowed upon her? Is it not deliberately anti-social, even inhumane, to choose death rather than take her place in family and society, continuing to love the son who means so much to her? For what seems above all perverse is that Ruth should, if not actually seek her own death, at least court it. This is a book of families; the Benson and Bradshaw households are placed against one another. Ruth plays a part in the character and fortunes of both of them, but finally withdraws into solitude, and, by nursing Bellingham, once again into her own past, as it were.

The idea of her isolation, at least, was not morally reprehensible to some of Mrs Gaskell's contemporaries. The *Christian Observer* indeed complained that Ruth should not be at all re-admitted to 'all the privileges of society':

> But we believe that society would sustain the deepest injury if, in virtue of this act of forgiveness, we were to rebuild the bridge of general intercourse between the guilty and the pure, and to re-admit even the true penitent to all the privileges of society which she has forfeited ... It is, we believe, far better for her to sit in her gate and mourn....[3]

It might be said in practical terms, of course, that Ruth does not have open to her the possibilities enjoyed by (say) a Margaret

Hale. However much Margaret may feel violated by over-
exposure of the self to an unmarried man, or by a necessary
untruth, she is still a virgin and may therefore reject the peace
of a nunnery or the death appropriate for her older friends
and relations. Having found and faced herself in life, she can
go on to blossom in love and marriage. But Ruth's son is growing
up; she will have no more children. The relief Mr Farquhar
feels at escaping an entanglement with Ruth shows how impossible any idea of marriage must be for her:

> His natural caution induced him to make a resolution never
> to think of any woman as a wife until he had ascertained all
> her antecedents, from her birth upwards. . . . (370)

The employment she eventually adopts perhaps signifies what
her role is to be. As a nurse she should be patient, gentle, calm
and self-sacrificing. She is to do menial tasks of servitude for
others. All this, as might be expected, Ruth gratefully accepts
as her lot and as part of the role she has lived herself into.
Moreover, contact with the sick and dying allows her to be a
spiritual as well as physical nurse: 'The low-breathed sentences
which she spoke into the ear of the sufferer and the dying
carried them upwards to God' (391).

All this, however, does not account for the apparently perverse manner of her death. A life of service to others would
surely be a suitable mode of redemption. She would still have
had the joy of motherhood, and would leave this life full of
years and approbation. But martyrs by definition meet untimely
deaths. As I have been at some pains to point out, moreover,
Ruth is a special person. Alone in the book she is, apart from
the one great fault, without sin. Apart from some initial low
spirits after arriving at the Bensons', which are quickly blown
away by Sally's downright advice to 'take a thing up heartily,
even if it is only making a bed' (174), she maintains absolutely
the virtues that are deliberately looked for in virtuous females.
She has no bad temper, no jealousy such as clouds Jemima's
life when she realises Mr Farquhar's attention is fixed upon
Ruth. The lie about her past is invented by the otherwise upright Mr Benson, and not by her. She feels awkward at wearing

the wedding ring Sally gives her as part of her 'disguise'. Mr Bradshaw, apparently the final paragon of absolute virtue, is in reality a moral shuffler. He does not wish to be associated with bribery, but realises it is necessary to gain his political ends, so turns a blind eye.

Mr Bradshaw is indeed a monster of oppressiveness, self-righteousness and inward corruption, to be seen not only as the patriarch condemned, but as a contrast with Ruth's truly spiritual absoluteness. The attention of all those around her is turned to life – to family, society, career and business. Her *raison d'être* lies in none of these things but in soul-making. Others are defined by worldly things, Ruth ultimately by death. If death is our ultimate goal, may it not also be our crowning glory? To live a good life may also imply dying a good death, and Ruth's death enacts the idea that our demise may be a positive – a completion rather than a taking-away, and to that extent a self-defining act with a life value of its own. Ruth could not be said actively to seek death any more than John Barton, Philip Hepburn or the many others in Mrs Gaskell's fiction who make a 'good end'. Yet one feels that her attitude is not merely unflinching but very close to courting death. Her closeness to mortality is poetically suggested in the crisis of her telling Leonard of her past:

> When she partially recovered, he helped her to the bed, on which she lay still, wan and deathlike. She almost hoped the swoon that hung around her might be Death, and in that imagination she opened her eyes to take a last look at her boy. (346)

> If she were away, and gone no one knew where – lost in mystery, as if she were dead – perhaps the cruel hearts might reflect, and show pity on Leonard. . . . (347)

But this would be a false death. She must wait for the moment when it will not be escape but a supreme sacrifice.

In a significant passage after she has obtained employment as a nurse, Ruth sees herself as the one unchanging person:

Everything seemed to change but herself, Mr. and Miss Benson grew old, and Sally grew deaf, and Leonard was shooting up, and Jemima was a mother. She and the distant hills that she saw from her chamber window, seemed the only things that were the same as when she first came to Eccleston. (392)

By contrast she observes an invalid next door who was a hearty and strong man when she first came, but must now be carried out into his garden. 'This told Ruth of the lapse of life and time' (392). The passage not only reasserts her association with death, but emphasises her stability, reserved for something in a decaying world. 'She felt just as faulty – as far from being what she wanted to be, as ever.' If she still feels the abiding sense of sin after all the reparations she has made, perhaps what she 'wants to be' is an angel – or at least to quit the mortal state.

Psychologically Ruth presents a remarkable combination of characteristics. She is at one and the same time the ultimately submissive woman, bearing all her sufferings and the accusations made against her humbly, as though they are entirely justified, and, as we have seen, extremely determined where matters of personal principle are concerned. Her resolution in taking upon herself the nursing of her erstwhile lover combines the two features and associates them with death, suggesting again the search for the 'good end':

> 'I can't! I can't!' cried she, with sharp pain in her voice. 'You must let me go, dear Mr. Davis!' said she, now speaking with soft entreaty.
> 'No!' said he, shaking his head authoritatively. 'I'll do no such thing.'
> 'Listen,' said she, dropping her voice, and going all over the deepest scarlet; 'he is Leonard's father! Now! you will let me go!' (440–1)

First she asserts what she *must* do, 'clenching her hands tight together' (440), then she becomes persuasive – 'speaking with soft entreaty'. She accepts that 'if he recognizes you, he will only be annoyed' with resignation. '"It is very likely!" said Ruth, heavily' and finally insists on her point with 'dull persistency'. It is a curious mood in which to do such an act. When Mr Davis asks her if she now cares for Bellingham she replies confusedly and evasively:

> 'I have been thinking – but I do not know – I cannot tell – I don't think I should love him, if he were well and happy – but you said he was ill – and alone – how can I help caring for him? – how can I help caring for him?' repeated she, covering her face with her hands, and the quick hot tears stealing through her fingers. (441)

She is not elated with conscious self-sacrifice, nor, for all her tears, moved with pity. He is indeed Leonard's father, but in physical paternity only. She has already rejected his offers of help, and Mr Benson, after Ruth's death, very firmly shows him the door, literally and metaphorically. Are we to believe that after all her experiences in the intervening years, her maturation, her dismissal of the man and his proffered love, her realisation of his worthlessness and lack of any real love for *her*, she would still feel the need to nurse him, putting her own life at risk and thus involving the happiness of her son and all her friends? The lack of real external motive highlights not only the idea of self-sacrifice, but the privacy and self-centredness of her decision.

In order to understand the nature of her self-sacrifice we must return to the idea of the expiation of sin. Clearly she has performed sufficient works to merit God's pardon, and wipe out a far greater sin than hers. Yet deep in certain areas of the Christian consciousness – more particularly associated with Nonconformity – is a belief in the ineffectiveness of works without grace. It is a spiritual mood captured in a stanza of Toplady's famous hymn 'Rock of Ages':

> Not the labours of my hands
> Can fulfil Thy law's demands;
> Could my zeal no respite know,
> Could my tears for ever flow,
> All for sin could not atone:
> Thou must save, and Thou alone.

The perceptive reader will rightly remark that such sentiments are almost diametrically opposed to the classic Unitarian stance. Far from relying on God's grace, especially in the form of Christ's divine mission, Unitarians emphasised the individual's reason and the importance of works. Far from being helpless wretches, we are capable of self-improvement in a strongly humanist manner. But Elizabeth Gaskell was not the woman to adhere to strict doctrinal principles when the question was the mystery of the human heart. Her treatment of Ruth's life is the debt she pays to her rational, humanist roots; her heroine's death reflects deeper and more unstable forces, in human psychology, sexuality and suffering. The idea of salvation through death is as fundamental to Christian thought as Christ's own sacrifice, and if Mrs Gaskell saw the Saviour primarily as an example of love in action, that side of her nature which was obsessed by death could not help being attracted to the sacrificial myth. In Ruth's case she can claim that she is saving Bellingham's life in the course of seeking her own salvation. It is a special kind of martyrdom; early martyrs bore testimony and died for their faith. This is not in question in Ruth's case, but it clearly has the Christian overtone of doing 'good to them who hate you, and pray for them which despitefully use you'.[4]

If Ruth's action seems perverse, it must be remembered that perversity in the form of self-punishment has been a feature of the Christian experience at least from the time that persecution ended:

> For by the tenth century and Hroswitha's day, the Christian struggle for perfection was no longer intelligible as a struggle against the authorities without. The Church had long ago triumphed throughout the known world. Christian struggle now concentrated on the enemy within. And concupiscence, as Augustine had defined it, was the root of sin, and one of its principal manifestations was lust. Virginity and martyrdom became complementary ideas, and the physical subjection of the body to the pains and ordeals of ascetic discipline was an integral part of sanctity.[5]

Sex and death do not need the sanction of Christianity for their association, as the concept of the *petite mort* suggests. With a different twist, loss of virginity is the 'fate worse than death'. We might look back one hundred years before *Ruth* to another lost virginity, and see an even more extreme and 'pure' version of this myth. Richardson's Clarissa Harlowe is raped, and thereafter consciously seeks death in a more unambiguous way than Ruth, having her coffin brought into her room and using it as a writing desk. For both Ruth and Clarissa it could be said that death is the only exit for a woman in their condition. But in neither case does this seem to be the real motive. Virginity and death share an absoluteness. Once the woman has lost her virginity she has entered the world of contingency and actuality, and only death can retrieve that wholeness she once enjoyed. Richardson's vision is far starker and grander than Mrs Gaskell's. He sees the absoluteness of virginity with greater purity and intensity. Clarissa achieves a single-minded vision as a result of her rape; her position is truly tragic because of the transcendence of the ideal she has set for herself as her life's values and its goal. And while her story thrives in a hothouse atmosphere, it is not the slightly foetid and hysterical air of *Ruth*. Moreover, *Clarissa* is not diverted from its central purpose by exerting a palpable moral purpose on the public. Clarissa has no child; her fate is truly self-centred. There could be no more telling contrast between the books than our last sight of the two gulty males. Lovelace, killed in a duel, raises his eyes towards heaven and cries 'LET THIS EXPIATE.' Bellingham goes off in a huff after his offer to bring up Leonard has been refused. Ruth is a ministering angel, sacrificing herself for her betrayer, Clarissa's betrayer himself gives up his life, and in death raises his eyes to the woman who may now, like the Virgin, be his intercessor.

Yet if *Ruth* lacks the single vision of its great predecessor, it has a vitality of its own which comes from the clash between the meliorative and absolute concepts of life's value. It is a confrontation between the naturalness of human life and the inexpiableness of sin, between virtue as a product of trial and failure and virtue as an inviolable wholeness. Elizabeth Gaskell was able to grasp both states imaginatively, though there can be little doubt that she sympathised with the contingent rather than the absolute, however much she admired the latter. Her problem is interestingly highlighted in her account of Florence Nightingale, whom she could not but praise for her single-minded energy, even as she felt alienated by it. She cites in a letter Miss Nightingale's alternate care and indifference to individuals:

> The mother speaks of F.N. – did to me only yesterday – as of a heavenly angel. Yet the father of this dead child – the husband of this poor woman – died last 5th of September, and I was witness to the extreme difficulty with which Parthe induced Florence to go and see this childless widow *once* while she was here; and though the woman entreated her to come again she never did. (L 319)

Mrs Gaskell herself was marked by her interest in and commitment to the individual – it is the leading feature of her artistic and moral realism – and she could not but mark the lack of it in Florence Nightingale. Of the famous nurse's declaration that she would put all her children into a crèche 'if she had twenty of them', she remarked:

> That exactly tells of what seems to me *the* want – but then this want of love for individuals becomes a gift and a very rare one, if one takes it in conjunction with her intense love for the *race*; her utter unselfishness in serving and ministering. (L 320)

Between the larger vision and particular attachment there seems no common ground, and this seems to be the case in *Ruth* also, but the articulation of this divergence is at the very centre of the novel's continuing vitality.

'Poor, poor Ruth!' (447). There can be no doubt that she is a victim throughout the book, but martyrs are certainly not victims, and there seems to be a case for viewing her death as something of a triumph, though not perhaps completely of the kind the author would have appreciated. The triumph is not only in her serene end – 'she displayed no outrage or discord even in her delirium'. (447) Her pathos is emphasised by her lying in the same attic room in which her child was born, stretched on the bed in utter helplessness, softly gazing at vacancy with her open, unconscious eyes, from which all the depth of their meaning had fled, and all they told was of a sweet, childlike insanity within. (448)

But the helplessness is deceptive, undercut implicitly by the renewed relationship with her seducer which has brought about her death. She watches through the night as she watched when he was ill in Wales many years before. But on that occasion she was outside the door, as she was outside society. His mother had claimed him, and when Ruth thanked God that he was well, Mrs Bellingham was outraged by the girl's claim on him 'as if, in fact, she had any lot or part in him' (85). His recovery is the beginning of her trials; his second recovery is the beginning of her peace. When she attends him the second time he is alone and friendless. No one can bar the door against Ruth, and it could be said that now, for the last and only time, she really has him. Her victory over him is not merely in possession, but in making a sacrifice which he does not deserve and which he cannot repay. His attempt to do so after her death is emphatically rejected. The spirit of such a 'victory' would scarcely seem to be Christian, but we might recall that we are enjoined to do good to those who have misused us in order that we may 'heap coals of fire upon their heads'.[6] It is a sacrifice of the self which implicates the person saved in its own fate, and I would with some trepidation suggest that if it is a strategy which owes a good deal to certain aspects of Christian morality, it is also an expression of a certain kind of female possessiveness and power. A similar message might be read in more than one of Christina Rossetti's poems – in the self-negating declarations of 'When I am dead, my dearest' whose apparent indifference ('And if thou wilt, remember,/ And if thou wilt, forget.') seems to betray a greater concern with the self than is made explicit. Or in the slightly morbid physical closeness of 'After Death', culminating in:

He did not love me living; but once dead
He pitied me; and very sweet it is
To know he still is warm though I am cold.[7]

Here the feeling seems to me almost vampiristic in its implied refusal of the dead to let the living go – indeed to attain the real fulfilment of love only after death. The self is denied as a reproach which thereby implicates the indifferent other – in some cases at least, an explicitly male other. Ruth's end is also a good example of the way in which Mrs Gaskell often presents her main characters with their pasts, giving them a chance to re-write their lives, to renew them or at least view them again. It is part of that strong sense of the total meaning of a single life which is one of her hallmarks, and is particularly seen in some of her shorter fiction.

5

Women, Death and Integrity 3: *North and South*

The two elements in this title, it may be noted, are allowed to stand beside each other – North *and* South, not North *or* South. The point is important because, as we so often find in Mrs Gaskell's work, we are not invited to make a final and absolute choice, but are given the opportunity to weigh both experiences, both sets of values, and give each its due. When Margaret returns to Helstone at the end of the book, she sees much to awaken memories – things which have not changed and retain their charm, though they also hurt her with their continuing, indifferent beauty:

> It hurt her to see the Helstone road so flooded in the sunlight, and every turn and every familiar tree so precisely the same in its summer glory as it had been in former years. Nature felt no change, and was ever young. (NS 385)

But much has changed too. The vicarage is now in the possession of an ardent teetotaller, his bustling, organising, well-meaning but insensitive wife, and their seven children. They are changing the house, and the kind of education given to the village children. 'And not before time', thinks Mr Bell, when he and Margaret are told of a cat's being roasted alive as a charm by the villagers. He first was opposed to the new educational plans, but later admits 'Anything rather than have that child brought up in such practical paganism' (390). 'There was change everywhere; slight, yet pervading all' (394). Mr Bell has the resignation of age towards the subject:

It is the first changes among familiar things that make such a mystery of time to the young, afterwards we lose the sense of the mysterious. I take changes in all I see as a matter of course. The instability of all human things is familiar to me, to you it is new and oppressive. (388)

But he speaks from the point of view of an old bachelor, living in scholarly obscurity with his manservant. For all his kindness he is maimed, spiritually, thinking of his own comfort, security, and, most grossly, his stomach. Change for Margaret is not something to be dismissed so easily. In one of the most crucial passages for understanding this book, and indeed some others of Mrs Gaskell's, she cries out to herself:

'I begin to understand now what heaven must be – and, oh! the grandeur and repose of the words – "The same yesterday, to-day, and for ever." Everlasting! "From everlasting to everlasting, Thou art God." That sky above me looks as though it could not change, and yet it will. I am so tired – so tired of being whirled on through all these phases of my life, in which nothing abides by me, no creature, no place; it is like the circle in which the victims of earthly passion eddy continually. I am in the mood in which women of another religion take the veil. I seek heavenly steadfastness in earthly monotony. If I were a Roman Catholic and could deaden my heart, stun it with some great blow, I might become a nun. But I should pine after my kind; no, not my kind, for love of my species could never fill my heart to the utter exclusion of love for individuals. Perhaps it ought to be so, perhaps not; I cannot decide to-night.' (400)

But she will not follow her parents whither they have recently gone (and where Mr Bell will shortly follow them). Absolute reconciliation is not for this world, and the gloomy thoughts that evening induces are balanced by her morning mood:

'After all it is right,' said she, hearing the voices of children at play while she was dressing. 'If the world stood still, it would retrograde and become corrupt, if that is not Irish.

Looking out of myself, and my own painful sense of change, the progress all around me is right and necessary.' (400)

I say 'balanced', not 'dispelled', because the essential value which is lived out in this book – particularly by Margaret – is admission that different things may exist together in our lives without destroying us. There is an openness to instability, uncertainty, changeableness and ambiguity. Her final words before she leaves Helstone are an acceptance of perpetual change as a condition of life:

> 'And I too change perpetually – now this, now that – now disappointed and peevish because all is not exactly as I had pictured it, and now suddenly discovering that the reality is far more beautiful than I had imagined it. Oh, Helstone! I shall never love any place like you.' (401)

When she has left the village she '[finds] her level' (401). At the beginning of the novel she is less experienced, and therefore less able to be assured that uncertainty is an acceptable state. She despises the trivial fussing over Edith's wedding arrangements and the superficial, cynical wit of Henry Lennox, but when the possibility of marriage comes into her own life, via this same man, she finds herself far from being settled and confident in mood. First 'the brightness of the sun' comes over her face, in the glad pleasure of renewing a London acquaintance (22). Her mother's complaints introduce a 'thin cold cloud' between her and the sun, but she and Henry set out 'in the merriest spirits in the world' (24), a mood which lasts through dinner. As he works himself up to his proposal, however, she becomes disturbed, only to overcome her disturbance by standing on her dignity. Yet when he takes her hand the disturbance of her inward calm returns, and she finds she is 'despising herself for the fluttering at her heart' (28). Once again she recovers her composure and refuses him, only to be reproaching herself a moment later for having given him pain. She puts him off by trying to close the subject entirely, but finds that this drives him into flippancy and her into a consequent return to annoyance and contempt. Finally she feels 'stunned' and 'unable to recover her self-possession enough to join in the trivial conversation that ensued between her father and Mr. Lennox' (30). On his departure, she reflects:

> How different men were to women! Here was she disturbed and unhappy, because her instinct had made anything but a refusal impossible; while he, not many minutes after he had met with a rejection of what ought to have been the deepest, holiest proposal of his life, could speak as if briefs, success, and all its superficial consequences of a good house, clever and agreeable society, were the sole avowed objects of his desires. . . . Then she took it into her head that, after all, his lightness might be but assumed, to cover a bitterness of disappointment which would have been stamped on her own heart if she had loved and been rejected. (32)

We may notice that her first, absolute judgement is modified by the end of the paragraph. Perhaps, indeed, men and women are not so dissimilar, but it is her uncertainty, and openness to the possibility of alternatives, that allows her to perceive this. When she comes to make the judgement on Helstone established in the course of her final visit she can encompass the whole experience. It is beautiful, but it is past; it is unchanging in her heart, subjectively, but in common with all things it is constantly changing. And on the larger scale, Milton and Helstone both exist. They cannot be denied, nor can they be made more than they are. The return to Helstone is crucial to Margaret at this point in her life. It gives her the opportunity to come to terms with what her life has been and will be – an experience shared by some older companions as a prelude to death, but one reserved for her as a final step into freedom.

In the passage of night-time musing I quoted above, Margaret regrets the instability of all things mortal, and that mortal yearning after our own kind which makes us cling to unstable, restless, troubled life. For a moment she feels the attraction of having her heart stunned with some great blow. It is reminiscent of the moment when her father first mentioned his doubts to her, and the whole painful process of change began: 'it was better to be stunned into numbness by hearing of all these arrangements, which seemed to be nearly completed before she had been told'. (36) Such a lament is not surprising, in view of the changes that have come upon her (and are yet to come) in the course of a year or so. It is not simply a matter of change in itself, however. The texture of experience suggests uncertainty, indecision, dividedness and the instability of discontent from the beginning. In spite of the easygoing nature of the couple who are about to marry, a faint note of discord is struck by Edith's mother's bemoaning 'constantly, though quietly . . . her hard lot in being united to one whom she could not love' (7). In this opening chapter Margaret herself is summing up an earlier phase of her life – her childhood – an experience which is a reconciliation to pain, involving self-repression. She hid her tears in childhood; is she to be condemned to the same experience again?

The character of the decision Mr Hale makes when he initiates the enormous change in his family's life and fortunes is typical of the man, but also characterises much of the 'feel' of experience throughout the book. His problem is, as Angus Easson observes in his notes, historical rather than a matter of strict faith (438). He feels he cannot subscribe to a Church which, it seems to him, compels men's belief. He must therefore give up his living and move the whole family to Milton Northern. It is scarcely his fault, since we cannot but believe that he is sincere in this rather abstruse point of conscience, but his act of integrity is perforce a rather negative one, involving doubt, uncertainty and withdrawal. Moreover his whole manner of avowal, when at last it comes, is about as far removed from a positive, clear declaration of some principle by which he would stand, as it is possible to be. After days of inward wrestling, and hours of sighing, he tells his daughter, being, as he admits, too much of a coward to break it to his wife himself. He plays with papers on the table in a 'nervous and confused manner', opens his lips to speak several times without beginning. His face when he has told her wears an expression of 'piteous distress . . . almost as imploring a merciful and kind judgement from his child' (33).

It is, of course, typical of this lover of 'speculative and metaphysical' problems that his one really active decision in the book, the decision which in fact impels all the rest of the story, should arise from abstruse doubt. Most of the practical consequences, in human and material terms, fall on his daughter, since his whole life appears to have been a retreat from the larger world into his parish, and from his family into his study. There are three deaths which affect Margaret closely. Her mother has never quite reconciled herself to the practical circumstances of her love and marriage. She cannot understand why her husband never sought preferment. She has not got his interest in books. Mr Hale's whole life has been in a sense a withdrawal from the world, and death completes that withdrawal. Mr Bell has not even attempted wider engagement with the world by marriage. His rooms in Oxford, closeted, lonely, self-centred, are the type of his last 'narrow cell'. Parallel with these three examples of lives which by their nature seem to anticipate the ultimate negative of death, Margaret encounters the pain of life as a means by which she can encompass experience and advance in maturity.

The doubt and negativity of Mr Hale's initial decision to give up his living is part of that general uncertainty which, as I have said, informs the whole book, and is seen characteristically in human gestures and features. Margaret views her father asleep on the train, his face in repose, but showing 'rest after weariness' rather than 'the serene calm of the countenance of one who led a placid, contented life'. The lines on his face speak 'plainly of habitual distress and depression'. When he wakens, after the first smile his face returns 'into its lines of habitual anxiety. He had a trick of half-opening his mouth as if to speak, which constantly unsettled the form of the lips, and gave the face an undecided expression' (16). But lest it should be imagined that uncertainty is confined to her father, we should note the many occasions on which Margaret herself feels changeable and undecided. To the world she appears 'superb', and assured even to the point of haughtiness, her habitual expression a direct contrast to her father's. This is how she first appears to Thornton:

> Margaret could not help her looks; but the short curled upper lip, the round, massive up-turned chin, the manner of

carrying her head, her movements, full of a soft feminine defiance, always gave strangers the impression of haughtiness . . .

She sat facing him and facing the light; her full beauty met his eye; her round white flexile throat rising out of the full, yet lithe figure; her lips, moving so slightly as she spoke, not breaking the cold serene look of her face with any variation from the one lovely haughty curve; her eyes, with their soft gloom, meeting his with quiet maiden freedom. (62–3)

Something of the unique quality of this heroine is suggested in 'soft feminine defiance', and I shall return to this in a moment, but what strikes the reader most forcibly here is the carefully composite detail in the picture, and the physicality, indeed the fleshliness, of this detail. Mrs Gaskell is not afraid of suggestions of the statuesque in 'massive'. It is sensual to the point of eroticism. She has 'taken off her shawl' to reveal further charms in her 'round white flexile throat'. Our attention is frequently drawn to her 'taper fingers', perhaps as a balance to any suggestion of cumbrousness, but one cannot escape the sense of weight and solidity in the description, and an accompanying sensuality. In part, of course, this is because a man is viewing her. The combination of provocativeness and appeal in 'soft feminine defiance', or the excitement suggested in the 'lovely haughty curve' of her lip betray a sexual engagement, but she has also the largeness of figure associated with (potential) maternity. She is, as one might say, 'all woman', and this womanliness is conveyed in her centred, self-assured poise. It speaks in her eyes, 'with their soft gloom, meeting his with quiet maiden freedom'. There is no confusion here, no falsity and no attachment beyond the necessary social intercourse. The feeling of 'togetherness' is promoted particularly by her being presented as a portrait – it is as though the eye travels over the subject, noting each point and drawing them together for a total impression. It is the visual embodiment of a 'powerful and decided nature' (48) but it suggests much more than simply strength of purpose.

The same sense of statuesque poise is apparent in Thornton's view of her at the dinner when their hands first touch:

> the curving lines of the red lips, just parted in the interest of
> listening to what her companion said – the head a little bent
> forwards, so as to make a long sweeping line from the sum-
> mit, where the light caught on the glossy raven hair, to the
> smooth ivory tip of the shoulder; the round white arms, and
> taper hands, laid lightly across each other, but perfectly mo-
> tionless in their pretty attitude. (161–2)

The 'long sweeping line' suggests the line of the artist's pen,
and again indicates unity and harmony. Thornton mentally com-
pares her favourably with his restless sister, 'now glancing here,
now there, but without any purpose in her observation' (161).

We certainly cannot doubt the essential strength of Margaret.
Dr Donaldson reflects on the literal strength of her handgrasp:
'Who would have thought that little hand could have given
such a squeeze?' (127). 'But the bones were well put together,'
he reflects, 'and that gives immense power.' He speaks of her
'backbone', another metaphor suggestive of inward strength
and well-composedness – a strength manifest in her handling
of domestic problems, the reception of news of her mother's
imminent death and the independence of her views on indus-
trial relations. There is a special kind of integrity in Margaret
which corresponds to the more obvious male integrity all around
her. However negative his decision may be, Mr Hale's integrity in making it is undoubted, as is the personal integrity of
his whole life. His son shows the same firmness in standing
fast against injustice, even though it costs him his career, threatens his freedom and forces him to live abroad. Mr Thornton is
self-made, clear-minded, determined, decisive; able (on the
whole) to compartmentalise his life; sure of his own rightness
in economic matters; incorruptible; the hard but just master. It
is not open to Margaret to compete with men in integrity of
their kind. All three of these men decide for themselves, and
thereby define themselves. Their whole lifestyle is their self-
definition, and as an inescapable result of the social order they
carry their women along with them (if they have any). Mrs
Hale must live in Milton; Fanny, and even the inflexible mother,

are carried with the man's success or fall with him. The accounts I have quoted of Margaret's appearance and personality are by men. Thornton's admiration is frankly sexual, even if he does not at first recognise it himself, and Dr Donaldson, too, reflects 'Such a girl as that would win my heart, if I were thirty years younger' (127). 'Integrity', involving wholeness, completion and untouchedness is perceived in Margaret, but she possesses it as an object rather than a subject – it might be called an 'integrity of the flesh' – the wholeness of a portrait, immobile, to be contemplated. Her untouchedness is her virginity – nothing has detracted from her absolute purity – but it means that she is seen as something already formed rather than filled with the instability that means also potentiality.

For in fact there is a deep irony in all this. Despite all the apparent composure of Margaret, her 'togetherness' and surety, her success in keeping her parents' heads above water, her comforting and encouraging the Higgins family and arguing confidently with Thornton and his mother, she is as much a representative of the pervasive uncertainty as anyone else. Margaret's completeness, exclusivity, untouchedness is apparent rather than real, and apparent to men, who wish to see such integrity there. For Mr Thornton her immobility is essentially of the nature of her virtue, but in fact, as we shall see, movement, uncertainty and instability are far more fundamental values for both him and Margaret when they see aright.

North and South is a book full of pain – not the pangs of hunger, as in *Mary Barton*, but the pain of stress and disturbance, of pangs of conscience and sexual torment. It is also the pain of loss, particularly for the heroine, and indeed it seems surprising on reflection that a happy ending could be retrieved from such unpropitious material. Those who are not suffering are the exceptions, and they are generally not admitted to centre stage, but rather used as foils to the more anguished characters. The most notable is Edith, who is first seen 'rolled . . . up into a soft ball of muslin and ribbon, and silken curls . . . gone off into a peaceful little after-dinner nap' (5). Her comfortable cocoon aptly suggests her sheltered existence, untroubled by any problems other than clothes and teething. Those whom we see in closer focus, of course, are always more likely to appear troubled than people we know distantly, but there seems little doubt that the sufferings of the Hales and John Thornton and his mother are real. The problems themselves are clearly enough stated, whether they be religious doubts, worry over illness or money, the consciousness of having lied, unrequited love, or bitter sorrow over the unhappiness of a beloved son. But the pain is embedded in the texture of the novel – in its kind of realism. Where *Mary Barton* is full of the stark shock of confrontation, *North and South*, with one notable exception, is diffusive. The weight of reality is borne much more by gesture and dialogue; two crucially repeated words are 'wince' and 'stun'. If the coin of experience in *Mary Barton* is moments, in *North and South* it is the rhythm of night and day.

Elizabeth Gaskell is very specific about times of day in this novel, and about what each of them means for her heroine. Mornings at the beginning of her story are a time of renewed hope for the future. Her face, as she watches her father wakening, is 'bright as the morning', speaking of 'boundless hope in the future' (17). After her father announces his planned change of life, sleep brings no refreshment. She drags herself up, 'thankful that the night was over, – unrefreshed, yet rested' (192). For most of the novel, life for Margaret is a matter of anxious activity by day and restless worry or watching through the night. When she first returns to Helstone, before her father has mentioned his doubts, she finds evenings 'rather difficult to fill agreeably' (19). After Henry Lennox's proposal she finds herself wishing bedtime were come 'that she might go over the events of the day again' (32). But it is not to bring her rest, since that very evening her father lays his doubts before her. At the end of the day she 'stole to bed after her father had left her, like a child ashamed of its fault'. 'Miserable, unresting night! Ill preparation for the coming day! She awoke with a start, unrefreshed, and conscious of some reality worse even than her feverish dreams' (43). Next day, after the news has been broken to her mother, Margaret rushes upstairs 'to stifle the hysteric sobs that would force their way at last, after the rigid self-control of the whole day' (47). She finds her daily life has changed immeasurably. In London there were few decisions left to her, but now 'every day brought some ques-

tion, momentous to her, and to those whom she loved, to be
settled' (51). She reassures her father that 'it is only that I am
tired to-night' (56) but the evening of their first day away from
Helstone 'without employment, passed in a room high up in
an hotel, was long and heavy' (57). On their first night in Milton,
Margaret feels 'inclined to sit down in a stupor of despair'.
She lies awake 'very long this night, planning how to lessen
the influence of Milton life on their mother' (89).

Few novels can have concentrated so much of their attention
on the hours of darkness. Sometimes the nights are simply described as wakeful or restless, on other occasions the experience of wakefulness is described in some detail – 'she was so
tired, so stunned, that she thought she never slept at all; her
feverish thoughts passed and repassed the boundary between
sleeping and waking, and kept their own miserable identity'
(191). Sometimes, by a reverse process, the nightmare is brought
into daytime experience as an image of terror or horror:

> The deep impression made by the interview, was like that
> of a horror in a dream; that will not leave the room although
> we waken up, and rub our eyes, and force a stiff rigid smile
> upon our lips. It is there – there, cowering and gibbering,
> with fixed ghastly eyes, in some corner of the chamber,
> listening to hear whether we dare to breathe of its presence
> to any one. (198)

This hysterical waking vision is the result of Thornton's proposal, following upon the scene before the mob of strikers. On
one occasion the subject of sleep and beds is actually discussed
in a half-comic way, Mrs Hale suggesting that beds are not
what they were in her youth, and that until she slept on a
water-bed she 'did not know when she had had a good sound
resting sleep' (201).

The detailed accounts given of the passage of days and nights,
and the constant marking of the beginning and end of the diurnal round gives a painful sense of the monotony of ordinary
existence – a life not threatened with the absolute finality of
starvation, but wearing in its demands on making-do, reconciling one's fellow-beings over trifles, feeling one's potential

circumscribed while one makes unrecognised sacrifices. It is the realism of gentility. When they settle in Milton they must find rooms suitable to their size of family, their income, their taste and their social standing. Any place to rest their head will not do. Margaret must soothe her mother's fears about health risks, and conciliate her to a new life in a strange town, as well as placate or put down the maidservant who believes that her mother threw herself away on Mr Hale. All these things are unspectacular, but essential to bearable family life. At the end of the first year of her trials, Margaret looks back and wonders how she bore them:

> If she could have anticipated them, how she would have shrunk away and hid herself from the coming time! And yet day by day had, of itself, and by itself, been very endurable – small, keen, bright little spots of positive enjoyment having come sparkling into the very middle of sorrows. (103)

'Where can we live but days?' asks the poet, and it is a question clearly endorsed in this novel. But we also live in nights. Night should be the time of rest, and it is rest that Margaret covets throughout the book, from the 'indescribable weariness' she feels at the preparations for Edith's wedding (11) to her lament at Helstone – 'I am so tired – so tired of being whirled on through all these phases of my life, in which nothing abides by me, no creature, no place' (400). She would seek 'heavenly steadfastness in earthly monotony'.

In its absolute form her desire for rest is the desire for death, an urge most clearly expressed here in Bessy Higgins' desire to view Paradise. The diurnal round which, for all its wearingness, is a source of strength to Margaret, is to Bessy simply a series of 'bits o' time' which are a distraction from Heavenly rest. 'Do you think such life as this is worth caring for?' gasps Bessy (90). Margaret urges her not to be impatient with her life 'whatever it is', but Bessy feels 'tossed about wi' wonder' (91). Margaret cannot enter into her affinity with death, shrinking from it 'with all the clinging to life so natural in the young and healthy' (89). Even revisiting Helstone, at her most exhausted, she desires calm and stability within, rather than be-

yond, life. Yet life seems to offer only insubstantiality and transience, as she reflects after a night's watching at her mother's
bedside:

> The dull gray days of the preceding winter and spring, so
> uneventless and monotonous, seemed more associated with
> what she cared for now above all price. She would fain have
> caught at the skirts of that departing time, and prayed it to
> return, and give her back what she had too little valued while
> it was yet in her possession. What a vain show Life seemed!
> How unsubstantial, and flickering, and flitting! (170)

In face of the possible loss of her mother she feels loss in everything – even the terible night just past. Monotony is assurance,
change means loss.

Margaret comes from a world that appears to represent stability and freedom. The stability is present in both her adopted
London home, with its wealth and monotonous ease, and apparently in Helstone also. Having always disliked the decorum
her aunt required of a woman walking the streets of towns,
she becomes free to adopt her own rhythm of the 'bounding
fearless step' in the woods about Helstone (71). In Milton she
finds this freedom curtailed in a new way. The townspeople
violate her space by bustling close past her and even making
remarks on her appearance. Yet it is out of this disturbance of
her privacy that she meets Higgins and his family. She is
'shocked but not repelled' by his words on his daughter (73),
and 'half-amused, half-nettled' by his invitation to their home
(74). The feeling of disturbance and the mixed response are
part of that uncertainty which is the quick of life and marks
the beginning of Margaret's new openness to possibilities.

The two most important men in Margaret's life – her father
and Thornton – seem respectively to represent, as sensitive specu-
lator and man of action, the undecided she finds so painful
and the decided and absolute she thinks she requires. Yet significantly she understands that 'the opposition of character . . .
seemed to explain the attraction they felt towards each other'
(80). It is an observation that suggests how difference may be
held in creative tension. For all that, she finds Thornton too

absolute, and is glad when he 'looks anxious' (166). He is 'as iron a chap as any in Milton' (163), and his ideas of the laws of economic life are rigidly hierarchical, Darwinian and determinist. They are the economic and biological equivalent of Bessy Higgins' religious predeterminism expressed just a few pages before. 'Margaret's whole soul rose up against him while he reasoned in this way' (152–3) but at almost the same moment she is forced to acknowledge another side to the man, and in doing so to feel again that anxiety, disturbance and uncertainty are of the essence of life:

> How reconcile those eyes, that voice, with the hard-reasoning, dry, merciless way in which he laid down axioms of trade, and serenely followed them out to their full consequences? The discord jarred upon her inexpressibly. (153)

They cannot be reconciled, in the sense of ironing out the differences and saying they are the same thing. They both exist, and must both be given their weight. Mrs Thornton, in her proud absoluteness, speaks a great truth when she says that 'South country people are often frightened by what our Darkshire men and women only call living and struggling' (116). Margaret is not afraid of seeing that to live is to struggle, but life is also change, unease, instability, and this is something Margaret could teach others as she experiences it herself. To acknowledge our own uncertainty and dividedness in the face of an uncertain, divided and mysteriously painful life requires the greatest integrity.

We constantly witness the crumbling of absoluteness, the clear becoming irresolute, the iron will a vulnerable flesh. The resolute Mrs Thornton has an 'uneasy tenderness' over her feebly self-centred daughter Fanny, but it is the only hint of a chink in her armour until, following a conversation with her son in Chapter XXIII, 'Her servants wondered at her directions, usually so sharply-cut and decided, now confused and uncertain' (187–8). The reason for this unwonted behaviour is her son's possible attachment to Margaret, and he himself, who has just been deciding on punishment for the strikers 'clean and sharp as a sword' (188) is a moment later reduced to indecisiveness by the apparent forlornness of his hope. He becomes exposed to feelings so disturbing and so mixed that he cannot form his ideas into any settled response:

> And it doubles the gladness, it makes the pride glow, it sharp-
> ens the sense of existence till I hardly know if it is pain or
> pleasure, to think that I owe it to one . . . whom I love, as I
> do not believe man ever loved woman before. (194–5)

Margaret finds her feelings changing the moment he has gone – from 'proud dislike into something different and kinder, if nearly as painful – self-reproach for having caused such mortification to any one' (196). The pain that both parties feel is part of the heightened emotional tension induced by passion, but pain, as I have said, is endemic in this work, particularly for the heroine. She is pained by leaving Helstone, by the death of her parents and Mr Bell, as well as that of Bessy Higgins, by false accusations and by her sense of wrongdoing when she lies to protect Frederick. Beyond all is that sense of daily pain involved in survival with an indecisive father, an ailing mother, a reduced income and an alien environment. The repeated references to 'flinching' and 'wincing' metaphorise the rawness of sensibilities open to acute pain. The complementary sensation is 'stunning' or 'numbing'. Taken together the words suggest a sensibility heightened to the extremes of sensation, which can only be relieved by some shock that deadens the nerves for a while and gives insensitivity to pain by a violent blow.

Two crises clearly stand out as being of supreme significance in Margaret's story. The first is the episode in which she challenges Thornton to face the mob and then throws herself before him and takes the blow meant for him. Her intervention may well, as Thornton says, have saved his life. In taking the blow, and indeed in her first facing the mob, she introduces that element of confusion and uncertainty which is a hallmark of this novel, into the 'man to man' confrontation. The presence of a woman turns the fierce determination of the mob into something more 'irresolute' in a moment. The role of the woman is the traditional one of conciliation and martyrdom as far as the public impression goes. She defuses the situation by taking the violence upon herself and becoming the injured body. But obviously, as both she and Thornton realise, the act has powerful sexual overtones. Her challenge to him to go downstairs is a sexual challenge, and her taking of the blow is a sexual reconciliation, marked by blood and wounding. Like so many encounters in this work it is notable for its self-contradictory nature. Having challenged him to go alone, she regrets the command and throws herself before him. In the light of this, how are we to take her avowal when she has recovered from the incident that she had been 'anxious that there should be fair play on each side' (190)? It is surely a defensive rationalisation. Is it only a change in sensibilities between two ages that makes her traumatised reaction seem extreme? Whatever she felt for him before, it is clear that the incident is an advance in intimacy of a sexual nature, as her reference to her 'maiden pride' (191) indicates. There is involved for her a real question of integrity. She will stand by her action, ambiguous though it may seem. But alone, she must test her *absolute* integrity, answerable only to God. There would seem to be two kinds of integrity – that we owe to our social and sexual beings, which is by definition not absolute, but a recognition of our own changeability, and a willingness to exist with it; and that we owe to ourselves alone, and which can only be measured in terms of that transcendent Absolute we call God.

Her second crisis is the lie she tells in order to allow her brother time to leave the country. At the moment she commits the sin there come together several elements we have already noted as crucially carrying meaning in the novel. First is Margaret's stillness; not here the stillness of repose, but the stillness and firmness of an indomitable will: 'She never blenched or trembled. She fixed him with her eye' (273). As so often the key word 'now' makes an appearance. Of course her apparent calm masks an agonising struggle only to be overcome by that 'stunned' condition which here amounts to an almost trance-like state in which she wears a 'glassy, dream-like stare' (274). The policeman 'thought to have seen her wince' (275), but it is not until she is alone that she falls in a 'dead swoon' – a reaction to unbearable tension, but also the horror of being forced into a lie. The chapter is called 'False and True'; Margaret is false to fact and to herself in order to be true to her brother, but even the clearly mitigating circumstances cannot relieve her from the feeling of having violated her own integrity. She rejects the comfort of sharing her secret: 'Alone she would go before God, and cry for His absolution. Alone she would endure her disgraced position in the opinion of Mr Thornton' (287). It would seem it is easier to admit one's fallibility to God than to man, but the seeds of that admission of dependency upon another which is the prerequisite of love have already been sown at the factory gates, although her heart cannot admit it.

When she finally comes to terms with the problem for herself, she has to go back to the nursery where:

> On some such night as this she remembered promising to herself to live as brave and noble a life as any heroine she ever read or heard of in romance, a life sans peur et sans reproche; it had seemed to her then that she had only to will, and such a life would be accomplished. And now she had learnt that not only to will, but also to pray, was a necessary condition in the truly heroic. Trusting to herself, she had fallen. (411–12)

Putting away childish things, she realises her dependence upon a transcendent truth with which she must engage if she is to establish her integrity. True integrity is not defensive self-enclosure and self-dependence, but outgoing and creative, realising our own natures and giving ourselves to the necessary instability and imperfection of things. This she discovers socially, sexually and transcendentally.

Anguish over a love relationship is not confined to the woman. When Thornton's belief in that 'integrity of the flesh' he observed in her is overthrown he suffers all the pangs of sexual jealousy. In a book of conflicting emotions and impulses, the dividedness of his feelings towards her is perhaps the most extreme and disturbing example of inward pain:

> He dreamt of her; he dreamt she came dancing towards him

with outspread arms, and with a lightness and gaiety which made him loathe her, even while it allured him. But the impression of this figure of Margaret . . . was so deeply stamped upon his imagination, that when he wakened he felt hardly able to separate the Una from the Duessa; and the dislike he had to the latter seemed to envelope and disfigure the former. (331)

Recalling the horrifying image of filth apparent when Duessa is revealed in *The Faerie Queene,* one cannot doubt the depth of feeling which can make the word 'loathe' appropriate to Thornton's feelings. Yet at a subsequent interview he would, for a look, 'prostrate himself in penitent humility'. To rouse that single glance 'he could have struck her before he left' (336). The mixture of self-abasement, loathing and erotically associated violence reveals not only Thornton's personal turmoil, but a classic male complex of sexual feelings, apparently reinforced to some extent by the woman's feelings about herself.

After the proposal of Henry Lennox, Margaret feels 'guilty and ashamed of having grown so much into a woman as to be thought of in marriage' (32–3). Initiation, with its loss of self-sufficiency, seems to be, for the woman, a source of guilt, like the loss of virginity which is its physical counterpart. Margaret thinks it possible, if only for a moment, that she could take the veil, were she in a different culture. But the implication of every aspect of the novel is surely, as I have been at pains to suggest, that we should not be alone. Certainly this is true for men. There is an interesting declaration by Thornton on the subject of 'a man', in which he touches on the essence of integrity as a lonely, self-sustaining state:

> I take it that 'gentleman' is a term that only describes a person in his relation to others; but when we speak of him as 'a man,' we consider him not merely with regard to his fellowmen, but in relation to himself, – to life – to time – to eternity. (164)

Margaret tells Thornton to go and face the rioters as a man, but she implies thereby the very opposite of self-sustaining alone-

ness. He is to 'speak to them kindly' (177). This is in fact what
he does, and later his relationship with Higgins shows this
same idea of manliness which sees communion with others as
the validation of a true human integrity.[1]

Margaret's story represents the classic journey from youth
to maturity, in which the novice must pass certain tests of initiation, involving self-discovery. She comes to understand the
necessary instability of all mortal things and in fact to see it as
a strength. She goes out into the world, surrendering her self-
sufficiency, her heart and her independence of God in finding
her own true self. She is involved in a process of steady loss
of family and friends. Even her one living, close relative,
Frederick, must live abroad, with no hope of any early return,
if indeed he still wishes it. 'It seems so selfish in me to regret
it' [his adoption of Spain], says Margaret, 'and yet he is lost to
me, and I am so lonely' (382–3). Her loneliness would seem a
paradox in the context of that sociability which I have suggested
as the essence of her maturity, but this is not so. She is the
hero-adventurer who must leave her own country in order to
begin a new life, and losing her family is part of that process.
Traditionally it is the young prince who is exogamous, found-
ing by his marriage a new dynasty. Here the hero is a woman,
who does not wait at home to be wooed. That life is left behind with the cocooned Edith and a final glimpse of the nursery on the opening pages. She gathers her past life together
to draw strength from it before striking out into a new phase.
Towards the end she returns with her Aunt Shaw to Milton
and takes stock again. She takes a cup to remind her of Bessy
– only memory is possible there. But with the living she must
settle accounts. She apologises to Mrs Thornton, while main-
taining her own point-of-view, and the proud lady acknowledges the concession, repeating twice that she is glad Margaret
has done her justice, to which Margaret responds by asking
that justice should be done to *her* in the shape of an acceptance of her integrity. Due weight is given by both sides to
experience, and neither is allowed to subsume the other. Higgins,
too, 'does her justice', and in return for the cup she has taken
she gives a Bible. And so Margaret finds herself alone and an
heiress. She can make her home anywhere, but where *is* her

home? She has returned to London, but this is a life she has
outgrown despite its temporary soothing comforts. The question is brought into focus for us by the deaths of her father
and Mr Bell.

Immediately before his death Mr Hale reviews his life and
the momentous decision of conscience he made, deciding that
'even if I could have foreseen that cruellest martyrdom of suffering, through the sufferings of one whom I loved, I would
have done just the same as far as that step of openly leaving
the church went' (349). He revisits Oxford, as though he too is
doing and receiving justice, and finally he entrusts Margaret
to Mr Bell, who in turn surveys *his* life, albeit with a gloomier
eye. In his return to Helstone he proposes to himself a return
to stability. He was born in Milton, but the orchards are gone,
and he now often loses his way. Only in dreams can he return
to his youth, where all was fresh and possible, but the dream
is now so real that 'his present life seemed like a dream' as it
is in the sense that a hotel room is not a home, a place of
peace and rest, but a temporary shelter:

> Where was he? In the close, handsomely furnished room of
> a London hotel! Where were those who spoke to him, moved
> around him, touched him, not an instant ago? Dead! buried!
> lost for evermore, as far as earth's for evermore would ex-
> tend. He was an old man, so lately exultant in the full strength
> of manhood. The utter loneliness of his life was insupport-
> able to think about. (382)

For these two men, as for Bessy and Mrs Hale, home is death,
the final resting-place. Their surveys of the vicissitudes, or, in
Bessy's case, the unbearable pains, of life enable them to leave
it. But Margaret is far from ready to die, and 'home' seems a
concept full of possibilities. Is it Heaven, our first home; childhood, to which so many return for solace; a new home; the
world of men? All, in fact, are true, and all require a different
finding of the self. Edith, we are told at the beginning, found
'anything of a gipsy or make-shift life was really distasteful to
her' (7). But while Margaret has all these possible kinds of home,
she has not one which can give her the peace she craves. Mrs

Shaw and Edith persist in calling Harley Street 'home', but it is, as the chapter title suggests, 'Ease not Peace'. Helstone she can give its due and lay to rest, Milton also. Yet could she but acknowledge it, this release from the ties of home and family is the escape she needs to show her that 'home is where the heart is' – not a concrete dwelling or specific place, but that realm in which we feel it is right for us to be. The dying turn to transcendent peace, the living turn again into life and make their home in the new heart's love, as of course do Margaret and Thornton.

6

Women and History: 'My Lady Ludlow'

Most critics have agreed in objecting that the interpolated account of events in the French Revolution which Lady Ludlow relates in order to prove the folly of teaching the common people to read and write, is an artistic error which unbalances the overall shape of 'My Lady Ludlow'. It could be claimed that there is less harm to be done to a tale which the narrator herself claims 'is no story: it has, as I said, neither beginning, middle, nor end' (EL 90). Yet the actual events and characters of the 'story within a (non) story' are scarcely of intense interest in themselves, and would seem rather to divert our attention from the business of Hanbury than develop any new themes or ideas. We know already that Lady Ludlow is opposed to universal literacy; do we need to have the point reinforced by a long and circumstantial account of doings in the French Revolution?

While it cannot be denied that the episode is over-long, and over-autonomous in its romantic interest, I do consider it of central importance to the whole tale, for two reasons. First, it is historical, and together with some other details, it gives a fairly careful context for the events in Hanbury. We are post-Industrial and post-French Revolution. The letter to Margaret Dawson is dated 1811; my lady dies in 1814. Now this feel for history, political and social, is important, because the particular disaster recounted in the story of the de Crequys is a type of the whole disaster of revolution which came upon France, but not upon Britain. For Lady Ludlow, every departure from tradition, but particularly any movement towards education for the masses, is a step towards the momentous act of 1792 – namely, royal decapitation. Nevertheless such a fate did not

119

then overtake the English monarchy, and in the person of Lady Ludlow there are suggestions of why this may have been.

'My Lady Ludlow' is not only a historical tale. As with many of Mrs Gaskell's works it represents an idyll. The narrator, as an old woman, opens her memories with the sense of change – from slow coaches to fast trains, from long letters to short notes, from an age with leisure to reflect to an age which has very little leisure for anything. She is referring to an idyll of her youth, and idylls are notoriously static. There is a vaguely medieval atmosphere about life at Hanbury Court when Margaret arrives there. The house was (according to my lady) once a priory, and while some of the young ladies marry, the quietness, sparsity of luxury and devotedness (even to death) of these girls to the lady of the manor might suggest the relationship of nuns to their Prioress. It is a self-enclosed life, always looking backwards, whether with nostalgia to a vanished youth or with fear to a violent past. The fort is being held, as it were, by this isolated household, but it is a dying cause, and indeed Lady Ludlow's own son dies in the course of the story. The sense of a historical context is reinforced by the description of the house itself, with windows like those at Hampton Court, its arches and stone mullions, and the Virginia Creeper said to have been first planted in England by one of my lady's ancestors.

Typically of the author, history is not simply dates, but is essentially a human phenomenon; one associated with natural growth. The subject of inherited predispositions is considered in the semi-comic belief held by Lady Ludlow that Hanburys have a special olfactory gift:

> 'So the old families have gifts and powers of a different and higher class to what the other orders have. My dear, remember that you try if you can smell the scent of dying strawberry-leaves in this next autumn. You have some of Ursula Hanbury's blood in you, and that gives you a chance.' (121)

For her, this is the meaning of history – inherited abilities of a subtle and mysterious character which are the preserve of a certain class and which must be maintained for the general wellbeing of society. Such natural faculties are exclusive and privileged, and look to unchanging tradition. The belief is humorously undercut a few pages later when we are told that Mr Gray, notwithstanding the supposed ability of the Hanbury hounds to recognise a Hanbury by instinct and reserve their affections for the favoured family, goes up to one of them 'and patted him in the most friendly manner, the dog meanwhile looking pleased, and affably wagging his tail, just as if Mr Gray had been a Hanbury' (127). A further association between Lady Ludlow and the past is suggested by the fragments of marble she has brought back from Rome. They are remnants of a vanished Empire, to which she pays due reverence – even to the earth itself:

> once when I thought of cleaning them with soap and water, at any rate, she bade me not to do so, for it was Roman dirt – earth, I think, she called it – but it was dirt all the same. (118)

For Mrs Gaskell a far more fundamental characteristic of the natural in history than attachment to the past, and genetic predispositions, is the tendency to change. The number and surprisingness of the changes in this little story are almost comic, considering the antipathy shown by the lady of Hanbury Court herself to any form of change whatsoever. The poacher literally becomes a gamekeeper; his ragged child becomes the local vicar, traditional pillar of the establishment. Captain James, introduced by my lady herself, and even more extreme than her in his Toryism, marries the daughter of a dissenting baker. Lady Ludlow's faith in 'blood' is hardly likely to prove a stop to such change. Nor, in general terms, is her own influence. She is maternalistic, operating a benevolent despotism over 'her' area by letting it be known what she approves and disapproves of. But Mr Gray points out to her that her influence with the villagers is not what she might like to believe:

> 'They would not do anything your ladyship disliked if it was likely to come to your knowledge; but if they could conceal it from you, the knowledge of your dislike to a particular line of conduct would never make them cease from pursuing it.' (204)

In practical matters she is behind the times and inefficient. The dissenting baker's land is far better-managed than her own. She extends patronage in a ridiculous manner by inviting a retired seaman to look after her estate on the death of Mr Horner. Nevertheless her methods have their virtues. The nature of maternalism means that one has the opportunity to judge every case on its merits and flout the letter of the law where the spirit dictates some quite other judgement. When Harry Latham the magistrate tells her that the offence of theft is not bailable, she replies that this is an extraordinary case and that she herself will go bail. On his objecting that it is against the law she magisterially dismisses such pettifogging excuses:

> 'Bah! Bah! Bah! Who makes laws? Such as I, in the House of Lords – such as you, in the House of Commons. We, who make the laws in St. Stephen's, may break the mere forms of them, when we have right on our sides, on our own land, and amongst our own people.' (113)

There is a curious paradox here. Lady Ludlow's appeal to the particular circumstances of each individual case promotes contingency over the absoluteness of the law. But the means by which she accomplishes this is a kind of absolutism, exemplified by her attitude to Mr Gray:

> 'But, my lady, it might convince him,' I said, with perhaps injudicious perseverance.
> 'And why should he be convinced?' she asked, with gentle inquiry in her tone. 'He has only to acquiesce.' (185)

The absoluteness of faith, she suggests, is preferable to the contingency of conviction by argument. And when Mr Horner protests that he could have trained little Harry Gregson 'to understand the rules of discretion' and not use his literacy to read private correspondence, she turns on him with:

> 'Trained! Train a barn-door fowl to be a pheasant, Mr. Horner! That would be the easier task. But you did right to speak of discretion rather than honour. Discretion looks to the conse-

quences of actions – honour looks to the action itself, and is an instinct rather than a virtue. After all, it is possible you might have trained him to be discreet.' (186)

Her professed stand on absolute values is turned upon her by Miss Galindo when the forthright spinster declares she is on Mr Gray's side:

> 'when I see a downright good, religious man, I'm apt to think he's got hold of the right clue, and that I can do no better than hold on by the tails of his coat and shut my eyes, if we've got to go over doubtful places on our road to Heaven.' (212)

Her shutting her eyes to 'leap over the ditch to the side of education' is a leap of faith, an absolute commitment that she makes for the man, rather than conversion by persuasion of what he advocates. Miss Galindo, an apparently ridiculous figure in some ways, is important as a commentator. She assumes a masculine role in becoming a clerk, and does it well, but retains a vigorous contempt for men themselves. She tells Margaret that she has been 'so curt, so abrupt, so abominably dull, that I'll answer for it he [the lawyer] thinks me worthy to be a man'. (223) The implication is that 'female' garrulity and liveliness are positive virtues. She sees things positively from a logical and reflective mind, despite her eccentricity, as when she sharply corrects Lady Ludlow's opinion that the landowner has never done anything to make the villagers follow her lead:

> Your ancestors have lived here time out of mind, and have owned the land on which their forefathers lived ever since there were forefathers. You yourself were born amongst them, and have been like a little queen to them ever since, I might say, and they've never known your ladyship do anything but what was kind and gentle; (213)

She perhaps represents what women can do if they are of a certain character and are 'given their heads'. She plays a notable part in persuading Lady Ludlow to reconcile herself to change. Perhaps most importantly she is a contrast to the lady herself, who has her own particular means of dealing with change, arising from the elusive quality of her own personality. For although we feel she is a little ridiculous in the extreme expression of her views sometimes, she is someone who claims and wins affection from all she meets. Above all she is gracious. This is a quality traditionally attributed to its possessors by virtue of birth – 'Your Gracious Majesty' implies the conferring of benefits within the gracious one's gift, and undoubtedly this sense of the word would apply to Lady Ludlow. People are given audience with her, and she is on her dignity. Nevertheless she has the ability to seem to beg a favour when she is conferring one. 'Will you do me the favour to allow your eldest daughter to supply her place in my household?' is the form in which her letter invites Margaret to join her at Hanbury Court. She has manners which are based on consideration for others and whose generosity of spirit may be embodied in gestures both formal and individually human:

> as she entered, she gave us all round one of those graceful sweeping curtsies, of which I think the art must have died out with her, – it implied so much courtesy; – this time it said, as well as words could do, 'I am sorry to have kept you all waiting, – forgive me.' (107)

The chair in which the crippled Margaret is allowed to sit, giving 'one's body rest just in that part where one most needed it' (117) seems to be a symbol of that gracious accommodating love which my lady stands for. For this graciousness is marked with the qualities of love, and a very high form of love. She is not self-centred, but genuinely concerned with the welfare of others. It is, to use Herbert's phrase, a 'quick-eyed love', that anticipates the needs of others and feels for them. Is this graciousness inherited or acquired? It certainly makes her maternalism far more appealing than the savage paternalism of her forefathers, as we realise when she tells the tale of her grandfather's forcing the parson of the day to eat a rook pie, and laughing uproariously at his own joke, although my lady 'could not look again, for shame' (131).

It would be folly to say that graciousness is confined to women,

but it undoubtedly goes, in this case, with a suggestion of vulnerability which is decidedly feminine. She is upright but frail,
undoubtedly makes wrong decisions; moreover her circumstances, with her property mortgaged and almost all her children dead, add to a sense of pity for her, reinforced by our
realisation that her age is past and she is bearing up against
the tide. After her son's death she seems 'altered in many ways
– more uncertain and distrustful of herself, as it were' (228).
Yet her graciousness is also a source of womanly power. She
is completely unshaken on discovering that Mr Gray has over-
heard her conversation with Harry Lathom, in which she repeated all the arguments she had rejected from her parson only
that morning:

> 'Mr. Gray and I did not quite part friends,' she continued,
> bowing towards him; 'but it so happened that I saw Job
> Gregson's wife and home, – I felt that Mr. Gray had been
> right and I had been wrong, so, with the famous inconsist-
> ency of my sex, I came hither to scold you,' smiling towards
> Mr. Lathom, who looked half-sulky yet. . . . (114)

Her graciousness here is a source of power because it disarms
criticism. She employs the mildest of understatements, which
also implies that she and the parson *are* friends, to account for
their disagreement, and admits her errors freely. The invoca-
tion of female inconsistency is disingenuous, since any suggestion of flightiness is clearly quite out of the case, and the urbane
manner of her speech shows that she is really in control, a fact
confirmed by her propelling Mr Lathom into her coach to carry
out the illegal course she has proposed. She has been diplo-
matic, but she has the self-knowledge to see herself in the wrong,
the honourable honesty to acknowledge it, and the courage to
put a wrong right. This is an example of reconciliation in personal terms, and it images the larger spirit of social reconciliation in the story. Priest and poacher, for example, are reconciled
through mutual respect: 'The poacher had a feeling of physical protection towards the parson; while the latter had shown
the moral courage, without which Gregson would never have
respected him' (216). Captain James and the Baptist baker are

reconciled over management of the estate. Time is the great agent in this work. If we are given, or give ourselves, time to know and understand, we cannot remain apart from others. Beyond all is death itself, which is the greatest reconciler. Lady Ludlow consents to the school when her son has died. It is only when he has died that Margaret realises what she has lost in Mr Horner. As so often in Mrs Gaskell, the absolute is used to define the relative – death giving perspective to life – 'the thoughts of illness and death seem to turn many of us into gentlemen and gentlewomen, as long as such thoughts are in our minds' (228).

I have proposed that My Lady Ludlow could suggest how Britain escaped the French Revolution. The reason is clearly that moderation, adaptability and mingling of classes marked a society which could adapt to new circumstances, given time. Miss Galindo employs her usual eccentric arguments to tell a truth about social mobility. While she is against the solid matters of industrialism, a baker may, she claims, rise in the world by his labour:

> I dare say he would have been born a Hanbury, or a lord if he could; and if he was not, it is no fault of his, that I can see, that he made good bread (being a baker by trade), and got money, and bought his land. (250)

The revolution which Lady Ludlow feared if education were granted to the poor is clearly avoided in part by the very fact of education. But Lady Ludlow herself grants the means to education, and, albeit unconsciously, plays a part in change whose roots are in the stuff of personal, everyday intercourse. She herself, in avoiding damaging social confrontation, is a means of reconciliation, and the natural graciousness which is her mysterious quality – perhaps, as she would claim, the product of hundreds of years of training and breeding – is deeply implicated in the larger process. The message is brought home comically at the end of the story when my lady confounds the small-minded snobs about her by behaving exactly as Mrs Brooke, the baker's wife, does:

She takes out her own pocket-handkerchief, all snowy cambric, and lays it softly down on her velvet lap, for all the world as if she did it every day of her life, just like Mrs. Brooke, the baker's wife. . . . (256–7)

At the beginning of her tale Margaret tells us that 'you will never meet with a Lady Ludlow in these days' (90). This is true in more than one way. She is of a specific historic age, a left-over from pre-Revolution times, her thinking influenced irremediably by that terrible watershed. She is also the product of a system now dead. Her special behaviour cannot be repeated in a different age because her manners are of her own time. She seems, regarded in one light, to have the stasis of a mythic figure. She looks back and regrets change. But because of her, quite directly, the future *is* a matter of change and reconciliation, and she herself is a leader in that change. We cannot and would not want to go back to her age, but it is not invalidated by this truth; on the contrary its values are vindicated in human terms, and as with all great fiction we feel the seamless unity of the fabric of life, stretching from individual to institution, moments to years.

I have referred to 'My Lady Ludlow' throughout as a 'story' or 'tale', but Margaret Dawson specifically denies this form to her narrative: 'It is no story: it has, as I said, neither beginning, middle, nor end' (90). In so doing, I think, she draws attention to the inconclusiveness of the action. It cannot really be said to be the 'story' of any particular character. We see some episodes in Lady Ludlow's life, but while, as I have said, she is crucial to the meaning, the events of her life do not give the narrative shape. Nor is it the story of Margaret Dawson's life. But the events selected have a shape, typically for Elizabeth Gaskell, conferred by a sense of value – suggested in the opening paragraph, where values of today are set against those of the past. In place of a 'beginning, middle and end' we feel a rhythm, a shift, the closing of a life and an age; but opening out from that life and age a new one, so the shift is one of loss and gain, decline and revival, ending and continuity at the same time. History has been lived, and though those who were a part of it are no more, the values their living embodied in a sense create all the ages that are to come.

7
Cranford and Economics

Cranford is a peculiarly rich book. It is an idyll, redolent of the eighteenth century, but it is as strictly realistic as any of Elizabeth Gaskell's novels. It is full of pain, loss and unfulfilled hope, but it is perhaps her most purely comic work. It is an old people's book, but celebrates the open eyes of childhood. It ranges from the pleasures and pains of sexuality to the fulfilment of providence.

For now, however, I would like to consider it as Mrs Gaskell's reflections on the idea of 'economy'. There are in fact three concepts involved here – first 'economics', the great (masculine) subject which involves banks, commerce and nations – that 'Political Economy' and 'theories of trade' of which the author of *Mary Barton* claimed to know nothing; second, economy as *domestic* economy, the way a home is run – not merely as a matter of money, but as the whole way that home governs itself as a social unit. Finally, and connected to this second meaning, is economy in the sense of 'thrift'. This is obviously very close to the 'business and bosom' of Cranford. Its general practice is referred to as 'elegant economy' (CR42), and goes hand-in-hand with straitened circumstances.

If one were to divide these three meanings into two groups, 'economics' would clearly form the first, as representing the philosophy of the great world. In Cranford this world is the 'great neighbouring commercial town of Drumble, distant only twenty miles on a railroad' (39). 'Drumble' is derived from a dialect word for the buzzing of bees, and the nearby town is clearly the place where work is done and commercial expansion is carried on in a serious way. Its only representative is Mary Smith's father, and he is an undoubted man of business. It was against his advice that Deborah originally invested in the Town and County Bank, whose failure ruins Matty, and

129

forces her into 'trade'. He scolds his daughter well for allowing Matty to give her five sovereigns away for a worthless
bill; his manner of calculating accounts when Matilda is ruined
is ruthless and incomprehensible to the two women: 'if we made
the slightest inquiry, or expressed the slightest want of com-
prehension, he had a sharp way of saying, "Eh? eh? It's as
clear as daylight. What's your objection?"' (195). His strictures
upon Matty's handling of the tea trade are severe, and clearly
based on good business sense. He wonders 'how tradespeople
were to get on if there was to be a continual consulting of
each other's interests, which would put a stop to all competi-
tion directly' (200). Even Mary can see that Matty will never
thrive if she insists on letting her heart rule her head, or, put
another way, her interest in her fellow-creatures overcome her
economic sense.

Matty's shopkeeping, in any serious economic sense, is surely
a joke. It works on a limited scale because she lives in an enclosed and 'primitive' society, where a rival shopkeeper kindly
turns customers off to her on the pretext that she supplies finer
teas, and where, because she gives good weight 'they, in their
turn, brought many a little country present to the "old rector's
daughter"' (205).

But are not Miss Matty herself, and certainly her fellow
Cranford ladies, a kind of joke, however indulgent the laughter? The humour in this book relies heavily on parody. The
ladies are all that tradition supposes their sex to be, but taken
to a parodic extreme. They are hopelessly unequal to any kind
of practical task. They find men too large and too loud, and
find they are '*so* in the way in the house!' (39). Alternatively
they are overawed by masculinity – even the pseudo-mascu-
linity of a Mr Mulliner. They are almost universally credulous,
even of 'Signor Brunoni' and his conjuring tricks. They love
gossip, retailing it to each other with a comic eagerness that is
openly admitted. But men too are the subject of parody. Mr
Mulliner himself is a caricature of male dignity and egotism,
looking, in his 'pleasantest and most gracious moods . . . like a
sulky cockatoo' (121). The rector, an old bachelor, parodies the
ways of a young spinster, 'as afraid of matrimonial reports
getting abroad about him as any girl of eighteen: and he would

rush into a shop, or dive down an entry, sooner than encounter any of the Cranford ladies in the street' (136). Even the
dog Carlo dies comically as a parody of the death which is
quite seriously in hot pursuit of most of the principal actors in
the book, being found 'dead, with his poor little legs stretched
out stiff in the attitude of running, as if by such unusual exer-
tion he could escape the sure pursuer, Death' (143).

Much of the comedy arises from the characteristics of the
young appearing as a somewhat grotesque parody of themselves in the old. Of nothing is this more true than of female
sexuality. Contempt for, and timidity of, men – perhaps charming in a young girl – appear bitter and hysterical or simply
ludicrous in later middle age. In the person of Miss Matty the
author even parodies that maiden modesty and reserve which
she most celebrates in younger heroines. In Mary Barton,
Margaret Hale, Phillis Holman, Molly Gibson such maidenliness
is one of the pivotal stances of womanhood. More than just a
state, it is a definition of a girl's selfhood and integrity, and at
the same time a statement of her sexuality and potential engagement with the opposite sex. But *old* maidenhood in *Cranford*
is a constant source of comedy, especially in the person of Matty.
She above all has a nervous fear of all things masculine. She
frets dreadfully over a gentleman even visiting the house. Her
sense of propriety, derived from authority, most notably her
deceased sister's, is almost exclusively sexual in orientation.
Now in male depictions of the Victorian old maid the leading
characteristic, apart from fussiness and gentility, is frustrated
sexual rapaciousnes. The cartoons of the age from *Punch* provide sufficient examples of this prejudice. Matty is of course
quite the opposite of rapacious. She is in many ways like the
children she loves so much. Yet she is not pre-pubertal. Were
she totally innocent of sexuality there would be no need for her
acute sensitivity to proper behaviour. Her development seems
to have been arrested at that first dawn of awareness, where
excitement is muted by fear of the unknown; where the opposite sex is filled with vaguely threatening wonder, and the girl
is fascinated but uneasy in their presence. Her confession to
jumping into bed, dating from her girlhood, surely suggests a
sexual fear, and the fact that she is no longer so active, with

the child's penny-ball contrivance, beautifully combines the images of advancing years and continuing childlikeness. It is also funny and touching, a kind of mixed response we often feel towards Matty, again suggesting that she herself is not a straightforward type, but a complex individual.

The parody in Matty's case is not necessarily a negative. It redefines the adolescent's qualities in terms of a longer life-span. No one is treated cruelly by Mrs Gaskell in *Cranford*, but compared to Matty the other ladies can appear blunt in sensibility, and self-enclosed. Matty quotes Miss Pole to the effect that 'one is never too safe' from marriage (157) but that lady's glib self-satisfaction, which implicitly polarises the sexes, is used by Matty as part of a sadly realistic appraisal of her own life and heart:

> But after all I have not told you the truth. It is so long ago, and no one ever knew how much I thought of it at the time, unless, indeed, my dear mother guessed; but I may say that there was a time when I did not think I should have been only Miss Matty Jenkyns all my life; for even if I did meet with any one who wished to marry me now (and as Miss Pole says, one is never too safe), I could not take him – I hope he would not take it too much to heart, but I could *not* take him – or any one but the person I once thought I should be married to, and he is dead and gone. (157)

Matty herself has had no shortage of safety in her life. Gentility, reinforced by the strictures of her authoritarian elder sister, has ensured her a life of extreme caution. But it has also been responsible for the event which has perhaps most shaped her life – or rather the non-event – since it was the disapproval of her family which prevented her from marrying Holcroft and having her own children. Of the time of this refusal we have but one pathetic glimpse from Mrs Fitz-Adam:

> And one day, I remember, I met Miss Matty in the lane that leads to Combehurst; she was walking on the footpath, which, you know, is raised a good way above the road, and a gentleman rode beside her, and was talking to her, and she was

looking down at some primroses she had gathered, and pulling them all to pieces, and I do believe she was crying. (194)

But her stability of place, and the uneventfulness of her subsequent life have meant that she is unusually able to place what has happened against what could have been. The tears of youth, awaiting the fulfilment of its destiny, are replaced by the 'tearless cries of old age' (207) when reconciliation finally comes – not with a lover, but with a lost brother. Poor Peter's 'lot in life', like her own, 'was very different to what his friends had hoped and planned' (93).

> 'My father once made us,' she began, 'keep a diary, in two columns; on one side we were to put down in the morning what we thought would be the course and events of the coming day, and at night we were to put down on the other side what really happened. It would be to some people rather a sad way of telling their lives.' (158)

This is the 'accounts ledger' of her life, and it does not balance. Life is not economics, in which we can add up symmetrical lines of figures and get them to balance out. Life is, for Matty and her brother at least, like the scales of her shop, already over balance before she gives the child another sweet 'to make up measure'. Yet this suggests a larger need, and in Cranford life's overplus would seem to be of sorrow, loss and frustration. The town is isolated, backward-looking, inhabited largely by women of limited means whose main occupation is surviving on those means. Wealth is not created by the ladies of Cranford. Their economy is a static one of parsimony on fixed incomes. In this 'primitive' economy, materials rather than cash are the main concern. Small economies are part of small economics:

> I have often noticed that almost every one has his own individual small economies – careful habits of saving fractions of pennies in some one peculiar direction – any disturbance of which annoys him more than spending shillings or pounds on some real extravagance. An old gentleman of my acquaintance, who took the intelligence of the failure of a joint-stock

bank, in which some of his money was invested, with stoical mildness, worried his family all through a long summer's day because one of them had torn (instead of cutting) out the written leaves of his now useless bank-book; of course, the corresponding pages at the other end came out as well, and this little unnecessary waste of paper (his private economy) chafed him more than all the loss of his money. (83)

Mary goes on with examples of string-hoarding and butter-rationing at the very table. Ridiculous as these examples are, they clearly are much more the matters by which people live than are stocks and shares, mortgages and columns of figures, as the behaviour of the gentleman with the bank-book shows. We live every day by minutiae. Our true pleasures and griefs, like our obsessions, are often small-scale. They *are* pleasures and griefs because they are lived rather than simply known. In becoming part of our lives they become values for life.

Economics in the Drumble sense of the word is essentially forward-looking, and this is characteristic of the nineteenth century, with its general belief in 'progress' and expansionist trading policies. Economics implies knowledge of the way the world works, in one limited field at least – but a field which is supposed to encompass all our lives. *Cranford* the novel, like Cranford the town, looks backward. It is, like 'My Lady Ludlow', a work that evokes the eighteenth century, both literally and by allusion. Hopes now dashed, expectations unfulfilled, loves lost, all once had their birth in the previous century. Miss Jenkyns' literary judgement is founded on that century's greatest critic; Matty relives its later years through her parents' and even grandparents' letters. Despite the railroad connection with Drumble, Cranford still employs a sedan chair. It is a town which has not lost its connection with the countryside on which it has depended for centuries. Even from a house on the main street one can smell the fragrance of the neighbouring hay-fields. Money in Drumble may be made in unknown places – even abroad – and it is on this kind of income that Matty has depended, but the fields of home are still bearing their 'wonted tribute' as the novel closes, despite the failures of banks.

And thematically *Cranford* is a novel of the eighteenth century. Its mixture of pathos and comedy could remind us of Sterne. Captain Brown is a classic figure of sentiment – upright, soldierly, strong-minded, but possessing a feeling heart – as indeed is his formidable rival Miss Jenkyns. This sentimental phenomenon, with its opposite, the reasoning but unresponsive head, is most manifest in the contrast between Matty and Mary's father, of which more anon.

Genteel poverty implies idleness. An eighteenth-century lady, just as much as a gentleman, would not be expected to work for her living. Betty Barker made money by trade, and even though she is retired from the pursuit of lucre, she knows her place is not quite one of social equality with the other ladies – though she draws the line herself at inviting Mrs Fitz-Adam. The lives of these ladies are a shared secret which gives them an *esprit de corps*. 'We none of us spoke of money, because that subject savoured of commerce and trade, and though some might be poor, we were all aristocratic' (41). Like other secret societies the members jealously guard their circle, including and excluding on the most judicious principles, though they are principles not easily defined. Gentility is a subtle concept, having its roots in that most mysterious of social phenomena, class. In the terms of Drumble life it is a sterile matter since, as I have said, it involves idleness. Activity in the world of trade is denied to the ladies, but they are no better provided for in terms of amusement: 'Miss Jessie sang "Jock of Hazeldean" a little out of tune; but we were none of us musical, though Miss Jenkyns beat time, out of time, by way of appearing to be so' (46). If she is not musical, Miss Jenkyns has at least some pretensions to literary attainment, but when Mary Smith tries to enumerate Matty's accomplishments, she finds herself on stony ground indeed. She has not even the minimal accomplishments of music and drawing which traditionally formed the cultural armoury of young ladies. Her needlework is confined to knitting garters, and her chief accomplishment is making spills. She has in fact, as Mary reluctantly acknowledges, nothing saleable, and to that extent, in economic terms she is worthless. Gentility is not merely secretive, self-enclosed and sterile – it is absolutely life-denying. The whole of Matty's life has been blighted for the sake of social demarcation. 'Cousin Thomas would not have been enough of a gentleman for the rector and Miss Jenkyns' (69). Compared with the reality of the things which were being cast away at that time – passion, sexual and maternal fulfilment, companionship into old age – the social strictures are of the flimsiest. She was the daughter of the rector, 'somehow' related to Sir Peter Arley. While she may not indulge in the destructive savagery of a D. H. Lawrence at the expense of the genteel poor in a story such as 'The Daughters of the Vicar', Mrs Gaskell is quite as aware of the destructive power of caste.

Outraged propriety is the cause also of Peter's departure. His misdemeanour is one which suggests sexuality and fertility. In his role as trickster he disrupts the social order, suggests confusion, and brings into conjunction inappropriate things. So he adopts the clothing of the opposite sex and suggests the image of the supremely upright, un-feminine Deborah with an unacknowledged baby. For this latter trick he is not only flogged by his outraged father, but as a consequence runs away and never sees his mother again. She is buried in the shawl he sends from India but the incident has been her death, and it denies Matty companionship for the greater part of her life, as well as that healthy subversiveness which could challenge authority and suggest change and vitality.

Miss Matty is, in short, a figure of ridiculous insignificance seen by any 'normal' standards. She is anomolous in society, an unproductive figure, stifled by fears of boundary-breaking, whether sexually or socially. She is timid, ignorant, easily flustered, inconsequential. Yet Mary closes the book with the assertion that 'We all love Miss Matty, and I somehow think we are all of us better when she is near us' (218). This silly little remnant from another age is the central figure of the novel, carrying its profoundest values, and living them for us in a way which excites not only our sympathy but our respect.

What are these values? She is plainly imbued with a strong sense of duty. It can overcome even that timidity which is so deeply ingrained in her personality. When it is proposed that they should run and hide if they were the subject of a burglary, 'Miss Matty, who was trembling very much, scouted the idea, and said we owed it to society to apprehend them, and that she should certainly do her best to lay hold of them and lock them up in the garret till morning' (142). Society for her is not merely an idea but a living entity to which she owes something of herself. We might contrast her determination with the selfish cowardice of Mr Mulliner, that self-satisfied caricature of masculine pride. Matty is truly humble. She will defer to almost anyone who has an ounce of knowledge, real or apparent, or any sort of authority. She does not underestimate herself, but clearly sees her talents, in the worldly sense, for what they are. Her obligingness and self-effacement are caricature features of the woman's, and even more so of the elderly spinster's role, but she also has dignity. The subtlety of this quality may be felt in her encounter with Mrs Jamieson, when the latter is insinuating 'pretty plainly that she did not particularly wish that the Cranford ladies should call upon her sister-in-law' (116):

> When she did understand the drift of the honourable lady's call, it was pretty to see with what quiet dignity she received the intimation thus uncourteously given. She was not in the least hurt – she was of too gentle a spirit for that; nor was she exactly conscious of disapproving of Mrs. Jamieson's conduct; but there was something of this feeling in her mind, I am sure, which made her pass from the subject to others in a less flurried and more composed manner than usual. Mrs. Jamieson was, indeed, the more flurried of the two, and I could see she was glad to take her leave. (116)

'Dignity' means that she senses the situation, appreciates fully its implications personally and socially, but so far from reacting in a way which would compromise the self by emotional involvement she turns the subject of conversation with composure from a matter painful to herself and her interlocuter.

Matty has courage, of her own kind, which is not public and aggressive, but private and stoical. In practical terms, she takes on shopkeeping when it becomes necessary. If a critic is tempted to point out that her business is scarcely an emporium, and that gentility is still the final arbiter in the enterprise, he should remember how little Matty has been prepared for such a venture,

culturally, educationally or indeed by temperament. Her supreme moment, in which she brings together all her qualities,
is her giving five sovereigns for the countryman's five pound
note, so enabling him to buy his goods. In choosing a new silk
gown, 'it would be really the first time in her life that she had
had to choose anything of consequence for herself' (173), and
this first independent act results in a much greater act of autonomous decision. She is childlike (Mary remembers 'my own
loss of two hours in a toyshop before I could tell on what wonder
to spend a silver threepence') and confused at the variety of
goods, which makes her subsequent firmness of mind the more
striking. Throughout the incident her quiet, gentle manner is
emphasised, and again her dignity is brought into play as she
refuses to be deflected by the 'nervous cowardice' of Mary which
seeks to keep the old lady's mind on the silks:

> But Miss Matty put on the soft, dignified manner peculiar to
> her, rarely used, and yet which became her so well, and lay-
> ing her hand gently on mine, she said –
> 'Never mind the silks for a few minutes, dear.' (176)

If she is childlike, she has a child's pertinacity when it knows
an adult is trying to divert it from its aim, yet she also has an
adult's restraint, whence springs that special kind of dignity
'peculiar to her'. Her constantly reiterated theme is that she
does not understand – 'I don't understand it', 'I don't understand you', I don't pretend to understand business'. This last
is her response to the shopman who whispers, doubtless to
correct her belief that 'I'm sure they would have told me if
things had not been going on right' (177). The truth is of course
that 'they' would certainly not have told her, since economic
reality in a capitalist society depends on confidence, and truth-
telling would undermine confidence. Her action in giving gold
for paper is a piece of scandalous naivety, financially speaking, but Matty refuses to recognise this. She ignores 'understanding', and relies on the immediate human response. In thus
relying on 'heart' rather than 'head' she returns to her roots in
the eighteenth century. As is well-known, for novelists such as
Sterne or Fielding the 'feeling heart' is always a final court of

appeal over the analytical head. Matty relies on that innate moral sense which is instinctive to the man or woman of true sensibility. She cannot ever understand a thing which is explained to her, as many discover, but she knows with fine discrimination what is the truth about really important human dilemmas.

Matty possesses special qualities of gentleness and sympathy which distinguish her from the other Cranford ladies, but her generous heart is shared by them all. When Sam Brown and his wife are discovered at the inn, he lying ill and the whole family without means of support, the ladies are immediately moved to find ways of helping. And their sympathy is not abstract but immediate and practical. Miss Pole looks out for lodgings, Matty sends the sedan chair, Lady Glenmire undertakes medical supervision, and Mrs Forrester makes some of her famous bread jelly. The general philosophy is aptly reflected in Matty's fine reply to Mary's rather unworthy inquiry 'if she would think it her duty to offer sovereigns for all the notes of the Town and County Bank she met with?' (179).

> 'My dear! I never feel as if my mind was what people call very strong; and it's often hard enough work for me to settle what I ought to do with the case right before me. I was very thankful to – I was very thankful, that I saw my duty this morning, with the poor man standing by me; but it's rather a strain upon me to keep thinking and thinking what I should do if such and such a thing happened; and, I believe, I had rather wait and see what really does come; and I don't doubt I shall be helped then, if I don't fidget myself, and get too anxious beforehand. (179)

The 'economics' of Cranford is not economics at all in the sense of barter, but the free giving of oneself. This true charity is even more remarkably expressed when Matty's money is lost and the ladies each secretly contribute a sum to help out. The fact that Miss Pole's reference to 'our mites' (191) is a slightly joking one should not blind us to the serious Christian implications of the word. It is reinforced a little later when Mrs Forrester's tiny contribution, necessitating 'many careful economies, and many pieces of self-denial' are said to be 'small and insignificant in the world's account, but bearing a different value in another account-book that I have heard of' (193).

Such free distribution of income is not worldly-wise, but Mr Smith is moved by it. Matty's unselfishness, and simple sense of justice call out the same good qualities in others. And when Mr Smith remarks that 'such simplicity might be very well in Cranford, but would never do in the world' Mary reflects that his own economic principles have not served him very well:

> And I fancy the world must be very bad, for with all my father's suspicion of every one with whom he has dealings, and in spite of all his many precautions, he lost upwards of a thousand pounds by roguery only last year. (201)

Mr Smith's scepticism and suspicion of his fellow men should be set against Matty's appeal for 'credulity' in her advice to Mary:

> But all this is nonsense, dear! only don't be frightened by Miss Pole from being married. I can fancy it may be a very happy state, and a little credulity helps one on in life very smoothly, – better than always doubting and doubting, and seeing difficulties and disagreeables in everything. (159)

It will be asked by a reader as sceptical as Mr Smith whether this appeal might not be Mrs Gaskell's also. Is she not trying to persuade herself and us of an idyllic, pre-lapsarian state of things when life was simple and good, and people's natural honesty meant that economics was a simple Christian matter? Such a reader will see the frequent looking back to the eighteenth century as a turning from contemporary realities to a dream-world. In partial answer to this one must again stress Mrs Gaskell's realism. These ladies are not angels. They are petty, gossipy, narrow, ignorant and obsessed with caste. If Cranford seems idyllic in its timelessness and intimacy, it is real enough in its boredom and enclosedness. The ladies' kindness is as real as the cash and the objects in which it is manifested. A significant point is in fact made about the importance of action in dispelling idle speculation. When the ladies become absorbed in helping Sam Brown and his family, the fears of robbery disappear. The point is made emphatically by Matty's putting to better use the little ball she had been wont to roll under her bed as a precaution against intruders. Mary finds her covering it 'with gay-coloured worsted in rainbow stripes' and explains that it is for the conjuror's little girl, who 'looks as if she had never had a good game of play in her life' (156). Matty herself is deeply realistic in conception. The subtlety of her personality, and her unique mixture of qualities suggests this, rooted as they are in the sad compromise she has had to make in a disappointed life. She is, in her dignity and integrity, that staple of realistic fiction, the 'small hero', whose low grade in the public view, unremarkable abilities, even ridiculousness, do not preclude nobility of a special kind.

In speaking of Matty's life, one cannot exclude love. I have mentioned already her sexual fears, but these would doubtless have been relieved had she married Holcroft and borne children. It must not be forgotten that *Cranford* is a comedy. It is comic in the most obvious sense of making us laugh, but it is also a book about romantic love. What is unusual is that it is told from an old person's point of view, so love is constantly seen as a fulfilment which might have been. Of course that fulfilment is not excluded from the picture. When Jessie Brown becomes Mrs Gordon 'with happiness something of her early bloom returned; she had been a year or two younger than we had taken her for' (61). In the same way Lady Glenmire is revitalised as Mrs Hoggins, while Martha, the other female to marry in the book, undercuts gentility with honest sexuality at one blow by her retort to Miss Matilda:

'And mind you go first to the ladies,' put in Miss Matilda. 'Always go to the ladies before gentlemen, when you are waiting.'
    'I'll do it as you tell me, ma'am,' said Martha; 'but I like lads best.' (68)

Yet there can be no doubt that the prevalent tone is one of loss and deprivation. Matty's effort at concealment of her feelings after the death of Holcroft leads to a permanent 'tremulous motion of head and hands' (81). Like a Shakespeare comedy, the book ends with a sort of celebration – the re-establishment of 'Signor Brunoni' in a special performance at the assembly room. But the customary marriage which would be celebrated is here a comic non-marriage. Peter, it would appear, is going to marry Mrs Jamieson and leave Matty alone once more. Such fears are dispelled, however, by Peter's obvious mocking of the lady, and instead he contents himself with reconciling her to Mrs Hoggins, the erstwhile Lady Glenmire.

So reconciliation is possible, but marriage is for a younger generation. But beyond question the uniting of man and woman in bonds of matrimony would have been the natural and best fate for Matty, and such unity is a fundamental human, social and economic value. Both Matty and Holcroft have devised domestic economies which suit their single lives, but the foundation of the economic state is the family, and alone they cannot make one. Matty is driven into secrecy, passivity and an exaggerated fear of men. Holcroft survives alone quite adequately, but secludes himself in poetry and natural beauty. He is eccentric, and pleases himself in a decided and masculine manner, as is the prerogative of bachelors. That the sexes were made for each other is hinted in her 'daintily' stuffing the 'strong tobacco' into his pipe. Mary's eye notes how the kitchen could 'have been easily made into a handsome dark oak dining-parlour by removing the oven and a few other appurtenances of a kitchen' (73). The best parlour is ugly, the country house pretty, but covered promiscuously with books. All his domestic arrangements could have been improved with marriage, and via children economics would be linked to human productivity and a sense of future fulfilment. Martha, though a servant, is able through marriage to offer Matty an arrangement which will help the old lady when hard times come upon her. Like all the arrangements devised at this crisis of her life, Martha's offer of accommodation combines the charitable, sociable and the economic.

Cranford, then, is a romantic comedy of an unusual cast. It deals with the old rather than the young, and its final harmony is symbolised by Peter's comic rejection of marriage and his satisfaction in being reconciled at long last to his dear sister. For her part Matty never fulfils her youthful romantic dream, but by her life redeems the concept of old-maidenhood from tragedy and loss to comedy and reconciliation. But the novel has a further comic dimension which refers us back once again to Matty's appeal for 'credulity'. It is a word which carries, in the novel, both a simply comic significance and some profounder overtones. The ladies of *Cranford* are deeply credulous. They sit wide-eyed before Signor Brunoni. They are also speculative in an idle, inturned way which takes the practical form of gossip. The most ludicrous and hysterical example of this is during the scare about robberies. Without any serious grounds apart from two men, an Irish beggarwoman and some footprints, they all work themselves into a state of terror, and even suspect Signor Brunoni of practising the Black Arts – 'he had apparently killed a canary with only a word of command; his will seemed of deadly force; who knew but he might yet be lingering in the neighbourhood willing all sorts of awful things!' (143). This rather vulgar credulity and fantasising is, as we have seen, swept away as the childishness it is when practical charity is required, but there is a credulity (and it is this, I think, that Matty is referring to) which is child-*like*; open-eyed and receptive to wonder. Miss Jenkyns gives it as her opinion that 'it was time for Miss Jessie to leave off her dimples, and not always to be trying to look like a child', but Mary modifies this to suggest that true childlikeness is a not an undesirable quality: 'It was true there was something childlike in her face; and there will be, I think, till she dies, though she should live to be a hundred. Her eyes were large blue wondering eyes, looking straight at you' (44). She also remarks of Sam Brown that it was 'wonderful to see what kind feelings were brought out by this poor man's coming among us' (155). And it is indeed wonderful if one thinks of the naive speculations over this poor unfortunate that had been preoccupying the minds of the ladies until only a day or two before. The implication of this appeal to 'credulity' is that life may confound and surprise us – certainly for ill, but quite as often for good, and we should be open to it, not, as Matty says, 'always doubting and doubting'.

The greatest source of wonder in the book is obviously the return of Peter. The opportunities for reconciliation have been missed in youth. Owing to circumstances, Peter's father and mother arrived too late to see their son at Liverpool. His mother's 'soft eyes never were the same again after that; they had always a restless, craving look, as if seeking for what they could not find' (99). And when Peter does come back, it is his turn to be too late. The shawl he has brought her is used for her interment. 'It is just such a shawl', says Peter's father, 'as she wished for when she was married, and her mother did not give it her. I did not know of it till after, or she should have had it – she should; but she shall have it now' (102). Such regrets and missed opportunities are the lot of mortal man – yet not entirely, for our links with the past are not purely negative ones of regret and bitter memories. Mary Smith is responsible for the largest and most practical piece of speculation in the book, when she sends a letter to Peter in India. The chance is faint; everything depends upon a frail slip of paper:

> I dropped it in the post on my way home, and then for a minute I stood looking at the wooden pane with agaping slit which divided me from the letter but a moment ago in my hand. It was gone from me like life, never to be recalled. It would get tossed about on the sea, and stained with sea-waves perhaps, and be carried among palm-trees, and scented with all tropical fragrance; the little piece of paper, but an hour ago so familiar and common-place, had set out on its race to the strange wild countries beyond the Ganges! (182–3)

At the beginning of the novel we have seen how letters from the past may convey on their frail sheets the pathos of human insubstantiality:

> There was in them a vivid and intense sense of the present time, which seemed so strong and full, as if it could never pass away, and as if the warm, living hearts that so expressed themselves could never die, and be as nothing to the sunny earth. (85)

Now the same means is used to cancel time and space in a reconciliation which is late, but not too late. This is one work in which Mrs Gaskell feels able to grant her heroine peace before her final rest – peace for a life obscurely but virtuously lived. In the context of a realistic work it introduces that note of wonder which suggests a providence in our lives – not as a glib miracle, denying all the intervening years, but asserting with Mr Holcroft's favourite poet that 'though much is taken, much abides'.[1]

8

Words and Values: 'Cousin Phillis'

Though by temperament and conviction Elizabeth Gaskell was drawn to the life of deeds, her writing shows her insistently dwelling upon the status of words, particularly as regards their opacity and autonomy. This is not just the creative language which it is the duty of every artist to employ, though she was not wanting in that talent. Beyond this she was conscious of the power of words, particularly as utterance. I have already mentioned 'what a single word can do' in *Mary Barton*, and the attention the author pays to explicating dialect words in the same novel suggests the concern she feels for what Sylvia Robson, referring to her mother's speech, calls the 'weight of words'. Again, Mrs Gaskell's concern with utterance is not merely a matter of a subtle ear for dialogue, though that too is one of her major talents. Words as utterance have an autonomous power and at times a seemingly independent existence. Again in *Mary Barton*, Mrs Wilson, when she is to be called as a witness against her son, says, 'If my words are to kill my son, they have already gone forth out of my mouth, and naught can bring them back' (339). They have the status of a deed committed. Of themselves, quite independent of intention, they can bring about a man's death.

Elizabeth Gaskell's fiction is full of words used as weapons – curses (sometimes with supernatural effect, as in 'The Poor Clare'), adjurations which control lives from beyond the grave (as in 'Half a Lifetime Ago'), words of forgiveness and its refusal. A search for words in a book is the means of turning old Mr Carson from vegeance to forgiveness. 'Never', says Kester to Sylvia, 'is a long word'. The absoluteness of her commitment

147

never to forgive has a binding force whose ties can be broken only at death. For Sylvia words have the function of self-declaration, even self-definition, and this is perhaps their greatest interest for Mrs Gaskell. The word 'witch' is an epithet used against Lois Barclay in order to define her in relation to her society and to God. So potent is it that the girl herself is led to question her own identity. Mary Barton commits, declares and defines herself by the self-revealing words of love she utters on the witness-stand at her lover's trial. Sometimes the meaning of whole lives may be declared in a few words, as at the climax of 'The Crooked Branch'. The texture of the discourse in *Wives and Daughters* demonstrates how words may evade as well as confront. Atrophied feelings, loss of social contact or despair at the intractability of the human condition may reduce articulacy even to the silence of a John Barton or the wordless misery of Squire Hamley and Osborne. Elizabeth Gaskell is concerned with all that makes words more than ciphers for conveying information. In this chapter I shall explore how words provide her with a metaphor by which she may explore values.

In some ways this long short story is at the very centre of Mrs Gaskell's achievement. In it she accomplishes something which evades easy classification as either comedy or tragedy; a love story where love is scarcely mentioned, let alone allowed to bloom; a story powerfully localised, yet universal in its implications; a work full of values yet in no narrow sense moral. It demonstrates more than any other of her fictions this author's peculiar ability to make us feel that the greatest matters in our lives may turn upon the smallest; that human feeling makes the trivial of immense moment; that to live is to change, but that no adaptation to circumstance can make us what we once were. Reflecting perhaps the loss of Mrs Gaskell's own dear son, cousin Holman has felt an 'aching sense of loss she [will] never get over in this world' (CP 327). There is no recompense for mortal loss. The pain is permanent though circumstances may change.

The interplay between stability and change is a leading motif in the story. It opens with the change in Paul's circumstances – a move from his parents' home to a new place, new work –

and ends with the resolve of Phillis to visit Paul's parents. This is the first hint of a move outwards from Hope Farm; hitherto others have always come from outside to visit, and it seems to symbolise the change which has taken place not only in Phillis, but in her family, and perhaps in life in general:

> 'Only for a short time, Paul! Then – we will go back to the peace of the old days. I know we shall; I can, and I will!' (354)

The railway is, as in so much nineteenth-century fiction, a symbol of change, and of course in reality too the precursor of enormous changes. Paul and Holdsworth are working on a branch line opening up an area hitherto unchanged for generations. When Paul is escaping from the practical realities of everyday life, from his new lodgings and tedious, narrow Nonconformist Sundays to go to Hope Farm, it might well be thought that the farm is the repository of stability and timelessness. Certainly it appears as something like this when Paul first views it and its occupants. Phillis herself stands at the door, her silence and immovability suggesting a permanent figure, as well as something stamped for ever on the memory:

> I see her now – cousin Phillis. The westering sun shone full upon her, and made a slanting stream of light into the room within. She was dressed in dark blue cotton of some kind; up to her throat, down to her wrists, with a little frill of the same wherever it touched her white skin. And such white skin as it was! I have never seen the like. She had light hair, nearer yellow than any other colour. She looked me steadily in the face with large, quiet eyes, wondering, but untroubled by the sight of a stranger. I thought it odd that so old, so full-grown as she was, she should wear a pinafore over her gown. (266)

The picture suggests an idyll of eternal untried youth and innocence, unmoving and undisturbed, a child unawakened to the sexual potency hinted at in Paul's reaction to her hair and skin and his wonder at her childlike clothing. Mrs Holman's first words suggest both length of time and time's standing still: 'To think of your being Margaret's son! Why, she was almost a child not so long ago. Well, to be sure, it is five-and-twenty years ago' (266). When Phillis waits upon him, Paul feels like 'somebody in the Old Testament – who, I could not recollect – being served and waited upon by the daughter of the host' (267). Much of these early encounters forms itself into pictures – of Phillis standing or serving or knitting, of Mrs Holman shading her eyes with her hand, of her husband standing with his workers bareheaded in the fields singing a psalm – and this reinforces the sense of stability and timelessness at the farm. When he is established there, Paul feels at times 'as if I had lived for ever, and should live for ever, droning out paragraphs in that warm sunny room, with my two quiet hearers' (282).

Yet nothing is as straightforward as it seems. Paul's father is an inventor, his mentor Holdsworth is an engineer. Both occupations suggest practicality and a positive search for technical change. Yet neither of these things is alien to the farm. When the minister and Paul's father meet there is an immediate rapprochement, and we should not be surprised at this if we have been attending to Mr Holman's personality and way of life from the first. The publican of whom Paul asks directions commends the minister's virtues as a practising farmer. But he is also interested in mathematics of a practical kind. His study is a type of the man – 'part study, part counting-house, looking into the farm-yard' (277). It has books of farming and farriery as well as of divinity; a box of carpenter's tools as well as manuscripts in shorthand. He is undoubtedly an idealisation, with his sober life, grave manner, industry, early hours and interest in everything. He is even a father-figure to neighbouring children; wise, kindly, just and practical, as we see in the incident with the little boys and the spilt milk (273–4). We may be reminded of Wordsworth's 'Michael' or those 'grave livers' of 'Resolution and Independence' who 'give to God and Man their dues'.[1] The figure of the priest/farmer (who is also lawgiver and executioner) suggests a complex of functions in an integrated society where religion and the practical are one. Nor is literature neglected:

'It's wonderful,' said he, 'how exactly Virgil has hit the en-
during epithets, nearly two thousand years ago, and in Italy;
and yet how it describes to a T what is now lying before us
in the parish of Heathbridge, county—, England.' (273)

His comments draw together past and present – unify and uni-
versalise experience – an appropriate response from a man whose
world appears satisfyingly integrated. Hope Farm is an Eden
of a particular kind. Its Edenic quality, its unspoiledness, is its
seamlessness. When the minister prays, his prayer comes directly out of the day's experiences (the only clue Paul can find
to link his impromptu ejaculations). He prays also for the cattle
and live creatures 'rather to my surprise' (279). The spiritual
and the practical, the transcendent and the immediate, are not
divided in his mind. The psalm sung in the fields is striking
not because it is bizarre, but because we feel its naturalness. It
certainly moves Paul, and it is a wonderful moment of harmony, literally and metaphorically. As a picture, however, it
asks to be read in its totality, and we may notice that *Paul* is
not integrated. He does not know the words, and so must remain silent, to Phillis's slight surprise. This faint air of exclusivity is characteristic of Paul's first visits to the farm. Why
should Phillis be surprised? She judges by her own life and
knowledge, and expects others to know what she does. Paul
later retaliates a little by mentioning his father's talent: 'I thought
everyone had heard of Manning's patent winch', only to be
slightly put down by the minister's 'We don't know who invented the alphabet' (276). A hostile witness might accuse him
of patronising his young relative, and he has an irritating habit
of giving his seal of approval to things which are a matter of
opinion:

'He is right to stand up for his father,' said Cousin Holman,
as if she were pleading for me. . . .
'Yes – he is right,' said the minister placidly. 'Right, because it comes from his heart – right, too, as I believe, in
point of fact. Else, there is many a young cockerel that will
stand upon a dunghill and crow about his father, by way of
making his own plumage to shine.' (276)

Yet his self-confidence in the world as he finds it makes the minister generous and charming in a way that Paul cannot resist, and there is no sense in which he and his family are narrow. The variety of their interests (or at least his and Phillis's) and their thirst for knowledge is all active. The energy and adaptability of the Hope Farm family is contrasted with the Sundays Paul has previously been spending 'up a dark narrow entry' listening to tedious prayers and sermons; the Holmans' openness is set against the views of the Misses Dawson of France, and those ladies' narrow acquisitiveness.

Yet a characteristic of Eden is that it is a bounded spot, and Hope Farm does not, in a quite literal, physical sense, go out into the world to gain its knowledge. Paul and his father and Holdsworth are all visitors. Were it not for them, the meaning of technical mechanical terms and difficult passages in Dante, not to mention the discovery of the new turnip-cutter, would never be vouchsafed. The close interlocking of everything at the farm means that there is no space for perspective outside practice, knowledge and prayer – and as we have seen, prayer in this household has a distinctly practical, even prosaic, cast. What this means in terms of daily life is that time is measured out by the clock in hours, each one a signal for a new activity:

> 'Your father up at three! Why, what has he to do at that hour?'
> 'What has he not to do? He has his private exercise in his own room; he always rings the great bell which calls the men to milking; he rouses up Betty, our maid; as often as not, he gives the horses their feed before the man is up . . . he looks at the calves, and the shoulders, heels, traces, chaff, and corn, before the horses go a-field . . .'. (270)

The same slightly obsessive parcelling-out is applied to the days of the week:

> At first, it seemed a kind of weekly diary; but then I saw that the seven days were portioned out for special prayers and intercessions: Monday for his family, Tuesday for enemies, Wednesday for the Independent churches, Thursday

for all other churches, Friday for persons afflicted, Saturday for his own soul, Sunday for all wanderers and sinners, that they might be brought back home to the fold. (277–8)

He mentions 'leisure time' only in order to point out how it may be filled. There are no gaps in this life on the literal level of time, but more significantly there is no room for admission of experiences not defined by that life. All is clear and direct. This is reflected in the manner of both the minister and Phillis to Paul. Both look at him directly. Any attempt by Paul to romanticise the family is ignored by its members:

'How old is cousin Phillis?' said I, scarcely venturing on the new name, it seemed too prettily familiar for me to call her by it; but cousin Holman took no notice of it, answering straight to the purpose. (267)

Phillis herself is calm, collected, and engaged, when Paul first sees her, in knitting 'a long, grey worsted man's-stocking'. She and Paul become 'practical friends' in an absolutely practical way, by finding their common liking for animals and then going round the farm to see them. Any idea Paul may have had of a romantic attachment to her is almost immediately crushed by her unselfconscious directness:

'But I may stay and help you, mayn't I?'
'Oh, yes; not that you can help at all, but I like to have you with me.'
I was both flattered and annoyed at this straightforward avowal. (283–4)

Self-consciousness is one of the major signs by which we understand that the serpent has entered this Eden. To describe Holdsworth as a serpent is unfair, of course. He never seeks to deceive, and Mrs Gaskell is typically unconcerned with moral fabulation of a narrow or doctrinal kind. It might be said that insofar as the Eden story is evoked, it is evoked in order to deny the original message. Not only is the man the 'betrayer', but we cannot really speak of 'betrayal' in any moral sense.

Nevertheless, Holdsworth is deceptive. By nature he is practical and decisive. He enjoys Paul's descriptions of the farm 'as much as he liked anything that was merely narrative, without leading to action' (286–7). But as a result of the illness, from which it is hoped that a visit to the farm will help him recover, he appears full of 'languid indecision' (297). He says of himself:

> 'I used to be as impudent a fellow as need be, and rather liked going amongst strangers and making my way; but since my illness I am almost like a girl, and turn hot and cold with shyness; as they do, I fancy.' (296)

Moreover he brings to the farm something it has not known before – idleness – or leisure, more indulgently speaking. He provides a space in which feelings not governed by practicality may grow. When they first arrive, Paul and Holdsworth take the occupants by surprise. The door, normally open as a symbol of trust, is significantly closed and they must go round to the back. Minister and mother are both away – the first time Paul has arrived and found Phillis alone. It is also the first time Paul has found Phillis shy. Holdsworth's presence and manners produce a blush of confusion, but blushing is also an indicator of shame and guilt. There is of course no sense in which Phillis should feel these things, but it is to be her lot as the woman to associate them with a consciousness of sexual arousal. The only reference to the world of sexual love prior to Holdsworth's arrival is in the following exchange:

> '– Phillis, I am thankful thou dost not care for the vanities of dress!' Phillis reddened a little as she said, in a low humble voice –
> 'But I do, father, I'm afraid. I often wish I could wear pretty-coloured ribbons round my throat, like the squire's daughters.'
> 'It's but natural, minister!' said his wife; 'I'm not above liking a silk gown better than a cotton one myself!'
> 'The love of dress is a temptation and a snare,' said he, gravely. 'The true adornment is a meek and quiet spirit.' (284–5)

The entire possibility of conscious physical attraction by women is wiped out for Phillis at a stroke by her father. As it transpires later, he has never seen her as a woman, but one might doubt whether he ever envisages womanliness in a sexual sense as being a part of the nature of things.

The first exchanges between Phillis and Holdsworth show Mrs Gaskell at her most subtle in evoking that evasiveness of discourse which has hitherto been entirely lacking at the farm, and which is another of the openings wherein love may grow. The words themselves are a kind of rhetoric behind which intuition senses truer things than may be expressed with the tongue:

> 'Father and mother are out. They will be so sorry! you did not write, Paul, as you said you would.'
>
> 'It was my fault,' said Holdsworth, understanding what she meant, as well as if she had put it more fully into words. 'I have not yet given up all the privileges of an invalid; one of which is indecision. Last night, when your cousin asked me at what time we were to start, I really could not make up my mind.' (298)

Holdsworth's phrases are elegant, faintly comic, self-depreciatory; but his intuition is direct and clear. Phillis herself is disturbed, unable to make up her mind. She is 'unconsciously' holding her basket in her hand. She is further disturbed by the obliqueness of Holdsworth's discourse.

> 'I am afraid you distrust me. I can assure you, I know the exact fulness at which peas should be gathered. I take great care not to pluck them when they are unripe. I will not be turned off, as unfit for my work.'
>
> This was a style of half-joking talk that Phillis was not accustomed to. She looked for a moment as if she would have liked to defend herself from the playful charge of distrust made against her; but she ended by not saying a word. (299)

Contrast this silence with her robust irony at Paul's expense

when they are first getting to know each other. Paul has determined to question Phillis rather than be further humiliated by
being questioned himself, and so when she enters with a basket of eggs:

> Faithful to my resolution, I asked –
> 'What are those?'
> She looked at me for a moment, and then said gravely –
> 'Potatoes.'
> 'No! they are not,' said I. 'They are eggs. What do you
> mean by saying they are potatoes?'
> 'What did you mean by asking me what they were, when
> they were plain to be seen?' retorted she. (280)

On that occasion she was totally unflustered. Her response indicates that she thinks him, at that moment, a fool. Their exchange is a variation on the question-and-answer which is the
general *modus operandi* of the farm, and her 'joke' requires only
the statement of the obviously *not* in reply to the obvious. But
Holdsworth is subtle; words are not merely a matter of elicit-
ing information; they are things to play with, to hide behind
with a power independent of a direct relation to reality. Words
are not 'potatoes' or 'eggs', but the repository of romance.
    When Holdsworth, teasing her, complains that her fetching
coats to keep them from the rain is 'an unchristian piece of
revenge' she is even more thrown off balance:

> His tone of badinage (as the French call it) would have been
> palpable enough to any one accustomed to the world; but
> Phillis was not, and it distressed or rather bewildered her.
> 'Unchristian' had to her a very serious meaning; it was not
> a word to be used lightly; and though she did not exactly
> understand what wrong it was that she was accused of do-
> ing, she was evidently desirous to throw off the imputation.
> (309)

Phillis is not unsettled by Holdsworth's words alone. After a
few minutes' work he is overcome by fatigue, and Phillis is
thrown into the interesting situation of being at fault. She is

'full of penitence', and blames herself for his indisposition. It is only a little thing, but surely significant, that as almost her first reaction she should blame herself in regard to the man who is to be the first to enter her heart. As with the blush he evoked earlier, the (perhaps desired) self-blame is an undeserved burden the woman seems destined to assume with her awakening to love. It certainly serves to make Holdsworth more interesting, and breaks down her defences momentarily, in a way never achieved by Paul. For his part, Holdsworth, once recovered from his faintness, takes up Phillis's Dante, and writes out translations for all her 'hard words' – an action which 'did not quite please' Paul, 'yet I did not know why' (302). It is an act of self-confidence which borders on intrusion. Paul would like to maintain the romantic ideal of the girl who would have to *condescend* to marry him; Holdsworth's boldness perhaps seems to set such idealism aside, but it is also the boldness which is part of a quite unconscious sexual strategy. In contrast to the 'slipperiness' of his conversation heretofore, he now produces a quite magically direct solution to the problem she had thought insuperable, simply by making a list of corresponding words – 'this equals this', as it were. Such linguistic directness is reinforced by his later contact with the minister, who forces him to 'make one's words represent one's thoughts, instead of merely looking to their effect on others' (303). In the case of Phillis and Holdsworth words never come to the point of representing thoughts. The internal life remains hidden, despite its turmoil and the profundity of the change it is effecting in the breast of one of the protagonists at least.

   To the world Holdsworth refers to Phillis as 'the minister's daughter', but privately she is 'Phillis'. The independence of 'Miss Holman' is denied her, since she is to be appropriated by either father or lover. The lover proposes giving her a copy of *I Promessi Sposi* in preference to the more difficult Dante. Paul wonders if her father will object to her being given a novel to read, but Holdsworth laughs off such scruples. He is quite proprietorial about her learning, and the title of his choice can hardly be missed as a wry comment on what is to follow. Holdsworth's evasiveness in regard to words is reinforced by his comment 'Why make a bugbear of a word!' (304). By contrast

the minister '[weighs] his words a little' as he confers quali-
fied approval on Holdsworth:

> He makes Horace and Virgil living, instead of dead, by the
> stories he tells me of his sojourn in the very countries where
> they lived, and where to this day, he says—but it is like
> dram-drinking. I listen to him till I forget my duties and am
> carried off my feet. (305)

Elizabeth Gaskell's sense of values is such that she can herself
give full weight to what Holdsworth represents. He is, to the
just man, like original sin – essential temptation. Yet he gives
life to the dead word. He is experience, and in a fallen state
we cannot live without experience. He does not sufficiently weigh
words; they do not always, with him, correspond to things.
And yet this is a part of the very charm which wins not only
the daughter's heart, but the half-unwilling attention of the father
too. For Mr Holman revises his opinion, as he confides to Paul:

> 'I miss him more than I thought for; no offence to you, Paul!
> I said once, his company was like dram-drinking; that was
> before I knew him; and perhaps I spoke in the spirit of judge-
> ment. To some men's minds everything presents itself strongly,
> and they speak accordingly; and so did he. And I thought,
> in my vanity of censorship, that his were not true and sober
> words; they would not have been if I had used them, but
> they were so to a man of his class of perceptions.' (328)

It is a generous tribute, which gives due credit to both the
speaker and his subject, and puts them in relation to each other.
For might not this elusive magic, this 'charm' be indeed the
profoundest use to which language may be put? It encompasses
all that the just man fears, but also all the world that eludes
him. Looking back, Paul can only say:

> It is many years since I have seen thee, Edward Holdsworth,
> but thou wast a delightful fellow! Ay, and a good one too;
> though much sorrow was caused by thee! (305)

In fact the very words which are, it would appear, at the very centre of the story – Holcroft's to Phillis in the storm – are not heard by Paul; thus the great event of the affair, the very commitment of the self which is to transform Phillis's life is no more than a breath. Or again it is the silent language of the eyes – a look from him to her which confuses her and forces her to leave the room. Paul feels that he must speak. Understanding something of the matter, but unable to bear the pregnant silence, he uses words 'stupid enough, but stupidity was better than silence just then' (311). Love finally becomes apparent in the 'language of flowers' when she gives him a nosegay. The blooms are old-fashioned, of such a kind as he had never seen 'since the days of his boyhood', suggestive of the homely, unchanging innocence of the affection she is bestowing upon him. They speak of home, childhood, of the days before travel had widened his horizons and made him the dangerously spellbinding figure the man is to her. They speak also, in this, of the hope that can never be fulfilled, the hope Paul has very little of when he says farewell to Holdsworth, since 'the same kind of happy days never returns' (314). Is there in this an implication that a *different* kind of happiness is a possibility? The heroine lives at Hope farm, and the word 'hope' is repeated several times in this crucial passage. Holdsworth sees Phillis as 'the sleeping beauty' waiting for him to return as a prince and waken to his love, but this is a complex image, and one not calculated to inspire confidence in his hopes for the future. It suggests that she will remain forever the same, which she cannot, though her heart would, and ironically contrasts his own fickleness. It unintentionally devalues their relationship to a fantasy which suggests a male power of awakening the woman from her sleep of inexperience, when in fact the sleep has already been broken. He arrogantly assumes the role of Prince, thereby subsuming the complexities of a dual relationship into his own personal power.

Phillis's 'peaceful serenity' of former days is replaced by a 'vivid happiness' in the spring of her trust in Holdsworth's love. Although she does not yet know it, it is the spring of a new experience of a quite different kind for her – the necessity of facing up to transience, contingency and change. But for this brief period she lives in secrecy, unwilling to acknowledge a sexual commitment, and therefore at first avoiding Paul until she is 'sure of there being no recurrence, either by word, look or allusion, to the one subject that was predominant in her mind' (326). She then returns to her 'sisterly' ways, reassuming her old mode of asexual innocence.

Paul's last visit to the farm is to witness and to break an idyll – one he has treasured up for himself but which now he must put behind him as a preliminary to the world of manhood. His desire to keep his innocence seems intertwined with a desire to keep his cousin in the state where she can deny the experience ever happened. In this he is colluding in the lie of her childish pinafore. He looks out of the window and sees the farm in the fulness of its natural production. Its cyclical rhythm is unchanging like all the images of Hope Farm, but on the stairs the unseen clock ticks on, telling off the seconds that change us irredeemably. The minister recites Latin verses to reinforce his belief that nothing in the realm of nature has changed, but his rhythmical beating-out of the Georgics is a profound irritant to Phillis's nerves, who has only recently felt the real force of change and decay in her life.

For the first time, says Paul, false communication comes into the household:

> Until now, everything which I had heard spoken in that happy household were simple words of true meaning. If we had aught to say, we said it; and if any one preferred silence, nay, if all did so, there would have been no spasmodic, forced efforts to talk for the sake of talking, or to keep off intrusive thoughts or suspicions. (340)

It is like the discord which comes into Eden after the fruit has been tasted. The Tempter there also spoke words not of 'true meaning' as did Holdsworth in his winningly indirect way, and we may be reminded that Paul is also implicated by the similarity with his forced words on more than one occasion.

Yet the values of the farm are scarcely those of the natural world they supposedly embody. They are an unchanging, simple ideal embodied in a generous, honest, but humanly incomplete patriarchy. Paul blames himself for raising his cousin's hopes, and is blamed also by the minister, but without hope she would never have gained the experience of vulnerability which comes with opening the self. Paul's attempts to protect the fact of Phillis's love from public view are justified by him in terms of 'secret', 'safe' and 'sacred' (344). The minister feels a profanity in even suggesting that his child should be considered in terms of marriage – for him it is associating sexual activity with a child – a violation of nature. He accuses Paul of 'spoil[ing] her peaceful maidenhood' (345) as though to deny (like Holdsworth) that nature had already planted the seeds of love in Phillis's heart. He would rather believe that she had been confused by an outside agent than acknowledge his daughter's sexuality. Yet acknowledge it he must when she speaks the simple words: 'I loved him, father!' By this confession the whole assumption of female reactive passion is overturned, and it is acknowledged that love may be self-initiated on the woman's part. He had never spoken of love to Phillis, yet she had allowed herself to love him. The convention of female passivity is violated, and the minister 'could not have believed it' (346).

At the moment of confrontation words are no longer of any value to the two. He is using them to distance her: 'Probably, the father and daughter were never so far apart in their lives, so unsympathetic' (347) – to cruelly expose her, out of his own hurt and disappointment. Under this strain, Phillis retreats into the non-communicative, secret world of delirium, and in the first moments her father feels that his words may have killed her. He himself cannot, when the time comes, overthrow his natural longings and accept the will of God. To hope is human, and he will follow what is contingent upon hope until resignation is required. Words for him must be real, relating directly to things and experience, so 'I cannot feel it; and what I do not feel I will not express, using words as if they were a charm.' Nor will the minister see a direct relation between sin and affliction. 'Charms' and the superstition of seeing sorrow as a 'visitation' are both alien to his sense of how the world works.

Throughout this tale words are a metaphor that accompanies the unfolding of experience, and measures value on a personal and a general human level, from Paul's clumsy overtures through Holdsworth's magically opaque discourse to the 'two or three faint words' Phillis speaks when she re-emerges into life. The undermining of the idea of 'true words' in the enclosed and seamless sense of the minister is a subversion of his world. Words are not simple correspondences to things any more than values are a static stereotype of experience. In the hour of thankfulness the whole household finds silence is the best praise they can offer. As the family kneels for prayer, the old servant John turns to the minister and says:

> 'Minister, I reckon we have blessed the Lord wi' all our souls though we've ne'er talked about it; and maybe he'll not need spoken words this night. God bless us all, and keep our Phillis safe from harm! Amen.' (353)

And Holman himself, the man who understood everything except a woman's heart, humbly goes to reinstate the feeble-minded Timothy. Where once he had simply desired to remove to another room so as to avoid the man, he now ventures to risk disappointment with patience in an imperfect world. The 'fortunate Fall' acts for father as well as daughter.

9

Tragedy, Topography and Choice: 'Sylvia's Lovers'

Mrs Gaskell's works reveal a strong commitment to life. This should not surprise us in a woman who lived her own life so fully, enjoying her children's growth and company, travel, food and drink and lively conversation. In her fiction this commitment is seen in the many examples of self-redemption, even in the jaws, as it were, of tragedy, loss and death. Susan Dixon, in 'Half A Life-Time Ago', would seem condemned to spending the remainder of her life bitter and regretful, cut off from the world in her lonely farmhouse, her youth and love wasted. But a snowstorm and a heroic effort on her ex-lover's behalf lead her to find renewed commitment to life in looking after his wife and family. Margaret Hale, alone and cast down by loss of her family and friends, contemplates retirement from life into a convent. She is rescued by love. Miss Matty's sad life is redeemed by her brother's return. Ruth's whole story might be said to be one of self-redemption.

'Sylvia's Lovers', however, is a rather different case, in that it presents us with problems to which there seems no solution, in this world at least. The reconciliation of the two main protagonists comes too late, when she is worn out with cares and loss, and he maimed and disfigured. The loss which is, even partially, made good in so many of her novels and tales, here appears irredeemable. There is a strong sense of entrapment running through the book, and seen in human terms in the hopeless pursuit of one human being by another. Sylvia desires Kinraid; Philip, Sylvia; Hester silently yearns after Philip and Coulson after Hester. At two extremes Kinraid and Coulson find a reconciliation with their desires – Kinraid by carelessly

marrying a wealthy and beautiful Southerner and turning his
back on his whole past life; Coulson by marrying a worthy,
dull girl 'as soon as he was convinced his object was decidedly
out of his reach' (244). But Sylvia, Philip and Hester are all
condemned to self-sacrifice, seclusion and regret.

As striking as the sense of powerlessness in the human state
is the way in which people are intimately bound up with place.
Seldom can a novelist's deliberate cultivation of a setting have
yielded richer rewards than Mrs Gaskell's decision to visit
Whitby and set her tale there. Her imaginative achievement is
one which combines an absorption of local history and cus-
toms, the sense of an age, both in domestic details and 'public'
history and a strong feeling for the topography of an area and
its metaphoric potential.

Time and place come together in such pervasive details as
the difficulty of travel, the self-sufficiency and parochialism of
small communities and the general slowness of life – at times
a slowness and inactivity which could induce boredom in the
shallow-minded, as when Daniel Robson is trapped at home
by bad weather. The importance Mrs Gaskell attached to historical perspective on human actions is witnessed by her remarks on human modes of thought:

> It is astonishing to look back and find how differently con-
> stituted were the minds of most people fifty or sixty years
> ago; they felt, they understood, without going through reason-
> ing or analytic processes, (SL 318)

This may be a Romantic myth, but it suggests that these people
are in a world more instinctive than our own, one less dis-
tracted by complexity of thought and manners, one in which
the heart is more open to other hearts, feelings are clearer and
stronger, affections simpler and more directly expressed. In this
it contrasts with the more evasive, subtle discourse of *Wives
and Daughters* or *North and South*. The distance in time gives a
further dimension to the question of knowledge also. Philip's
literacy is not to be taken for granted. He has a special power
in a society which functions well without 'book-learning' most
of the time, but is pathetically vulnerable when the distant and

alien authorities come into their lives. Instinctive communication is no use to Bell and Sylvia when Daniel is apprehended;
they are thoroughly disorientated and need Philip's intervention. His special faculties and attainments lead to lawyers, York
and business of trust in London; Sylvia's to the open heights
and the sea.

The leisurely opening account of Monkshaven and its sur-
roundings demonstrates the importance Mrs Gaskell attached
to the local topography. The houses of the town itself are 'pent
in', the bleak moors 'shut in' Monkshaven, but within these
desolate wastes are a few fertile valleys where small farms nestle.
Beyond all is the 'vast ocean that blended with the distant sky'
(1). 'For twenty miles inland there was no forgetting the sea'
(4–5). Economically speaking, it is the source of the town's wealth
and independence, but emotionally and spiritually it represents
a freedom from constraint and authority, an openness of possibility to the infinitude of human imaginings. Robson and
Kinraid swap stories of the mighty denizens of the deep; the
latter claims even to have seen the mouth of Hell.

The metaphoric richness of the setting is fully exploited in a
great set-piece early in the book, the occasion being the burial
of the sailor Darley, shot by the press-gang. On that day the
population toils out of its enclosure in the diurnal security of
the little town to witness, high and exposed, the last rites of
an adventurous life and courageous death. Looking down to
the town and out to sea they are able for a while to encounter
at the same time 'types of life and eternity' (63).

> Homeward-bound sailors caught sight of the tower of St.
> Nicholas, the first land object of all. They who went forth
> upon the great deep might carry solemn thoughts with them
> of the words they had heard there; not conscious thoughts,
> perhaps – rather a distinct if dim conviction that buying and
> selling, eating and marrying, even life and death, were not
> all the realities in existence. (63–4)

The stones in the churchyard bring to mind those distant re-
gions where so many inhabitants of the little community have
perished:

'Supposed to have perished in the Greenland seas,' 'Ship-wrecked in the Baltic,' 'Drowned off the coast of Iceland.' There was a strange sensation, as if the cold sea-winds must bring with them the dim phantoms of those lost sailors, who had died far from their homes, and from the hallowed ground where their fathers lay. (64)

The aged pause and take a seat at the end of each flight of steps on their way to that place which will soon receive their own remains, and below them, the others coming up are reduced to the inhabitants of a busy ant-hill. Everyone, even the little children, is carrying a *memento mori* in the shape of mourning ribbons or a little 'rosemary for remembrance.' (65) The agony of Darley's father – 'How came God to permit such cruel injustice of man?' – has been soothed by the service into acceptance that 'it is the Lord's doing'. At this moment of solemn overview of lives and destinies, Sylvia obtains her first glimpse of Kinraid, 'a ghastly figure that, with feeble motions, was drawing near the open grave' (70). Immediately after, Philip 'press[es] to her side, with an intention of companionship and protection' (70). The eventual role the specksioneer is to play in the lives of the two people before him is grimly hinted at by Molly's greeting:

> 'Well, Charley, a niver was so taken aback as when a saw yo' theere, like a ghost, a-standin' agin a gravestone. How white and wan yo' do look!' (71)

And indeed the scene is a type of the roles played by all three major protagonists – Sylvia excited to sympathy by the pale figure of the specksioneer, but pressed upon by the over-solicitous care of Philip. About them stretch the moors and the sea, open, wild and challenging; between them stand the gravestones, final symbols of retreat, enclosure, security. While she is young and careless Sylvia feels no disjunction between these two modes of being. From the warmth and security of a loving home to which

> the short crisp turf came creeping up to the very doors and

windows, without any attempt at a yard or garden, or any nearer enclosure of the buildings than the stone dyke that formed the boundary of the field itself (35)

she confidently goes out upon the moors. Her parents step out on to the bank top to anticipate her coming. The last, moving words with her father take place outside the house. Security and adventure are integrated, as they are in the differing natures of her parents.

But from the time when the authorities, penetrating that safe retreat even as far as the bedroom to pluck her father forth for execution, Sylvia is forced to choose between the open spaces and the dark little shop – between dreams and a necessary commitment to reality involving the oppressiveness of a narrow street, the dark fustiness of the shop, the stifling of spontaneity attendant upon the ideas of propriety which make her have to dress up to sit at home every day.

Choice, instead of being an enabling, creative matter, is here a source of entrapment. Sylvia makes a crucial choice for the direction of her life when she decides to marry Philip, and its gravity is highlighted by the kind of innocent choices we see her make when she is still a young girl. Stopping on the way to Monkshaven to bathe her feet, she thoughtlessly leaps on to a stone, only to find herself stranded:

> 'But if I put on my stockings and shoon here, and jump back into yon wet gravel, I'se not fit to be seen,' said Sylvia, in a pathetic tone of bewilderment, that was funnily childlike. She stood up, her bare feet curved round the curving surface of the stone, her slight figure balancing as if in act to spring. (13)

Here is a situation she can retrieve. Her 'balancing as if in act to spring' captures her poised for a moment with all the careless buoyancy of youth, unmoved by the down-to-earth Molly's declaration that she's 'getten no gumption.' – 'Thou shall have all the gumption, and I'll have my cloak' (13). This cloak is the more serious choice she must make that day. Should she choose the sensible grey or the more attractive red duffle? Again scorning sensible advice, more especially since it is given by

Philip, she of course chooses red. Thus she exercises a free choice – to follow her own desires, to be youthful and make errors yet overcome them, to define herself in relation to her parents and also to her cousin:

> 'I wish mother hadn't spoken up for't gray.'
> 'Why, Sylvia, thou wert saying as we topped t'brow, as she did nought but bid thee think twice afore settling on scarlet.'
> 'Ay! but mother's words are scarce, and weigh heavy. Feyther's liker me, and we talk a deal o' rubble; but mother's words are liker to hewn stone. She puts a deal o' meaning in 'em. And then,' said Sylvia, as if she was put out by the suggestion, 'she bid me ask cousin Philip for his opinion. I hate a man as has getten an opinion on such-like things.' (12)

By contrast, the choice of Philip as a husband is made in a context of restriction, necessity, a sense of indebtedness. In vain she asks Kester if it is possible Kinraid has survived. All he can do is put both sides of the question. The choice must be hers, and she stands 'quite still, thinking, and wistfully long-ing for some kind of certainty' (325). Certainty is what she cannot have. Some evil attaches to either course of action. She may live out her life in hardship for a man who is dead, or ensure her mother's ease for her remaining days by breaking her trust. Kester exhorts her 'dunnot go and marry a man as thou's noane taken wi', and another as is most like for t' be dead, but who, mebbe, is alive, havin' a pull on thy heart' (325). But she is already committed further than she has acknowl-edged, and at Philip's call she decides to 'try t'make him happy', even as she wishes 'that the grave lay open before her, and that she could lie down, and be covered up by the soft green turf from all the bitter sorrows and carking cares and weary bewilderments of this life' (326). The unhappy choice has the absolute irrevocability of death for her. While she has not chosen she is painfully uncommitted but is nevertheless open to pos-sibilities – doors which are forever closed when, deprived of certainty in circumstance, she makes her own certainty, af-ter which 'the deed was done, the choice taken which comes to most people but once in their lives' (351).

Philip, too, has an unenviable decision to make. His confused feelings in approaching Kinraid as the sailor lies on the
sand foreshadow the uncertainty he will shortly feel over his
rival's message:

> Philip was coming towards them slowly, not from want of
> activity, but because he was undecided what he should be
> called upon to do or to say by the man whom he hated and
> dreaded, yet whom just now he could not help admiring.
> (218)

If he passes the message to Sylvia she will reject him in favour
of a man who is, he believes, his inferior in human worth; a
man who will never remain faithful to her. But if he does not
mention the matter he will get the girl, if at all, only at the
cost of his own conscience. He feels the terrible irony and burden of his 'having been chosen out from among all men to
convey such a message as Kinraid's to Sylvia' (221).

Sylvia makes her decision in the form of a self-defining action, however her hand appears to be forced. Philip, faced with
uncertainty, decides to leave the matter uncertain, and by a
piece of sophistry – 'a promise is not given when it has not
been received' – enables his conscience to tolerate his guilty
inaction. It is a matter of some irony, painful to both, that Sylvia
and Philip find themselves acting against their true natures.
Sylvia is, or was when we first see her, constitutionally unhappy at being captured, pinned down, even by Kinraid. Philip
is the epitome of uprightness, clearness, decision, of giving every
man his due. He it is who particularly prides himself on his
conscience. She gives up her freedom, he abandons honour and
principle when these things are most needed and most difficult to live out. Yet we feel nothing but sympathy for both of
them, for it is in the nature of this tragedy that people should
find life insoluble at the moment when it demands most of
them.

These choices, crucial as they are, embody in terms of action
an aspect of irreconcilable opposition which also lends its weight
to the novel's tragedy, and which informs the whole book as
image and theme. It is no very obscure truth that the choice of

lovers faced by Sylvia is not simply between two men, but between two quite different ways of life. Their values are expressed in their employments, their speech, their very physical appearance. Kinraid is lively, active; his trade is adventurous, fought for by his own hands on inhospitable seas. He is constantly in motion – six months at sea, staying with the Corneys, visiting in Newcastle, returning to his ship. He has, by reputation, already abandoned a girl who loved him, yet he blithely sings his song and entices Sylvia Robson to commit her heart. Yet he too, like Sylvia and Philip, finds that he plays an unaccustomed role; he remains faithful to Sylvia's memory and comes back to her. 'I niver thought you'd ha' kept true to her!' says Philip (431) but the reason for his return is not hard to seek. His nature calls to hers, and her deepest instincts answer it. Kinraid, Sylvia and her father represent one side of a duality that runs as psychological type and image throughout the book. In Sylvia we see the type in its most detailed, individualised and attractive form. She is a child of nature, from the moment we first see her stepping out barefoot to sell her butter and eggs in Monkshaven, and pausing to play in the stream. If she is childish in her petulance and wilfulness she is also childlike in her wonder, innocence, love of pleasing and spontaneity. She is

> ready to smile or to pout, or to show her feelings in any way, with a character as wilful and undeveloped as a child's, affectionate, wilful, naughty, tiresome, charming, anything, in fact, at present that the chances of an hour called out. (24)

To Molly, whom she has splashed, she is 'quiet, not to say penitent, in a moment' (12). Her lament at the predicament she finds herself in, having jumped into the middle of the stream, is given in a 'pathetic tone of bewilderment, that was funnily childlike' (13). She is, of course, pretty, but her attractiveness is not skin-deep. She has 'that impressible nature that takes the tone of feeling from those surrounding' (18). On the one hand this suggests a passively weak personality, but on the other it implies the feeling that responds instinctively to others. She does not act from duty where she feels sympathy, but the feeling is nonetheless genuine, and has the additional virtue of the warmth of her whole personality's commitment. This quality is felt very strongly by comparison with the long-suffering rectitude of Hester Rose

> Sylvia had leisure in her heart to think 'how good Hester is for sitting with the poor bedridden sister of Darley!' without having a pang of self-depreciation in the comparison of her own conduct with that she was capable of so fully appreciating. She had gone to church for the ends of vanity, and remained to the funeral for curiosity and the pleasure of the excitement. In this way a modern young lady would have condemned herself, and therefore lost the simple, purifying pleasure of admiration for another. (75)

Sylvia is in the fortunate position of naturally attracting people. Hester must work at it:

> Hester, who had craved for the affection which had been held from her, and had from that one circumstance become distrustful of her own power of inspiring regard, while she exaggerated the delight of being beloved, feared lest Sylvia should become jealous of her mother's open display of great attachment and occasional preference for Hester. But such a thought never entered Sylvia's mind. (347)

The terrible self-repression of the plain Hester is poignantly captured when she looks in the shop mirror as the unthinkingly vain Sylvia has just done: 'What did she see? a colourless face, dark soft hair with no light gleams in it, eyes that were melancholy instead of smiling, a mouth compressed with a sense of dissatisfaction' (118). She patiently turns back to 'serve all the whims and fancies of purchasers'. Where Hester is good, Sylvia is nice. Sylvia has no cause for dissatisfaction – the assurance of love and her own charms have given her a deep security in herself, and Hester's morality will never match in human terms that secret, mysterious attractiveness. And no matter how she admires her, Sylvia can never warm to Hester. A large part of Sylvia's attractiveness derives from her changeability and elusiveness. It is imaged in her movement between light and shadow:

> Kinraid's eye watched her as she went backwards and forwards, to and fro, into the pantry, the back-kitchen, out of light into shade, out of the shadow into the broad firelight where he could see and note her appearance. (97–8)

and in the varying opinions the world holds of her:

> In fact, her peculiarity seemed to be this – that every one who knew her talked about her either in praise or blame; in church, or in market, she unconsciously attracted attention; they could not forget her presence, as they could that of other girls perhaps more personally attractive. (121–2)

Even the grim Alice Rose responds to her, while the unfortunate Hester's virtues are made to seem monochrome beside the glowing warmth of Sylvia's natural spontaneity:

> then Sylvia turned to Hester, and, with the sweet grace which is a natural gift to some happy people, thanked her; in common words enough she thanked her, but in that nameless manner, and with that strange, rare charm which made Hester feel as if she had never been thanked in all her life before; and from that time forth she understood, if she did not always yield to, the unconscious fascination which Sylvia could exercise over others at times. (340)

Alas for Philip, he too must recognise the virtue of her natural self when he has lost it:

> 'I don't want yo' to be grateful, Sylvie,' said poor Philip, dissatisfied, yet unable to explain what he did want; only knowing that there was something he lacked, yet fain would have had. (336)

She is 'gentle and good', but he wants her to be 'tender and shy' with him (334). She looks at him straight and composedly.

That essential sexual allure is not to be a part of their marriage. He has gained her body, but not her soul, and he begins to feel that 'the fruit he had so inordinately longed for was but of the nature of an apple of Sodom' (334). Her allure is not wanton. If she is not like Hester, she is even less like the increasingly coarse Molly Corney. She has a strong sense of her own worth and likes to keep men at a distance. The kiss Kinraid steals at New Year is resented because it has not been freely bestowed but snatched by a ruse which makes their relationship one of sexual play, and for all her wilfulness Sylvia, with one exception, never teases, but is always genuine and straight in her affections. And the proprietorial manner of Hepburn and his insistence on closeness is understandably unpleasant to the girl.

Sylvia's natural habitat is the open uplands, and her natural heart's companion her father, however much she might respect her more cautious, less garrulous mother. She recognises that her mother's words 'weigh heavier' than her father's, but as with all her human intercourse the spontaneously attractive, the irrationally beloved, dictates the strength of her affections. The special relationship between herself and her father goes deeper than the wife's and husband's:

'Well! missus, and who's to pay for t' fettling of all them clothes?' as Bell came down with her arms full. She was going to answer her husband meekly and literally according to her wont, but Sylvia, already detecting the increased cheerfulness of his tone, called out from behind her mother –

'I am, feyther. I'm going for to sell my new cloak as I bought Thursday, for the mending on your old coats and waistcoats.' (50)

The teasing she would never grant a lover is bestowed on her obstinate but warm-hearted father. It is she who thinks up and puts into practice the plan of bringing Donkin to entertain her father, 'For Bell, good and sensible as she was, was not a woman of resources' (46). She is ignorant, but she is sensitive, shrewd, creative and persuasive in essential domestic ways where her family affections are invoved. Her ignorance is most obviously expressed in her illiteracy, and this is both a bond and a source of conflict in her relations with Philip. Reading and writing, the means of advancement, the signs of public acceptability to him, are puzzles, if not completely worthless matters for her. When Philip tells her that Daniel is 'ta'en up for felony' (300) she seizes on the word as a kind of talisman:

> 'Felony,' said she. 'There thou're out; he's in for letting yon men out; thou may call it rioting if thou's a mind to set folks again' him, but it's too bad to cast such hard words at him as yon – felony,' she repeated, in a half-offended tone. (300)

It does indeed, in its mystery, represent the unfamiliar world of authority which, indifferent to her and her family, comes and with apparently arbitrary power seizes her beloved father. Neither of them can understand 'how fearful sometimes is the necessity for prompt and severe punishment of rebellion against authority' (308).

The arbitrary and circumscribed nature of the book-learning that Philip tries to convey to his young cousin reflects one aspect of a personality which is diametrically opposed to Sylvia's. His virtues are most clearly registered by the person who is best placed in terms of physical proximity, temperament and inclination to appreciate them. Hester 'had seen how devoted he was to his master's interests, had known of his careful and punctual ministration to his absent mother's comforts, as long as she was living to benefit by his silent, frugal self-denial'. (119) His virtues are careful, narrow, methodical, derived from and acknowledging tradition and authority. He prizes knowledge of the kind which is cultivated and nurtured – cultivated through many tedious hours of slow acquisition in Philip's case. His affectionate nature makes him try hard to do what will please, but he lacks Sylvia's spontaneity, and cannot win hearts. He is the instructor, the preacher of caution when buying new cloaks; the man who decides that certain people should not be mixing with her. He is the repository of formal knowledge, and offers to teach Sylvia 'Arctics, and tropics, and equator, and equinoctial line' but *her* closing words are a request to 'tell me about t' Greenland seas, and how far they're off' (79).

What for her is a boundless realm of the romantic imagination is seen by him in terms of superimposed piecemeal knowledge. Alice Rose tells him 'it's noane schooling, nor knowledge, nor book-learning as takes a young woman. It's summat as cannot be put into words' (243). But Philip is bound by the limits of the word, and his and Sylvia's complementary limitations later provide touching images of their belated and fruitless attempts at communication. He writes from York:

'Sylvia, will you try and forget how I used to scold you about your writing and spelling, and just write me two or three lines. I think I would rather have them badly spelt than not, because then I shall be sure they are yours. (309)

and when her husband has left for ever, as it seems, Sylvia humbly begs Alice Rose to teach her to read.

When Sylvia's thoughts turn to the Greenland seas she is of course half-consciously thinking of Kinraid, but she is also turning to her father's past, and to the freedom of spirit that past represents. In the social sphere Philip's role is that of the conformist to established authority. The impulsive Sylvia would go to help the sailors taken by the press-gang, but Philip is emphatic: 'Sylvie! you must not. Don't be silly; it's the law, and no one can do aught against it, least of all women and lasses' (28). Daniel Robson has no restraining mentor, and with his daughter's impulsiveness plunges into actions fatal to himself and his whole family.

The problem of the relation of freedom and independence to 'necessary authority' was clearly one which concerned Mrs Gaskell. It arose in her first novel and is treated on more than one level in *North and South*. As the struggle of a lone female against an oppressive and misguided male authority it recurs in 'Lois the Witch'. In 'Sylvia's Lovers' her attitude is typically undogmatic, though her point of view makes it impossible for her sympathies to be other than with the individual, and the matter gives a further dimension to the tragic opposition of temperaments we have seen in Sylvia and Philip. Daniel's domestic situation is an example of authority arrived at by mutual consent between individuals. Bell is altogether more sensible

and responsible, but cedes authority to her husband 'for th'
Bible's sake' (46). '[T]h' feyther's feyther, and we mun respect
him' (46). 'Niver gie a woman t' whip hand o'er yo'!' says
Daniel. Yet everyone in the household knows where authority
really lies. It is upon such assumptions that Daniel judges larger,
more public questions of authority:

> 'And when did I say a word again King George and the
> Constitution? I only ax 'em to govern me as I judge best,
> and that's what I call representation.' (40)

> 'Nation here! nation theere! I'm a man and yo're another,
> but nation's nowhere.' (41)

The whole family are ignorant of the rigid and implacable nature
of this public authority. Philip's four words 'It is the law' comprehend its absoluteness and the uselessness of looking to it
for human attributes.

The book is set in a time and place where individual and
local independence is particularly prized. Local landowners see
the press-gang as a useful means of reminding the *nouveau riche*
of their allegiance. Smuggling is a widely practised and re-
spectable trade. The author herself can find only one word for
the power of the press-gang: 'Now all this tyranny (for I can
use no other word) is marvellous to us' (6–7) and she blames
the government itself for the prevalence of smuggling, since
their unreasonable duty on such articles as salt 'did more to
demoralise the popular sense of rectitude and uprightness than
heaps of sermons could undo' (99). The sense of injustice is
particularly aggravated in the case which prompts the burning
of the 'randyvoo house' by the government's preying upon
natural human kindness. They ring the fire bell and thereby
draw out able-bodied seamen eager to help their fellow-townsfolk
who may be in danger. The confused, human mixture of hatred
and kindness which makes Daniel Robson rescue Simpson's
cow and give him all the money he has about him is the very
antithesis of the unrelenting 'justice' which sees only an af-
front to authority. Robson, far from being ashamed, or fearful
of the consequences of his actions, is stupidly boastful. In his

self-centred confusion he sees himself as the hero, and to the
very last, far from showing a fitting remorse, boasts of his readi-
ness to repeat the exploit.

Despite her sympathy with the individual over a tyrannous
government, it is typical of Mrs Gaskell's even-handedness, her
willingness to give every circumstance its weight of value, that
she is able to appreciate the necessity of the force used by outraged authority to suppress mob violence. 'So the authorities
were quite justified in the decided steps they had taken, both
in their own estimation then, and now, in ours, looking back
on the affair in cold blood' (283). But the individual victim of
these measures is nonetheless a human being, and that human
selfness has its values too. Before he is taken away, Robson
asks his daughter's forgiveness for his harsh speech to her the
night before:

> 'Nay, nay, my wench, it's thee as mun be a comfort to mother:
> nay, nay, or thou'll niver hear what a've got to say. Sylvie,
> my lass, a'm main and sorry a were so short wi' thee last
> neet; a ax thy pardon, lass, a were cross to thee, and sent
> thee to thy bed wi' a sore heart. Thou munnot think on it
> again, but forg'e me, now a'm leavin' thee.' (280–1)

The moment's importance lies not just in the humility of its
request, and its emphasis on human and individual qualities,
but in the bond of love it rehearses between father and daughter. Like Sylvia, though in a coarser guise, Daniel has a mysterious quality which draws love to him:

> With all his many faults, however, he had something in him
> be dearly loved, both by the daughter whom he indulged,
> and the wife who was in fact superior to him, but whom he
> imagined that he ruled with a wise and absolute sway. (247)

As a free girl, Sylvia's heart inclines to Kinraid as the man
associated with her father by profession and nature. Deprived
of the male principle by Daniel's death, both mother and daughter are left with no centre to their lives, and Sylvia turns to
Philip for authority. But the compromise reached by a lifetime

of love and tacit forbearance at Haytersbank cannot be recaptured behind the shop in Monkshaven.

The touching scene between Sylvia and her father has a symbolic function, also. Insofar as the principles of authority and freedom are irreconcilable, the pursuit of the loved one hopeless, and the loss of life, youth and natural fulfilment irredeemable, this novel is essentially tragic. On the day Sylvia, his child in her arms, lifts up her face to kiss him, Philip 'reached the zenith of his life's happiness' (353). Kinraid's return ruins his life and Sylvia's, deprives the child of a father, and shortly thereafter of a mother, leaving the stoical, disappointed Hester Rose to found almshouses as her only legacy to future generations. In the face of this bleak mortal destiny, forgivenes is an important consolation. Robson's last words with his daughter are the more moving for being on such a slight point – a cross word which would, in the normal course of things, have dissipated itself in normal daily intercourse – but their importance lies in the principle of love which they embody, and the eternity against which that love is about to be measured.

Words of forgiveness are required from Sylvia on other occasions. When Simpson, the main accuser of her father, is dying, Sylvia refuses her forgiveness with verbal absoluteness:

> 'I've a mind to break it off for iver wi' thee, Philip.' [who has brought the request] ... 'Ay, there's some things as I know I niver forgive; and there's others as I can't – and I won't, either.'
> 'But , Sylvie, yo' pray to be forgiven your trespasses, as you forgive them as trespass against you.'
> 'Well, if I'm to be taken at my word, I'll noane pray at all, that's all.'

> ... 'I tell thee my flesh and blood wasn't made for forgiving and forgetting. Once for all, thou must take my word. When I love I love, and when I hate I hate. (332–3)

Her words are almost a repeat of those uttered to Kester a few pages before:

'Them as was friends o' father's I'll love for iver and iver;
them as helped for t' hang him . . . I'll niver forgive – niver!'
(319)

'Never', as Kester says, is 'a long word', and words can bind
ourselves and others to them, but their absoluteness is out-
matched by Sylvia's flexible, responsive humanity, and she
repents her refusal to offer forgiveness to Simpson. Philip assumes that her words mirror herself – another instance of tem-
peramental unlikeness leading to misunderstanding – and so
never learns 'how her conduct might have been more gentle
and relenting than her words.' Words, which enabled Robson
and Sylvia to communicate their love, are a barrier to communication of the heart when they become large and absolute,
concerning themselves with abstract principles, rather than
addressing the suppliant human being. The first words (in the
chapter entitled 'First Words') spoken to Philip by his child
are words of pity and charity. They are accompanied by physical
sustenance delivered by the child's own hand. In a renewal of
possibility, speech comes to him via the untainted child, which
opens the way to ultimate reconciliation with Sylvia. The seemingly final and absolute acts on both sides are modified. Philip
returns, Sylvia forgives. Yet reconciliation is a prelude to death
– indeed comes with death itself – in a way for which we have
been prepared by a change of tone in the last quarter of the
book.

The suggestion of death and transcendence is established, as
we have seen, as early as the burial of Darley. The ocean, and
the moorland which is never far from its piping, salt winds,
are both symbols of freedom for Sylvia. From the enclosure of
the shop she goes out to gaze at the 'mother-like' sea. It represents for her a freedom from the constraint of purpose which
the busy-ness of others seems to impose upon her. Despite her
happiness in her child, she is oppressed by the irrevocable nature
of her marriage. The darkness and confinement of the shop
sucks out of her the vital spirit, and to that extent anticipates
the confines of the grave. After Philip has left, Sylvia, not wanting
to appear as an abandoned wife, scarcely goes out at all, acting out her conviction of the end of all future possibility.

Philip is of course from the first associated with enclosure. For his temperament and values an indoor life is natural; it means security, order, shelter, caution. His slight stoop speaks of his trade, and also suggests a pressure upon him, preventing an outward-looking stance. He leaves the shelter of Monkshaven twice. His visit to London on business – a matter of trust, secrecy and cautious financial investigation – is the occasion of his great lie of omission. The second occasion is his enlistment as a soldier, in despair at that lie having been discovered. This is a wild and desperate action, a decision made when he is, for once in his life, drunk and out of control, but it frees him for a pilgrimage to the Holy Land where he is, as Alice Rose puts it, 'suffered to enter Jerusalem, which is a heavenly and a typical city at this time'. (450–1)

His rescue of Kinraid appears to the seaman 'too like a dream, too utterly improbable to be real' (431). The sailor who searches unsuccessfully for Philip says 'Maybe it was a spirit' (433). We are here in the realm of miracles, of redemptive wonders, and it is consonant with a transcendent note asserted most fully in the last chapters, but already, as we have seen, introduced as early as the burial of Darley.

From the moment she says farewell to Kinraid for the last time, Sylvia's thoughts are inclined to the immortal part of herself:

> He's spoilt my life, – he's spoilt it for as long as iver I live on this earth; but neither yo' nor him shall spoil my soul. It goes hard wi' me Charley, it does indeed. I'll just give yo one kiss – one little kiss – and then, so help me God, I'll niver see nor hear till – no, not that, not that is indeed – I'll niver see – sure that's enough – I'll never see yo again on this side heaven, so help me God! (383)

She fears that her mother 'knows what I said to him [Philip] where she's gone to' (403). His words withheld, hers given, can never be said or unsaid, and the finality of this doom drives her into the refuge of transcendence, just as Kinraid's words in the icy dairy find her 'driven into a corner' (183) and 'driven to bay' (184), and Philip's whistle and call decides her to enter into marriage with him for security. She is terrified by Jeremiah Foster's suggestion to little Bell that 'thine earthly parents have forsaken thee, and I know not if the Lord will take thee up' (412), and regrets her words:

> 'I niver told him to go, sir.'
>   'But thy words sent him forth, Sylvia.'
>   'I cannot unsay them, sir; and I believe as I should say them again.'
>   But she said this as one who rather hopes for a contradiction. (413)

His words make her think of 'the unknown region from whence both blessing and cursing come' (418–19). To this gradual ac-climatisation of vision, the stern Quaker doctrine of election plays an important counterpoint, not only in the subtle per-sonality of Jeremiah, but unconsciously through Alice Rose. She is 'unconsciously to herself . . . touched by the filial attentions she constantly received from the young mother, whom she be-lieved to be foredoomed to condemnation' (418). This under-mining of doctrine reminds of the book's prevailing theme of opposition between rigid authority and the human heart. The old Quaker's belief in 'the vanity of setting the heart on any-thing earthly' is contradicted by the affection she gradually feels for Sylvia, and the latter's tentative attempts at learning to read suggest a dawning reconciliation with the husband she has dis-carded 'for ever'.

Yet we cannot miraculously become a spiritual creature united with a transcendent absolute. The importance of contingent re-ality is suggested by two slight accidents which enormously change the course of events for at least two human beings. In the first, Sylvia's baby is carried into the parlour of Jeremiah's house – 'and much of her after-life depended on this trivial fact' (408) since she thereby wins the heart of the old bachelor. In the second, a gleam of sunlight – 'a strong clear sunbeam' – catches Kinraid full in the face as he lies dying at Acre, and 'that strong clear sunbeam had wrought his salvation' (431). It saves Philip too, in the sense that he pays his debt. It is the climax of that pilgrimage to the self that he embarks upon when, leaving Monkshaven in despair, he loses himself for once in drink.

The shrine of Philip's pilgrimage, his 'heavenly and typical city', is the Holy Land. It is a landscape similar in general topography to the North East coast of England he has left behind, with the 'eternal sea', a town, and hills beyond. But essentially it is an alien scene. In place of the greys and greens, the mists and piping winds of Monkshaven, the colours are blue and white, the 'clear eastern air' makes everything sharp and glittering; the sky is 'literally purple with heat' (425). Reinforced by Biblical references, this open, blazing landscape is clearly visionary, as far removed as is possible from the huddle of houses and streets and the dark little shop in Monkshaven. His debt repaid, Philip bears the scar, the fruit and sign of his ordeal, back into seclusion, first in a cottage at St Sepulchre's, thence into a tiny cottage room at home, before he attains his last 'narrow cell' where he will finally behold the celestial city for all eternity.

It is Philip's fate never to find the key to his wife's heart, always to be the observer, as he observes the abduction of his rival in a torment of indecision and stands watching the circus procession as it passes him by on his return to Monkshaven, unable to reveal himself to his wife and little daughter, so happy do they seem and so worthless and poor himself. It is her fate to find too late the words that correspond to what her heart secretly knows. They are bound together in the child who symbolically reconciles them and actually survives them both. It is easy to find localised points of blame for this tragedy, but it is rather to be traced in the nature of human desire. Sylvia's uniqueness, her elusive sexual femaleness, is what she *is*, not what she chooses to be, and the rival desires of her lovers are as natural as each other and as their object's charm. That these things should be destructive when they were designed as part of nature's creative force is a paradox too mysterious for solution. It is embedded in the texture of mortal life, and will be known only in the realm of truth 'behind the veil'.

This is Elizabeth Gaskell's only thoroughgoing tragedy, in which no sense of self-discovery and self-definition leads to a renewal of life-commitment or a newly-created, active potential. We may feel that 'Sylvia's Lovers' anticipates some aspects of Hardy's work, though her evocation of the transcendent gives an alternative dimension to the problem not allowed to him. There is the same general belief in the potential destructiveness of sex, the triangular relationship so frequently explored by Hardy, and the parody of an idea of 'survival of the fittest' in the destinies of Kinraid and Coulson, like the role of Arabella and Vibart in *Jude the Obscure*. Most importantly, for all the Christian faith of the earlier writer, both express the feeling that there is something out of joint in this mortal state which denies our sense of justice and providence, and which is incapable of resolution, despite all human love and belief.

10

'It is not long to bide':
The Shorter Fiction and
the Meaning of Lives

Though each story has its own peculiar character, three features serve particularly to distinguish Mrs Gaskell's shorter fiction
– its concern with the past, the interest in family and blood
ties, and its exploration of the meaning of an individual's life.
Such matters are not confined of course to her shorter fiction,
but a special focus is given to them by the more compact form.
The past is met with in the novels as a precondition for present
circumstances, or as the actual setting for some works – a period
within living memory but romantically distant by at least a
generation. In her shorter fiction, however, the sense of the
past has a peculiar oppresiveness. This is in part because it is
felt in generations and families, and in part because of the secrets
the past contains. Many of these stories detail family relations
– marriages, births and deaths – for more than one generation
before narrating the central action of the tale. 'A Dark Night's
Work', for example, describes the rise of Mr Wilkins senior as
an attorney, passes on to the career of his son, before finally
passing to that son's daughter Ellinor, whose guilty secret forms
the main point of the story. 'The Poor Clare' might leave the
reader wondering for much of the story when the title was to
be justified, as it pieces together a web of familial, generational
and social relationships, beginning with a Jacobite follower of
James II and ending with his servant's granddaughter being
released from a curse. In 'The Doom of the Griffiths' we are
taken back nine generations to the time of Owen Glendower,
that we may understand the original curse which the main action

shows being worked out in modern times.

In part this is simply a matter of that most essential feature of storytelling, the business of cause and effect. But cause and effect is obviously not merely mechanics; in part we need the density of the sense of the past which is conveyed in marriages, families, careers, births and deaths, in order to convey an idea of the complexity of the circumstance which now binds the protagonists. But centrally these stories are about ways of handling the past – a past for which we may be guilty or over which we could have no control. Are we gradually or suddenly reconciled? Do we carry the burden to our graves? Do we find ourselves overtaken by events? However the problem is resolved, there is no escape from the burden of the past for those who act out their lives in these fictions.

In these stories we also see most clearly the debt Elizabeth Gaskell owed to the fairy tale. Their situational energy derives from premature deaths of one or both parents, remarriages to cruel or indifferent step-parents and romantic and sibling rivalry. Despite the particularity of their location in county towns, the fells of Northern England, the Welsh borders or Antwerp, the claustrophobic sense of family, marriage and blood ties is the real medium, and its narrow confines suggest the schematised life of the fairy story. A good example is to be found in the little tale entitled 'The Half-Brothers'. Gregory is the son neglected as a result of his mother's remarriage. The stepfather wants her to love him more, but also to love her child less. She, on the contrary, never smiles after the day of her marriage to William Preston. The stepfather's rough words bring on the premature birth of Gregory's half-brother, but Preston blames Gregory. After his mother's death Gregory, who is lumpish and awkward, is trained as a shepherd. The favoured son, in common with most people, baits Gregory. But it is the cast-off son who goes out in a snowstorm to rescue his half-brother, thereby perishing himself. The rather schematised relationships, and the theme of the obscure hero, together with the bare narrative prose all suggest the kind of ritual enactment we associate with fairy tale. But Mrs Gaskell's treatment is richer in particuar human interest. Instead of an out-turning into the world of tough experience this is a tale that turns inward for the reassurance of blood ties. This inturning and humanisation is greatly dependent on the fact of the story's being told by the son whose birth has, as it were, usurped Gregory's place. The narrator is by his existence guilty of the story's tragedy, but he is also essentially, humanly, blameless. The cause lies somewhere in the interstices of circumstance and character – that the mother married young, and chose an older second husband for security; that the stepfather is impatient and frustrated. We are told that William Preston could have loved the mother if she had had no past to be jealous of. When Gregory is born, his mother lies in bed with the two brothers, and smiles at the father 'almost her first smile at him; and such a sweet smile! as more besides aunt Fanny have said. In an hour she was dead' (MM 195). By this gesture she tries to draw a family together in love, and it is recalled as Gregory and the narrator lie down in the snow together:

> 'Thou canst not remember, lad, how we lay together thus by our dying mother. She put thy small, wee hand in mine – I reckon she sees us now.' (201)

But the tragic dénouement turns the bed into a grave, Gregory being laid by his mother in a gesture of unavailing remorse by the stepfather, whose last words are 'God forgive me my hardness of heart towards the fatherless child!' (202).

The theme of the obscure hero is treated again in 'The Sexton's Hero', but in this case the hero is more clearly to blame, in scorning a man for refusing to fight. The sexton-narrator gets the girl, who also scorns Gilbert Dawson for his supposed cowardice. Gilbert dies in rescuing them both from the advancing tide, but there is a curious paradox in the case which may remind us of the 'vengeful death' of Ruth Hilton. Letty, the wife, is never the same after Gilbert's death. Their child dies and the mother declines soon after. The events the sexton narrates are more than forty years in the past, but they have affected his whole life, leaving him to reflect on the dead until the day death releases him. There is in both these stories, but particularly in 'The Half-Brothers' a paring-down of human experience to love and death, bed and grave. Words are few, gestures are sparing – a single smile in a three-year marriage – hair turns white overnight, because the well of emotions is so deep, yet so repressed, that it can only be manifest in great actions, or, as we shall see, typically in words, whether of cursing or forgiveness or self-commitment and self-recognition.

In both these stories the legacy of the past is tragic. In 'The Doom of the Griffiths' tragedy seems to be peculiarly stark because the fate that overtakes the protagonists is so arbitrary. A curse is acted out hundreds of years later, resulting in a father killing his son's child and the son killing his father. In the finale the son and his wife, with the body of the father, sail away in a little boat and are never seen again, while 'The house of Bodowen has sunk into damp, dark ruins; and a Saxon stranger holds the lands of the Griffiths' (MM 86). The intensity of love between Owen and his father (when his father is drowned he lies with him in the boat as they lay in bed together when he was a boy), Owen and his wife and Owen and his son only makes the mysterious hold of past over present more poignant. At least in 'The Old Nurse's Story' the cry of Miss Furnivall – 'Alas! alas! what is done in youth can never be undone in age!' (CP 56) suggests a plain responsibility for one's own fate. This is one of the few stories in which Elizabeth Gaskell directly invokes the supernatural. The old nurse tells of how she took a little orphan to stay at Furnivall Hall , and how the child is lured into the snow by a phantom girl. Apart from servants, the only inhabitants of the Hall are the elderly Miss Furnivall and her companion. The ghostly child, it transpires, belonged to Miss Furnivall's sister, the fruit of her marriage with a foreign musician. The family's pride was notorious, and when the younger Miss Furnivall, in jealous rivalry, betrayed her sister to the old Lord, he struck the child a violent blow and turned mother and daughter out. Next day the child was found dead and the mother mad.

In an apocalyptic scene the guilty secret repressed so long bursts out in full ghostly manifestation:

All at once, the east door gave way with a thundering crash, as if torn open in a violent passion, and there came into that broad and mysterious light, the figure of a tall, old man, with grey hair and gleaming eyes. He drove before him, with many a relentless gesture of abhorrence, a stern and beautiful woman, with a little child clinging to her dress. (55)

The previous occasional glimpses of the guilty past had seemed to suggest that it was only temporarily repressed. A lifetime of denial was not enough for Miss Furnivall to lay to rest emotions of such extremity and violence. Her isolation serves for many years to hide from the truth, but the fresh sensibilities of a little child respond to its counterpart from the past, just as Miss Furnivall had begun to be stirred again by feelings of tenderness towards the little orphan. It would seem that the real affection blossoming again in the present carries with it the demand for pity from the little ghost of the past. Miss Furnivall's attempt at renewed love is literally haunted by her old hate, just as Lucy carries a mocking double for her purity, inherited by her grandmother's curse, in 'The Poor Clare'.

The final acknowledgement of a repressed truth is treated in a totally different manner in 'The Crooked Branch'. As the title suggests, the family, and blood-ties grown awry are once again the central themes, but whereas 'The Old Nurse's Story' involves Gothic and supernatural images – the melodrama attendant on high-born ladies marrying poor musicians and being turned out in the snow for their pains; the pathos of ghostly children and mad mothers – 'The Crooked Branch' is all domesticity, quietness and understatement. It is a story which could have come from suggestions in Wordsworth's 'Michael'. But Benjy, the hoped-for son of old age, unlike Luke, comes back to bring his troubles and shame with him. Nathan Huntroyd's marriage to Hester Rose is made in middle-age, some years after her family had rejected him as a social inferior. She, a 'hardworking, homely-looking (at thirty-seven) servant' (CP 195) is greeted by him in his Sunday-best at the door:

Her former lover fell into no ecstasies. He simply said to himself, 'She'll do'; and forthwith began upon his business. (196)

Out of this practical, affectionate arrangement comes a son, Benjamin, who, though he is their dearest joy, contradicts in every part of his being those solid virtues of trust, affection, thrift, quiet, proper pride, honesty and uprightness that his parents have cultivated. But Benjy is handsome and imperious. He not only has his parents' love, but holds in thrall their young ward Bessy. He callously exploits her devotion for his own ends, but both she and the old couple remain devoted to him. Having fled to London to escape the consequences of his scrapes at home, he returns briefly to take £200 from his father in payment for a law partnership. Not content with this he demands the remaining few pounds,which are kept in the home. This his father refuses, and the climax comes when thieves break into the house. One of them is locked into a cupboard downstairs, and while Bessy is left to guard him, he reveals himself as the abjectly defiant Benjy, demanding his release. She opens the door and he escapes into the night, never to return. This final encounter with the despicable son who had posed as her lover for so many years is painful enough for Bessy, but it is as though she has acted out a kind of cornering and dismissal of the illusions treasured in her past life. She is thus freed to marry the worthy John Kirkby, son of a local farmer.

But for the old couple, facing the truth is more terrible. They are summoned to the trial of Benjy's two accomplices to testify that there was a third person involved in the robbery. Under questioning Hester is forced to concede more and more about her son's part in the crime, until finally, when asked what the 'third person' downstairs said:

> Her face worked – her mouth opened two or three times as if to speak – she stretched out her arms imploringly; but no word came, and she fell back into the arms of those nearest to her. (238)

and Nathan, forcing himself into the witness-box, tells the whole court that 'It wur my son, my only child, as called out for us t' open door, and who shouted out for to hold th' oud woman's throat if she did na stop her noise' (238). Before night the mother lies on her death-bed, stricken with paralysis. For her, confrontation with the long-suppressed truth about the child she has borne cannot be uttered; even acknowledgement of it produces such trauma that she is paralysed. All three have poured their worldly goods, their hope and their love out, and it is as though it had been swallowed without trace by indifferent circumstance. Bessy's life is not over, but for the parents the courtroom is a public declaration of the meaning of their whole lives. Disappointed in their early years, they begin the latter part of their lives together, and place their trust in Benjamin as they place their trust in their own union and in future generations. Yet finally they are forced to acknowledge the baselessness of this hope for which their patient, monotonous, hardworking lives were lived.

This same concern with the meaning of a life is found in a tale whose setting and ambience are not dissimilar to that of 'The Crooked Branch'. The title, 'Half a Life-time Ago', hints at the theme, as do its closing words: 'And so it fell out that the latter days of Susan Dixon's life were better than the former' (CP 102). It is a tale, like many others, of a secret life, obscurely lived in itself, but concealing human truths which are at the heart of what the meaning of the individual's life may be. Like 'The Crooked Branch', it may be indebted to Wordsworth – for some of its names, one of its characters, who is an 'idiot boy', and the lyrical opening, describing the setting of Susan's cottage. The house is 'yet to be seen', like Michael's sheepfold, and a brook runs by it, like Greenhead Ghyll. In place of the 'clipping tree' stands a 'funereal umbrageous yew, making a solemn shadow, as of death, in the very heart and centre of the light and heat of the brightest summer day' (59). And obviously reflecting the dark themes that shade Susan's earlier years.

We are introduced to Susan in the manner of Wordsworth, as outsiders, viewing her as many travellers did, in her middle years, 'tall, gaunt, hard-featured, angular' (60). Her manner to passing strangers is, if not hostile, at least 'stony' and monotonously 'indifferent' in its refusal to yield warmth of welcome and encouragement to intimacy. We are then taken back to the days fifty years before, when Susan, living with her family, had been 'a fine-looking girl, bright-spirited and rosy; and when the hearth at the Yew Nook had been as bright as she, with family love and youthful hope and mirth' (60).

On her deathbed, Susan's mother lays on her one of those

fatal injunctions we so often find in Gaskell – that she should look after her delicate, sensitive brother, Willie. In the fulness of love for her dying mother Susan makes a promise which is to colour almost all her life, and 'Henceforward she was all in all to her brother' (64). Her lover, Michael Hurst, despises Willie from the first, and Susan is torn between them. But after typhus has struck down her father, and left Willie an idiot, Michael forces her to choose between sending her brother to an asylum and losing the chance of marriage. Susan of course remains faithful to her trust, and looks after Willie until his death some years later, Michael meanwhile marrying a rival girl and gradually sinking into drunkenness and squalor, together with his family, until he is found dead in a snowstorm by his former sweetheart. She takes the news of his death to his wife and children, suffers a stroke, and after she is nursed back to health takes Michael's widow and children to live with her 'and fill up the haunted hearth with living forms that should banish the ghosts' (102).

Told thus baldly, one understands the starkness of the story, but misses the ambience of a work which is one of the most profoundly realistic of all Mrs Gaskell's fictions. If her statesman family is independent, just, hospitable, sensible and shrewd, the author does not flinch from conveying to us the darker side of lives lived remotely in self-enclosedness. Occasional drunkenness is a matter of course, and is taken indeed as a sign of manliness. Violence seems almost equally routine, the by-product of a physical existence demanding strength and endurance. Michael Hurst, stung by a blow from Susan, in turn kicks Will. When told by Susan that 'that lad's motherless but not friendless' (66) he retorts that 'His own father leathers him, and why should not I, when he's given me such a burn on my face?' to which she coolly replies, 'His father's his father, and there is nought more to be said.' The situation in which she is placed requires her to be strong by the combination of a variety of emotions – defiance of Michael while feeling the 'thrill' of his voice as he calls to her, pity for Willie even as she bids him 'be a man'. In fact she herself must 'be a man' ultimately, in looking after the farm following her father's death, and controlling the rapidly-growing but feeble-minded Willie. For, like

Wordsworth's treatment of his idiot boy, Mrs Gaskell is not sentimental. Willie is an unrewarding trial of body and spirit, shared with no one, and assuming the status of a *raison d'être* for his sister:

> The one idea of taking charge of him had deepened and deepened with years. It was graven into her mind as the object for which she lived. The sacrifice she had made for this object only made it more precious to her. (92)

Her life is reflected in her face and body. The lines in her face are 'strong, and deep, and hard'. 'The wrinkles at the corners of her mouth and eyes were planted firm and sure; not an ounce of unnecessary flesh was there on her bones' (91). The obsessive pursuit of this talismanic bond between herself and her dead mother, her day-to-day living and the absolute meaning of that living, leads to her turning thrift into miserliness for Willie's sake. In the same way she hoards her emotions for another, living to a vow and only allowing herself one, depressing glimpse of the possibility that might have been – Michael beating his horse in savage drunkenness – until the living relict of that vow is taken from her, and she lives from habitual strength, privateness and parsimony alone.

As with all great works of realism, metaphoric power is generated by an acute grasp of the physical and of the bonds it may have with human emotions and values. When she is told that Michael may be paying court to another girl, Susan says to herself, 'I can bear it without either wincing or blenching' (84) but when Willie comes running to her, the sight of him makes her burst into tears. He brings with him his cherished paper windmill, and 'thrust it into Susan's face, her hands, her lap, regardless of the injury his frail plaything thereby received' (85). But sobered by her hopeless gaze he now needs comfort, and Susan tries to comfort him by twirling the toy. Alas, it is broken:

> 'it made no noise; it would not go round. This seemed to afflict Susan more than him. She tried to make it right, although she saw the task was hopeless; and while she did

so, the tears rained down unheeded from her bent head on the paper toy.

'It won't do,' said she at last. 'It will never do again.' (85)

The pathos here is the more striking because it is so rare, and because it contains her whole life, as it appears, in one stark and simple phrase. When, a few pages later, she finally dismisses Michael, she turns to making clap-bread, 'one of the hardest and hottest domestic tasks of a Daleswoman' (88). As she works, beating the cakes thin 'with vehement force' she feels a touch on her mouth. It is a cup of tea proffered by the old servant Peggy, and held to her lips at exactly the right time. The simplicity, homeliness and tenderness of the gesture reduces Susan to tears, and leads Peggy to deliver her own bleak comfort: 'It is not long to bide, and then the end will come' (88). This is certainly one form of comprehending the whole meaning of one's life, but it is essentially a denial of meaning bestowed upon the young by the very old, and it cannot serve the human needs of Susan, who continues for some time to mourn the loss of her lover, drinking 'the delicious cup of poison, although at the very time she knew what the consequences of racking pain would be' (89). As years go on she succeeds at farming, and keeps to her old ways, not wishing change, because it would seem like a betrayal of Willie and all her life has meant. It is only when she confronts the past that she can open into the future. It is a confrontation that requires all the strength she has built up over years of denial and effort:

> How Michael Hurst got to Yew Nook no one but Susan ever knew. They thought he had dragged himself there, with some sore, internal bruise sapping away his minuted life. They could not have believed the superhuman exertion which had first sought him out, and then dragged him hither. Only Susan knew of that. (99)

In fact the internal bruise is Susan's, and greater even than the physical strength she shows over the body of her dead lover is the strength of heart and will needed to go to the widow, tell the news and confess all that her own heart has held for so many years:

'Alas! alas! It would not have brought him to life. I would have laid down my own to save his. My life has been so very sad! No one would have cared if I had died.' (101)

The stroke she suffers puts her in a state of dependency. For the first time in many years she must cede responsibility and be as a child. The widow diverts her grief in caring for Susan, and out of the mutual bond, life begins a second time.

If 'Half a Life-time Ago' represents an extreme of sombre realism, 'The Poor Clare' is, in essence, wildly romantic, but it is a work which suggests vividly the power of long-past events and actions to influence lives remotely distant in time and place and, as much as the realistic story, is concerned to establish the meaning of an individual life. The narrator's detective-like search for the links between the principal actors in the story enhances the feeling that there is a focus of significance for the disparate strands, and that the destinies of many lives are mysteriously involved with that of a single powerful personality. He plays a part in the tale not only as investigator, but as lover of the young girl Lucy, who is the innocent victim of a curse. The events are approached from two directions. First we are told from the outside, as it were, of the return of the Roman Catholic Starkey family to their home in Lancashire at the beginning of the eighteenth century. They are accompanied by an Irish servant, Bridget Fitzgerald, and her daughter Mary. Mary leaves to seek service abroad, the Starkey parents die, the son is taken by guardians, and Bridget is left alone in her primitive cottage on the estate. Despite their passionate love for each other, she and her daughter had parted in anger, so Bridget resolves to seek out her child. After a long absence she returns alone, looking as though she had been 'scorched by the flames of Hell'. Her solitude and general appearance have earned her the local reputation of a witch, and in a moment of rage she curses a certain Mr Gisborne who has accidentally shot her little dog.

In the second section the narrator introduces himself and describes how, by a series of events, he meets Bridget, and discovers her granddaughter Lucy, now a victim of the curse in the shape of an evil 'double'. Finally Bridget, now a 'Poor Clare' in Antwerp, rescues Gisborne from the midst of fighting and takes him to her cell, expiring soon after as she declares her grandchild freed from the curse.

Elizabeth Gaskell needs her supernatural element in this story to give validity to one of her most extreme examples of the power of words. Such, it would seem, is the force of feeling, the suppressed rage against and love for her daughter, turned on to the cult of the Sacred Heart and her pet dog, that when she curses Gisborne the words are given actual power.

'The Poor Clare' is in some ways a supernatural counterpart to 'Sylvia's Lovers', the former taking the latter's simple refusal of forgiveness and turning it into the more intense and transcendent form of a curse. Both stories use the metaphoric structure of wandering and enclosure. 'The Poor Clare' parallels this metaphor with a general sense of bringing disparate elements from various lives into a final focus. Bridget is a solitary figure, enclosed in her faith and her love. The inwardness of her life is mirrored in her face, 'wild, stern, fierce, indomitable' (MM 151). From her search abroad she retreats first to her hovel and finally to her cell in Antwerp. But meanwhile the narrator has travelled from land to land accumulating the evidence which brings all lives back to the curse. One image at the dénouement captures brilliantly the spiritual dimension of this tale (and it is this dimension which rescues it from melodramatic fantasy). The narrator is in the starving city of Antwerp, in the midst of battle, when:

> Suddenly there was a sound of many rushing feet past our window. My landlord opened one of the sides of it, the better to learn what was going on. Then we heard a faint, cracked, tinkling bell, coming shrill upon the air, clear and distinct from all other sounds. 'Holy Mother!' exclaimed my landlord, 'the Poor Clares!' (MM 187)

The bell has been rung that is only sounded in the extreme need of the Poor Clares, and suddenly all men, women and children, friends and enemies alike, are borne along on a tide of human love and succour:

We met the first torrent of people returning with blanched and piteous faces; they were issuing out of the convent to make way for the offerings of others.'Haste, haste!' said they. 'A Poor Clare is dying! A Poor Clare is dead for hunger! God forgive us and our city!' (188)

More than the charity of the act, it is the cataclysmic nature of the surge of humanity, like all human feeling rushing to undo evil, which makes this image so overwhelming – or, to reverse the idea, the secret retreat of the Clares opening up as the human heart opens up after years of inturnedness and self-obsession. Bridget Fitzgerald, as 'Sister Magdalene', like the parents of Benjamin in 'The Crooked Branch', relieves her soul of its burden in public, as though she makes her declaration of what her death means to all mankind before she is released.

The lifting of the curse is not arbitrarily linked to Bridget's death. She has dedicated herself to good works for many years before the bell rings for her death, and the idea of reparation is never far from Mrs Gaskell's mind where forgiveness of sins is concerned. But this is only part of a process by which at her death the protagonist can feel a justification which gives meaning to her life. It is that sense of having paid debts, made peace and confronted oneself which we found in *North and South*. Bridget's last years in the convent are not only appropriate because they serve to exorcise the curse, but because they are the culmination of a life lived narrowly, inturnedly, but with intense devotion. She is devoted to her child, her family, her faith. Her husband abuses her, her child leaves her, her dog, the only object left on which she can lavish affection, is shot. But out of this instability and rejection she finds a way which gives meaning to her life and death.

The meaning of lives, and the allied themes of the past, secrecy and expiation are given their fullest expression in 'A Dark Night's Work'. In this novella the author has room to move at a more leisurely pace. Although Ellinor's is the main life to be delineated and measured, those of others join to make the total effect more complex and expressive of 'life' in general as much as 'lives' in particular.

If the telling is more leisurely, the central act is more serious and devastating than most of those events which change people's lives in her fiction. The 'Dark Night's Work' is the inadvertent killing of a lawyer, Mr Dunster, by his partner, the well-to-do attorney Mr Wilkins. The only witnesses to the body, though not the act, are his old servant Dixon and his beloved daughter, Ellinor. These two share complicity by helping to bury the body in the garden. Mr Wilkins takes to drink and becomes morose and depressed. Ellinor, painfully aware of her guilt, shields him until his death, and then, in reduced circumstances, moves to a distant part of the country. Some time later she is recalled from Italy by news that the servant Dixon is condemned to death for Dunster's murder. In an exciting and moving climax, Ellinor returns to England, seeks out the judge, Ralph Corbet, once her suitor until her father's insults and his own ambition made him break off their engagement, and by telling the truth simultaneously saves Dixon, frees herself from her conscience and inadvertently makes her one-time lover consider his life and career in a new and sadder light. Ellinor is finally married to a worthy Canon Livingstone, who has remained faithful in his attachment to her since the day he made his first proposal – the very day of the 'murder' which changed Ellinor's whole life.

Viewed in one way this story is one of *hubris*. Edward Wilkins' father had built up his practice upon the solid inheritance of *his* father. He is naturally kind, generous and loving, but by a combination of circumstances overreaches himself, lives beyond his means, and is forced to take Dunster into partnership, from which the latter's unlooked-for death arises. His money disappears, and his daughter is forced into a life very different from that which his hopes and her childhood might have led either of them to expect.

Yet despite these implications, and despite the undoubted adverse reflections on Corbet's lack of faith, and worldly ambition, this is no more a tale with a moral purpose than any other of Mrs Gaskell's fictions. What we feel most strongly is the movement of lives, particularly in terms of expectations and disappointments. This note is struck in the very opening pages when Edward's father decides that his son will not study for the bar, since the business is too lucrative to be allowed to pass out of the family. The self-indulgence which is to lead to Edward's ruin is born here, since his father 'tried to compensate him for the disappointment by every indulgence which money could purchase' (DNW 2) though 'if it had done him an injury the effects were at present hidden from view'. The death of his wife, and of Ellinor's baby sister, throw the father and surviving daughter together. Ellinor feels assured of her lover and her future life as they sit with Mr Wilkins on a favourite spot in the garden a few days before the catastrophe occurs. Yet even in the very moment when actions immediately below her room are shaping her destiny in one disastrous direction, she is also in receipt of Mr Livingstone's proposal, which she has taken upstairs to read. The next morning, when she is shocked into numbness by the death and burial of the night before, Livingstone comes to urge his suit and retire discomfited. The final shape of Ellinor's life is mysteriously embedded in the events which seem to her at that moment to be delivering a blow from which she will never recover. Corbet, by contrast, feels himself in control of his future. It is planned while he is still a very young man. He is always in control of his feelings. He decides with cool self-assurance when he should tell Ellinor of his love, weighing in the balance his family's possible reaction, and coming down on the side of prudence. Livingstone, by contrast, is so taken by Ellinor that he could wait no longer than the next day after meeting her to propose. This openheartedness, shared by Ellinor and her father, is not just generosity, but an openness to events which is a kind of humility. She instinctively cuts through the veils of self-deception which Ralph has cast about himself when he is losing interest in her.

> She bent a little forward, and looked full into his face, as though to pierce to the very heart's truth of him. Then she said, as quietly as she had ever spoken in her life, –
> 'You wish to break off our engagement?' (89)

– only to admit immediately after that she was probably wrong. The secret she has to hold turns her life inward. She moves to a Cathedral town with her one-time governess, and feels such calm and security that she does not wish to leave. But as a kind of facing of lost possibilities she insists on attending Corbet's wedding. When she receives a letter from him, 'Her life rolled backwards, and she was a girl again' (123). She deposits it in a box of treasures:

> among the dead rose-leaves which embalmed the note from her father, found after his death under his pillow, the little golden curl of her sister's, the half-finished sewing of her mother.
>
> The shabby writing-case itself was given her by her father long ago, and had since been taken with her everywhere. To be sure, her changes of places had been few; but if she had gone to Nova Zembla, the sight of that little leather box on awakening from her first sleep, would have given her a sense of home. She locked the case up again, and felt all the richer for that morning. (123)

Thus she keeps her life contained, under lock and key, possibilities never to be fulfilled. She sees Corbet once more, unobserved by him as he hurries on with his wife and child. 'Such were the casual glimpses Ellinor had of one, with whose life she had once thought herself bound up' (128).

Their final meeting is a masterpiece of understated confrontation. Before him in his study sits the woman who might have shared his life, across the way in the dining room is the one who in fact occupies that position. The former has come to unburden herself of a secret which reopens all the lost possibilities of his youth, while the latter, complaining loudly of intrusions of strangers who keep him from his family, confronts him with the actual outcome of the choices he made so confidently then. The awkwardness he anticipates in introducing the two leads to 'a wonderful relief' when she excuses herself from joining them at breakfast. He is still able, even at this moment, to keep separate in his sharp, cautious mind his thoughts, feelings and calculations:

> All the time that he said this he had other thoughts at the back of his mind – some curiosity, a little regret, a touch of

remorse, a wonder how the meeting (which, of course, would have to be some time) between Lady Corbet and Ellinor would go off; but he spoke clearly enough on the subject in hand, and no outward mark of distinction from it appeared. (159)

There is a terrible, bitterly comic undertone in the conjunction of confession and kedgeree, as the Judge's wife complains from the other room of tiresome callers who detain the judge from his breakfast. But there is no comedy about Ellinor's final blow, which is to show Corbet her father's letter, found under his pillow after his death. Incoherent and unconcluded, it is yet generous and loving, like the man, and addresses Corbet, 'From my death-bed I adjure you to stand her friend; I will beg pardon on my knees for anything – '(99). I say 'blow' because, although Ellinor comes as suitor to the man of power and authority, wealth and family, her position is, throughout, stronger than his. She has already freed herself of emotional ties to him, and in confessing her secret she frees herself from guilt and another oppressive link with the past. He is by turns moved, piqued, curious and aware of his own deficiency. Finally he is forced to face the implications of the choice he has made and find further cause for regret:

He had obtained the position he had struggled for, and sacrificed for; but now he could not help wishing that the slaughtered creature laid on the shrine of his ambition were alive again. (162)

The man who at 18 had determined his life's span, measures it in middle age and finds it wanting. But Ellinor has a just measure of her life. Talismans of her values she preserves in her writing-case; what oppresses her from the past she faces and overcomes. Dixon understands his life by circumscribing it – seeing it complete. He has decided where he is to be buried, next to his sweetheart, the pretty scullery-maid:

'I put this stone up over her with my first savings, ' said he, looking at it; and then pulling out his knife, he began to clean out the letters. I said then as I would lie by her.' (125)

Edward Wilkins puts himself right with the world as far as he is able, in his deathbed note. Even the governess, Miss Monro, is able to put her life into practical perspective after the disappointment of not receiving a hoped-for legacy

> Miss Monro looked very blank. Many happy little visions faded away in those few moments; then she roused up and said, 'I am but forty; I have a good fifteen years of work in me left yet, thank God.' (102)

There is in all this a kind of poetic justice which embodies Mrs Gaskell's characteristic ability to give a proper weight to all experiences, even where, as in the case of Ralph Corbet, the experience is a source of regret. At its best her shorter fiction draws on fabular shape for a measure of the overall meanings and values of lives, and combines it with the passion of melodrama, the transcendence of the supernatural and the realism of personal bonds and inherited obligations.

Conclusion

It is my hope that the foregoing chapters speak for themselves, and will provide the material for readers to draw their own conclusions, but it may be helpful to review some matters and to try to point up what is special about the author, particularly in regard to her values, her beliefs about women and her status as an artist.

An assumption that has underpinned all that I have written on Elizabeth Gaskell is that she is a deeply poetic novelist. It did not take her long to realise that she was not a poet herself, but, as I have suggested at various points there can be little doubt of the importance of Wordsworth's influence upon her writing. He was the impetus for her sense of the poetry of 'common things' and ordinary lives, for the value she put upon endurance and the human heart, for her belief in the power of natural objects, the tragedy of loss, the idyll and the significance of childhood. The extent of her more pervasive debt is marked by her use of names, quotations, allusions and echoes. Donald D. Stone has remarked that 'Wordsworth was the one major Romantic poet congenial to the tastes even of Evangelically minded Victorians, brought up to a life of duty and self-denial and suspicious of imaginative literature',[1] and her realism essentially takes its form from his, not only in local features, but in its meaning. Wordsworth's more challenging sense of the 'other' features in Mrs Gaskell's work as a Christian concern with the life beyond and all the moral values that this implies. In this, poetically speaking, she is more indebted to another poet she admired – Alfred Tennyson, from whose *In Memoriam* she (or rather her daughter) borrowed the epigraph for 'Sylvia's Lovers'. The very morbidity of this poem's direct confrontation with the personal emotional loss caused by death could not but appeal to a woman who was in many ways the absolute product of her age.

Her own poetic nature is not specially manifest in 'the joy

of words in tuneful order', though she can occasionally produce an eloquent or moving phrase, and she has an ear for the
nuances of everyday speech. It is most apparent in her handling of objects and human gestures – the minutiae of ordinary
life that speak to us. She also has a sense of the shape of life
and its issues – of rhythms and patterns – which gives to her
fiction a dimension other than that of simple cause-and-effect
action. She thinks in parables, in themes and ideas experienced
as images. The Bible, for instance, is a living experience, not
merely the Word; its aphorisms and examples are the mythic
life-blood of a novel such as *Mary Barton*. Life is an individual
pilgrimage whose stages are spatial metaphors for the growth
of the self. Often the underlying form of a work may be
suggested by the mood implied in a word or two – 'wince'
and 'stunned' in *North and South*, 'morbid' in *Ruth*, 'never' in
'Sylvia's Lovers'. Themes and motifs, differently handled, expressed in the context of other concerns, recur throughout her
many novels and short stories, and it is not always easy to
subject her to a critical analysis which will capture her whole,
as it were, without repetition and without dissecting the poetry out of her. Realism, values and gender all affect each other,
and are constantly interacting. Realism, morally speaking, dictates values; values are qualities inhering in life and as such
are part of the fabric of her realism. Gender colours the values
she is most concerned with, and realism dictates the sober assessment of the woman's place in relation to man and society
which makes an assertion of human values possible.

Her most pervasive structural impulse is one of duality.
Alternatives, sometimes opposed, sometimes complementary,
abound in her work: North and South, night and day, enclosure and freedom – spatial and temporal metaphors reflecting
more abstract pairings: stability and insecurity, authority and
independence, repression and spontaneity. Gender of its very
nature contains a duality, and upon it depend yet others – witch
and martyr, angel and serpent, chastity as religious ideal and
as sexual weapon, sex itself as nature and perversion – rich
ambiguities for a writer possessed with both a deep religious
conviction and a concern for the lives of women. And beyond
all lies the most crucial opposition – between the contingent

and the absolute, the mortal and the eternal. Nothing could illustrate more aptly the way in which Elizabeth Gaskell's concerns are imaginatively of one piece than the complementarity of this pair of ultimate opposites in her work. As realism, contingency feeds back into life as a preference for spontaneity, charitable action, over a fruitless desire for perfection, or narrowly authoritarian, doctrinaire faith. Looking the other way, out of life, glimpses of the eternal, which can only be achieved through death, put our lives into perspective. Death itself is so crucial a factor in her art because it is a sounding-board catching echoes of eternity in our everyday lives. It gives life meaning even as it terminates our existence. Mrs Gaskell has not the sense of death's otherness belonging to Emily Brontë – she has felt its pain, but not imaginatively grasped it as a real presence – but if sex is '*the* subject of a woman's life', death is *the* subject of life in general. The number of deaths that occur in her work, sometimes beginning, sometimes ending, always changing, the story of a life, is of a part with a heightened sensibility typical of her time. It is further reflected in the more melodramatic episodes and moments that punctuate almost all her work. Many commentators have felt uneasy at this note in a writer who seems at her best when dealing urbanely with the flow of provincial life or stoically with the trials of urban poverty – in short with the reality of the everyday. I would refer the reader again to the passage from 'A Dark Night's Work' in which the life of Ellinor is reviewed:

> There are some people who imperceptibly float away from their youth into middle age, and thence pass into declining life with the soft and gentle motion of happy years. There are others who are whirled, in spite of themselves, down dizzy rapids of agony away from their youth at one great bound, into old age with another sudden shock; and thence into the vast calm ocean where there are no shore-marks to tell of time. (DNW 115)

Here is a story which classically sets one melodramatic incident involving a violent death in the context not only of a mundane lifespan, but of some generations past. Again, in *Ruth* she speaks of our lives dwindling into the 'practical and tangible' until 'it seems to require some great storm of the soul before we can again realize spiritual things' (R 201). Gaskell's placing of mundanity against crisis, one life rhythm against another, is a way of articulating values in the lives of her protagonists. A key word she returns to is 'now'. It is repeated as Mary Barton makes her decision to acknowledge publicly her love for Jem Wilson:

> The present was everything; the future, that vast shroud, it was maddening to think upon; but *now* she might own her fault, but *now* she might even own her love. Now, when the beloved stood thus, abhorred of men, there would be no feminine shame to stand between her and her avowal. (MB 390)

This is not the everyday, commonsense 'now' of Molly Gibson's 'this is now, not some time to come a long way off' (WD 140). It is the 'now' of the crisis moments in our lives when we must commit ourselves, when life will not allow us to drift any longer, but demands some clearer definition of its meaning. It makes its appearance when Margaret Hale tells the lie to secure her brother's escape. The ultimate juxtaposition of life and death, and the urgency with which one defines the other is captured in the last moments of Philip Hepburn's existence:

> now, the strong resolve of an ardent boyhood, with all a life before it to show the world 'what a Christian might be;' and then the swift, terrible now, when his naked, guilty soul shrank into the shadow of God's mercy-seat, out of the blaze of His anger against all those who act a lie. (SL 499)

The 'now' of life and the 'now' of death bring together the contingent and the absolute, diurnal living and crisis living, and they comprise the fundamental form by which values are given expression in the individual's life.

Two central questions require some consideration: what *are* these values, and how far are they values peculiarly implicit in being a woman? While I have emphasised Mrs Gaskell's inclusiveness, her exploratory rather than didactic tendencies, there can be no doubt that her work contains implicit judgements about the worth of the lives her characters live. We may easily recognise 'local' values. The fact that *Mary Barton* is an articulation of the values of one faith, vivid though the articulation may be, is an indication of a comparative narrowness which she did not repeat. Lovingkindness, neighbourliness, pity, charity are all endorsed in ordinary lives, as we have seen. But in later work the implications are wider and the values less tangible. What she celebrates may be recognised in part by what she dislikes. She clearly despised the narrow authoritarianism represented by Mr Bradshaw, and the tyranny of the government which supported the operations of the press-gang in 'Sylvia's Lovers'. Similarly suspect are the rigid economic principles practised in Drumble, the cruelty of a local magistracy which will send a man to prison as a compliment to a local landowner's first appearance on the Bench (in 'My Lady Ludlow'). But even here, typically, it is not easy to pin the author down. In the case of authority, she recognises its need in a practically functioning society. The evil in Salem which she documents so vividly is not easily ascribed to any simple or single cause. It is a compound of blindness, lack of human feeling, lack of sober authority, precarious social conditions, a hot-house theocratic state and natural human faults of jealousy, mischief and self-delusion.

The question of evil itself raises an interesting problem about Mrs Gaskell's art. Angus Easson has claimed that she 'finds it difficult to think of anyone as actively bad', and cannot manage 'the full creation of unpleasant characters or the free play of evil'.[2] While there are examples of full-blown ingratitude or cold-bloodedness in her work, these features are not found in the foremost of her creations. One might think of the wastrel son in 'The Crooked Branch', the brother Edward in 'The Moorland Cottage'. What we do not find is a thoroughly metaphysical vision of evil such as Dostoevsky is capable of imagining. There are some parallels between *Mary Barton* and *Crime and Punishment* – the isolated, essentially good murderer, his confession induced by lonely despair, the power of pity, especially for children, the place of desperate poverty in breeding extreme feelings and actions, the pressure of urban life, the Christian ethos. What the English novel lacks is the kind of corruption of heart – selfish, sordid, sensual, exploitative, of a Svidrigailov. Such a creation, it might be said, is beyond most writers, but Mrs Gaskell's sense of human wickedness simply does not include this dimension. The nature of her realism is such that she is bound to see evil in terms of simple failings of the human heart. She is at home with the spitefulness of a Sally Leadbitter, and can capture shrewdly the elder-brother arrogance of Edward towards Maggie in 'The Moorland Cottage':

> 'I wonder how men make their boats steady; I have taken mine to the pond, and she has toppled over every time I have sent her in.'
> 'Has it? – that's very tiresome! Would it do to put a little weight in it, to keep it down?'
> 'How often must I tell you to call a ship "her"; and there you will go on saying – it – it!'
> After this correction of his sister, Master Edward did not like the condescension of acknowledging her suggestion to be a good one; so he went silently to the house in search of the requisite ballast.[3]

Mrs Gaskell's sensibility is far nearer in this respect to Tolstoy's than to Dostoevsky's – people are guilty of moral stupidity, blindness, egotism; they are essentially rational beings going (perhaps temporarily) wrong. It might be said that this is yet another characteristic she shares with her mentor Wordsworth, who speaks positively of the 'little, nameless, unremembered acts / Of kindness and of love'[4] and negatively of 'the sneers of selfish men, / Nor greetings where no kindness is, nor all / The dreary intercourse of daily life'.[5]

Most of Mrs Gaskell's negatives are to do with coldness of heart, and naturally enough her positives are associated with warmth and generosity. But it is clearly insufficient to leave analysis at the charitable acts of *Mary Barton*. Human warmth is deeply associated with the self, its growth, creation, assertion and integrity. Cynthia Kirkpatrick retreats from full self-discovery, from the danger of commitment. Margaret Hale's great achievement is that she is open enough to establish her self fully; it is in this that virtue lies. The attendant question is how far this self-orientated system of values is also a peculiarly female affair.

It is obvious that Mrs Gaskell is not a feminist at all in the late-twentieth-century sense of the word. Fulfilment of the self for her women, in normal circumstances, implies marriage, childbearing, the duties and pleasures of the mother. These clearly formed the author's own major *raison d'être*, and she was sufficiently of her time and class to accept this as an adequate norm. Yet as the well-known passage in her letters indicates, she was aware that the self may not be as singular a phenomenon as we would like to think, and reconciliation of disparate roles not a straightforward matter:

> One of my mes is, I do believe, a true Christian – (only people call her socialist and communist), another of my mes is a wife and mother, and highly delighted at the delight of everyone else in the house, Meta and William most especially who are in full extasy. Now that's my 'social' self I suppose. Then again I've another self with a full taste for beauty and convenience whh is pleased on its own account. How am I to reconcile all these warring members? (L 108)

In these early letters she presents a 'mission-led' concept of self-fulfilment:

> I do believe we have all some appointed work to do, whh no one else can do so well; Wh. is *our* work; what *we* have to do in advancing the Kingdom of God; and that first we must find out what we are sent into the world to do, and define it and make it clear to ourselves, (that's *the* hard part) and then forget ourselves in our work, and our work in the End we ought to strive to bring about. (L 107)

There is a clear-cutness here, a sense that self-understanding is something to be wrapped up and put aside, which is quite at variance with the development of the self as we see it in her fiction. The most strikingly 'feminist' aspect of Mrs Gaskell's fiction depends on the fact that her heroines are by definition, and often also by special circumstance, situated where self-discovery and self-creation are essential. By contrast, men are certain of themselves, however erroneously, and to that extent are largely enclosed. We need not appeal to the example of that monster of self-satisfaction, Mr Bradshaw, to support the point. John Thornton, initially at least, feels himself defined by his worldly success, and it seems he need seek no further. *His* appointed work' *is* work in the public domain. That is his relation to others and the meaning of his life until he meets Margaret. The fact that she can force him to consider his life again is a measure of the power of women, but this power would not be apparent were she not herself involved in painful self-discovery.

At the same time there is an inescapable sense that women, for all the power they may command, are victims. The repeated situation in which a woman's integrity is questioned implies a female ripeness for guilt and self-doubt which the ethos of her society makes it possible for men (and occasionally other women) to exploit. Sylvia is pulled apart by two men's demands (or three, if her father is included), Ruth and Lois can only be themselves at the cost of their lives, Phillis is nearly destroyed by the world of Hope Farm – embodiment of her father's life and beliefs. The relationship with a father who is in some way inadequate is of course a recurrent motif in the fiction, perhaps related to the author's feelings about her own father. As figures of male authority, they fail, betray, inhibit, alienate themselves from their daughters, but are nevertheless bound to them by a special affection. Often the fathers do not know the special qualities of the child whose love they accept as their natural due. Holman would deny the totality of Phillis by shutting his eyes to her sexual maturity, Mr Hale throws all the burden of his woes upon Margaret. It takes a foolish marriage to make Mr Gibson value Molly fully, and even then he can doubt his own child's integrity. Perhaps what is most notable of all in Elizabeth Gaskell's treatment of women is that she is capable of feeling the special and unique quality of her heroines. Every one is felt to have some mysterious quality which is their personal dynamism, and which, while it reflects on gender, is manifested as an attribute of the individual woman. So Lady Ludlow's graciousness derives from a special combination of personality, experience and social position, as does Matty's intuitive knowledge of the meaning of economics. Margaret Hale has an inward strength expressed for the world in her bodily solidity and integrity, her unhurried hauteur, Phillis an un-tried fragility and eagerness for the complexities of human intercourse beyond her family, Sylvia a natural warmth and charm, Cynthia the power of sexual attraction, Molly a simple, commonsensical, practical affection.

The variety and uniqueness of her women confers a special and individual quality on all Mrs Gaskell's major fiction. Her themes and situations are repeated and reworked, but their fresh articulation relies on the values of the human heart, which were established where her own heart seems sometimes to have lain, in the eighteenth century. For if her writing most obvi-ously recalls Wordsworth among poets and Jane Austen among novelists, *Cranford* evokes the sentimental ethos of Sterne, and the questions raised in *Ruth* about female integrity, sexuality and death recall the Richardson of *Clarissa*. Her belief in good-heartedness and her rational, undaemonic conception of evil look back to the age of Enlightenment. Yet there is no way in which we can feel she is caught in the time-warp of a previous age. She is solidly Victorian as much in her concern with the social and political issues of her age, her evangelism and con-cern with the family, as in her less admirable traits of melo-drama, love of the supernatural *frisson* and, in slacker moments, clichéd versions of female sensibility.

The variety of the elements in her writing matches the variety of her women as a crucial factor in the vitality and interest of her work. She embraces the contemporary, the recently past and the historic; generations and individuals; the transcendent, the supernatural and the solidly real; the public and personal; sex and religion. The richness and variety of *North and South* can make a Charlotte Brontë look monomaniacal. The warmth and delicately dense realism animating a fully-realised social milieu in *Wives and Daughters*, and comprehending the whole *comédie humaine* even up to and including death, can make *Middlemarch*'s earnestness look clumsy and two-dimensional. Yet paradoxically it is a lack of this narrowness, this earnest-ness, in *artistic* terms which can betray her as a writer in her weaker moments. There is, it must be admitted, at times a failure of artistic nerve which will not allow Mrs Gaskell to let the word, the image, the story, speak for itself. It leads to a lack of restraint which makes religiosity out of passionate faith, a lack of rigour that allows a too easy path into Heaven. It is peculiarly unfortunate when it is manifested as a desire to spell out an image for the reader or to refuse the implications of an open ending, since restraint, understatement and an openness which can wait to hear the answering echo of her own words are her very strongest suits as an artist. But when she writes at her best – with the bare, compassionate realism of the Flaubert of *Un Coeur Simple* in 'Half a Lifetime Ago', with Chekhovian perfection of understated richness in 'Cousin Phillis' or with Hardy's tragic sense of inescapable human passionate perversity in 'Sylvia's Lovers', we have no need to apologise for ranking her with the foremost writers of her age.

Notes

Preface

1. Edgar Wright, *Mrs. Gaskell: The Basis for Reassessment* (London, 1965), p. 1.
2. Angus Easson, *Elizabeth Gaskell: The Critical Heritage* (London, 1991). (Hereafter CH.)
3. Coral Lansbury, *Elizabeth Gaskell: The Novel of Social Crisis* (London, 1975), p. 7.
4. Patsy Stoneman, *Elizabeth Gaskell* (Sussex, 1987), p. 206.
5. Jenny Uglow, *Elizabeth Gaskell: A Habit of Stories* (London, 1993), pp. 601–2. (Hereafter 'Uglow'.)
6. David Lodge, *Nice Work* (1988; Harmondsworth, 1989), p. 80.

Introduction

1. Uglow, p. 7.
2. Ibid., p. 96.
3. William Wordsworth, 'The Ruined Cottage', ll.513–24.

1 Realising Christianity: *Mary Barton*

1. Unsigned review in the *Inquirer*, CH, p. 74.
2. Matthew 25: 40.

4 Women, Death and Integrity 2: *Ruth*

1. John Relly Beard, in *Tait's Edinburgh Magazine*, CH, p. 262.
2. James Joyce, *Ulysses* (London, 1960) p. 866.
3. Unsigned Notice, CH, p. 314.
4. Luke 6: 28.
5. Marina Warner, *Alone of All Her Sex: The Myth and Cult of the Virgin Mary* (London 1976, 1985), p. 70.
6. Romans 12: 20.
7. *A Choice of Christina Rossetti's Verse*, selected by Elizabeth Jennings (London 1970), p. 37.

5 Women, Death and Integrity 3: *North and South*

1. Robin Gilmour, in *The Idea of the Gentleman in the Victorian Novel* (London, 1981) has pointed out (p. 85) that Mr Thornton is being

213

'less daring than he thought', since 'manly' already had by the 1850s the overtones of meaning that he ascribes to it.

7   *Cranford* and Economics

1. Alfred Tennyson, 'Ulysses' 1.65.

8   Words and Values: 'Cousin Phillis'

1. William Wordsworth, *Resolution and Independence* 1.105

Conclusion

1. Donald D. Stone, *The Romantic Impulse in Victorian Fiction* (Cambridge, Mass., 1980), p. 134.
2. Angus Easson, *Elizabeth Gaskell* (London, 1979), p. 198.
3. Elizabeth Gaskell, 'The Moorland Cottage' ('World's Classics', London, 1934), p. 270.
4. William Wordsworth, 'Lines Written a Few Miles Above Tintern Abbey', ll.5–6
5. Ibid. ll.130–2.

Index

215